ВЕСНА РУССКАЯ
"Russian Spring"

William Sutherland

Printed in Victoria, Canada

National Library of Canada Cataloguing in Publication Data

Sutherland, William, 1965-
     Becha pycckar = Russian spring / William Sutherland.

Includes bibliographical references.
ISBN 1-4120-0418-7

     I. Title. II. Title: Russian spring.

PS3619.U84B42 2003   813'.6   C2003-903540-9

TRAFFORD

This book was published on-demand in cooperation with Trafford Publishing. On-demand publishing is a unique process and service of making a book available for retail sale to the public taking advantage of on-demand manufacturing and Internet marketing. **On-demand publishing** includes promotions, retail sales, manufacturing, order fulfilment, accounting and collecting royalties on behalf of the author.

Suite 6E, 2333 Government St., Victoria, B.C. V8T 4P4, CANADA

Phone	250-383-6864	Toll-free	1-888-232-4444 (Canada & US)
Fax	250-383-6804	E-mail	sales@trafford.com
Web site	www.trafford.com	TRAFFORD PUBLISHING IS A DIVISION OF TRAFFORD HOLDINGS LTD.	
Trafford Catalogue #03-0787		www.trafford.com/robots/03-0787.html	

10   9   8   7   6   5   4   3   2   1

Dedications

ВЕСНА РУССКАЯ – "Russian Spring" is dedicated to my grandmother Irene J. Sutherland (1913-1988), my grandfather John E. Sutherland (1906-1985), my brother Don Sutherland who has always been there to give me support and encouragement on this endeavor, Veronica San Lucas (1975-2002), Claude Brown (1969-1997), Valerie Williams (d. 1999), each of whom will always remain dear to my heart, Mr. D. Schirmer my high school writing teacher, Aaliyah Dana Haughton (1979-2001), Selena Quintanilla Perez (1971-1995) for their inspirational examples and the benefits they had left this world, and most of all to God whose countless blessings made this novel possible.

Table of Contents

William Sutherland

<u>Chapter 1</u>

The whitish-pink storm-colored night sky gradually brightened into a silvery-gray with the approach of dawn. The blinding New Year's Eve blizzard slowly departed and the opaque curtain of swirling flakes lifted. A majestic winter wonderland emerged in the storm's wake.

The gray cobblestones of Красная Площадь [Red Square] were buried under an inch of thick ice topped off by a foot-and-a-half of white, powdery snow. The colorful onion-domed spires of St. Basil's Cathedral and the golden onion-domed cupolas of the Kremlin Cathedrals were all coated in white. Likewise, the redbrick Kremlin fortress walls and towers and the yellow-hued Kremlin buildings were clothed in white. The snow covered city blended picturesquely with the silvery-gray sky. The temperature hovered around 4° Fahrenheit, expected to drop below zero during the coming evening.

For a moment, as Muscovites celebrated the New Year 2014, they directed their thoughts away from their daily struggles to make ends meet. Some Russians openly downed vodka in the streets offering shots to all who would take. Children skated through Красная Площадь [Red Square] under the watchful eyes of protective mothers and babushkas. Two lonely soldiers

ВЕСНА РУССКАЯ

stood in front of Lenin's Mausoleum, the only reminder of their country's past prestige.

"Reminds me when I was young like you," Natalya Kalinina, a Muscovite at birth teased her 13 year-old Belarussian cousin, Tatyana Ivanovna, playfully pushing her. Prior to the holidays, Natalya had not seen her relatives for nearly four years. The 12-hour trip from Minsk to Moscow had become virtually impossible to make. Train service was frequently halted due to constant fuel shortages. In addition, Natalya's aunt Sofya, plagued by asthma since childhood, found the smoke-filled trains too harrowing for her respiratory system. "I'll race you to the museum," Natalya challenged her younger cousin, momentarily escaping back to her youth when her mind was not troubled by the worldly problems plaguing her country and the other former Soviet States.

Born in Moscow on April 16, 1991, Natalya Kalinina was too young to remember the waning days of the Soviet Union, when her country was one of the most powerful nations on earth. The story of the two coups that led to its demise were mere events out of the history books.

Just four months after Natalya's birth, a group led by then Vice President Gennady Yanayev with military and KGB (the State Intelligence and Security force) backing seized control of the Soviet Government. Fearful that the Soviet Union was about to unravel with the expected implementation of a new "Union Treaty" that transferred many of the Kremlin's powers to the various republics, the group placed then President Mikhail Gorbachev under house arrest and declared a state of emergency. They were determined to save their country, but ironically, their actions had the opposite effect. The Soviet Union's demise was accelerated when during the putschists brief

2

rule, virtually every republic, including conservative and loyal Belarus, declared independence.

Unlike in past decades, because of the effects of Perestroika and Glasnost (the opening of Soviet society and granting of greater freedoms) Russians had lost fear of the authorities. Concerned that the Yanayev Government would strip them of their newfound rights, Russians vigorously resisted the coup. Crowds defiantly stood up to the tanks that had been dispatched to intimidate and disperse them. People erected crude barricades around the Russian White House where Republic President Boris Yeltsin (the equivalent of a U.S. State Governor) and his staff were holed up to protect it from a possible assault. These Republic officials refused to recognize the new Soviet Government and its decrees.

During the chaos, three persons were killed, accidentally crushed by maneuvering tanks that attempted to escape when cornered by an angry mob that set several fires. Within 72 hours, because of the peoples' heroic actions and the putschist's incompetence, the coup collapsed and Mikhail Gorbachev was restored to power.

Unknown to everyone at the time, Boris Yeltsin has secretly conspired with the other Soviet Republic leaders to sabotage the Union Treaty. Yeltsin held this meeting just prior to the August coup with designs of destroying the Soviet Union so that he could elevate himself from the equivalent of a governor to the status of "world leader." The other Republic leaders also agreed. The temptations of greater power and riches were too much for them to resist.

During this tumultuous three-day period, the Western powers led by the United States denounced the putsch in the strongest terms and refused to deal with the new Government. Although they demanded the

ВЕСНА РУССКАЯ

restoration of the "legitimate Soviet Government" they had other ambitions. Their desire was to gain influence and control over the Soviet sphere and this goal came to light in December 1991 when Boris Yeltsin staged his own coup.

With Yeltsin in power, the West had their long-awaited chance to exert influence and control over the Soviet sphere. Therefore, no one protested when Gorbachev was overthrown and forced in humiliation, from the Kremlin. Shortly thereafter, the Soviet Union was officially dissolved on December 30, 1991. Each Soviet Republic became an independent nation and with this division, the West had the opportunity they had dreamed of for more than 40 years – the chance to conquer, subjugate and colonize their one-time rival with a strategy of manipulation and exploitation under the slogans of "democracy" and "capitalism." Within a matter of months, a first-class State under Czarist and Soviet rule was reduced to a third world country devoid of much global influence.

It was during this period of colonialization that Natalya Kalinina grew up. Her school years were filled with watching her mother country slowly whither with each new capitulation, and with each new capitulation, the Kalininas found life increasingly more difficult. Russia was being impoverished through the repeated rape of her precious resources. The cancerous exploitation was humbling a once proud country.

Despite promises of a better life under "Western-style" democracy, goods became increasingly scarce to ordinary Russians. Lines became longer. The once peaceful streets became war-zones as rival organized crime groups fought for economic and political control.

The new elite class of tycoons, the so-called "entrepreneurs" grew rich from their connections at the expense and misery of their fellow citizens. Wealth and material goods were their gods. Things once considered sacred to Russians were desecrated.

For a day at least, concerns and worries about this bleak situation were far from Natalya Kalinina's mind, as she focused on the joy of the Ivanovna's visit. She could hardly wait to taste the hearty meal of fish and Russian Закуски [zakuski --hors d'oeuvres] that her mother, Katya and her aunt Sofya were preparing. It was quite a change from the usual meager portions of wilted cabbage and beets, bruised potatoes, bread and emaciated Western-imported reject chicken they were accustomed to eating. She cherished the thought of sipping a glass of fine wine instead of the usual cups of steaming tea or shots of vodka.

The special dinner was a luxury the Kalinina's could rarely afford since the introduction of capitalism. The "closed stores" and special privileges once handed out to State officials like Natalya had long vanished. Natalya received virtually nothing for her dedicated service to the country while the tiny "entrepreneurial class" with their illegitimate wealth rode around in stretch limousines, dined in the best restaurants and wore the finest Western imports.

"No running," Tatyana set the rules as her long dark-hair drifted in the slight breeze.

"No running," Natalya agreed.

Before Natalya could finish her words, Tatyana was off, slipping and sliding along the snow-covered ice.

"I'll get you for that!" Natalya called after her cousin.

"Only if you can catch me," Tatyana shouted back weaving in-and-out of small pockets of startled Western

ВЕСНА РУССКАЯ

tourists who stuck out with their fancy clothing and awkward, rigid steps. They were in constant fear of slipping on the thick snow-covered Moscow ice. They were unaccustomed to the hazardous wintry conditions in Russia. Unlike in the West where snow was plowed and ice broken and removed, the former Soviet Republics could ill afford to engage in such projects. As a result, it was expected that everyone traverse ice and snow with reasonable prudence.

While awkwardly making their way through Красная площадь [Red Square, the Western visitors cowered in heavy coats and hid their faces under scarves and hats. It was as if they were making a conscious effort to show their disdain for the Russian winter.

"Girl, watch where you're going," a middle-aged American tourist cursed and swore in his native tongue as he wildly flailed about, sliding uncontrollably along the ice after being brushed by the Belarussian girl. Then just as he appeared to be regaining his balance, Natalya glanced off one of his outstretched flailing arms. In a renewed flurry of curses, he went falling in a heap into the soft Russian snow. "That's what's wrong with you damn people – you have no respect for others," he angrily chastised Natalya who had momentarily spun around to make sure he was all right.

A small group of elderly babushkas quietly chuckled as the American vigorously shook the snow from his clothing. As he beat the snow from his clothing, the American tourist continued swearing and cursing.

"С новым годом [Happy New Year]," Natalya warmly wished the fallen tourist with a patient smile, upon seeing that he was not hurt. She then resumed the race.

"All you can do is shout insults," the uncomprehending American yelled back as a group of tipsy Russian men, reeking of their daylong celebration, heartily laughed at the spectacle as a small protective group of Americans rallied around their angry compatriot.

Despite her efforts, Natalya, having suffered a considerable loss of time from her encounter, had no chance of catching her younger cousin who joyfully slid into the redbrick wall of the Museum of History. "I won!" she shouted with happiness.

"So you think," Natalya replied, playfully wrestling her cousin in a snowdrift.

"No fair. Let me go!" Tatyana protested.

"Not until you give up," Natalya demanded.

"No way," the Belarussian defiantly answered.

"Very well, have it your way," Natalya replied, taking a handful of snow and playfully sifting it over her cousin's face.

"Okay, okay, you win," Tatyana surrendered.

"Are we still friends?" Natalya then asked in a more serious tone of voice as she lifted her cousin from the drift.

"Friends," Tatyana replied shaking Natalya's hand. "One more race," she then challenged, having brushed the snow from her clothes.

"To St. Basil's" Natalya agreed as they set off.

Tatyana immediately skated out in front, partly due to her elder cousin's generosity. She continued to expand the lead until they reached the rectangular, red and black granite structure of Lenin's Mausoleum. Once there, Natalya, fully aware that they had reached the halfway point, began to skate with all of her strength and energy. She aggressively closed the gap, and before long both were in a virtual tie with the Muscovite beginning to pull ahead.

ВЕСНА РУССКАЯ

As Natalya was on the verge of overtaking her cousin for good, she was suddenly grabbed. "Let go," the startled Muscovite demanded, quickly pulling herself free. By the time Natalya had extricated herself, Tatyana had surged ahead with a renewed burst of energy. Natalya, upon seeing this, became overanxious to make up for the lost time. She skated more recklessly in haste to catch up until she suddenly lost her balance and went sliding into the snow. With her fall, the race was over. Tatyana had won again.

Infuriated by her loss, Natalya set out to exact revenge. She grabbed he unsuspecting captor by the arm and demanded to know why he had hindered her efforts.

"I couldn't let you win, not after the humiliation you put her through in that snowdrift," Jim Keating, a youthful New Yorker declared in fluent Russian. "I felt sorry for her," he added recounting the episode he had witnessed when Tatyana was forced to endure torture at the Museum of History."

"This is a family affair," Natalya countered, trying her best to sound stern upon learning she had been obstructed in good taste. Понимала [Do you understand?]" she demanded to know taking him by the coat after the American had extricated his arm from her grip.

"Yes."

"Very good!" Natalya sternly replied, maintaining her composure. "And don't you forget it!" she added before releasing him from her grip and turning away. Then without warning, she attacked the American, pulling him into the snow.

Unwilling to resist, Jim refused to fend off the Muscovite's attack. Natalya then firmly planted herself on

8

him and grabbed a handful of snow and playfully inundated him with it. "Now we're even!" she declared trying to maintain a serious composure as she ruffled his hair with her mittoned-hands. "I couldn't just let you get away unscathed," Natalya added with smile as Tatyana skated up to them. Afterwards, she lifted herself from the American and extended her hand in a gesture of friendship.

"Why should I take your hand after what you did to me?" Keating playfully protested.

"Because I won't let you go if you don't allow me to help you," Natalya playfully countered gently nudging him back into the snow.

"Have it your way. You drive a hard bargain," the American playfully surrendered with resignation, taking the young Russian woman's hand and allowing her to assist him to his feet.

"С новым годом [Happy New Year]!" Natalya then wished him.

"С новым годом!" Jim returned the greeting before they went their separate ways with Natalya playfully warning that he might not have seen the last of her.

"So I won again," Tatyana teased her Muscovite cousin.

"Not without a little help!" Natalya warmly retorted putting her arm around her Belarussian cousin. "But I'll still treat you to some ice cream," she offered taking Tatyana to a small, glass and plastic kiosk behind GUM Department Store.

"Who was that?" Tatyana inquired as Natalya surrendered two 5000 Ruble notes and took their cones.

"I don't know. I never asked him. Must've been a secret friend of yours since he made sure you won," Natalya countered.

9

ВЕСНА РУССКАЯ

"I would've beaten you anyway," Tatyana protested between slurps of ice cream.

"Sure you would have," Natalya warmly answered taking her younger cousin's hand. "I'm just giving you a hard time," she added as they walked hand-in-hand to the metro station, eager to get home before dark.

Although it was only half-past three in the afternoon, darkness had already begun to set in. Sporadic explosions of firecrackers echoed through the city as the crowds gradually thinned out. A few flurries softly drifted to the ground from the leaden Moscow sky as a cool breeze kicked up.

Chapter 2

The light flurries gradually moderated into a steady snow, silently filling the footprints and sled tracks left behind during the day. With the winter darkness, the bone-chilling temperature silently slipped below zero. A biting wind cut into the skin of a few stragglers making their way home, as they passed through the dark slippery park across from a cluster of empty kiosks outside Красные Ворота Metro Station. Many had their ears covered by fur hats. A few carried shopping bags.

The dark roads around Natalya's residence at Лунковой Е.О. were virtually deserted. Only an occasional trolley passed by as it mechanically kept to its schedule along with the sparsely crowded subways that came and went from empty stations every five minutes.

At the Kalinina residence, only a block from the metro, the family sat down at a large retractable table set up in the study that served as a small living room during special occasions. Like many Russians, the Kalinina family lived in a tiny apartment consisting of a kitchen (which held two small wooden cabinets, an ancient gas stove whose burners had to be lit by a match or the cracking of two flints, and a small refrigerator that periodically required manual defrosting), a bedroom

11

(shared by Natalya's mother Katya and grandmother Anna), a small study (which served as Natalya's bedroom and as a living room when guests were present), and two half rooms that made up the bathroom. One of these rooms held the toilet while the other consisted of a shower, a bathtub that resembled a large, elongated metal pot on stilts, a sink, and a towel rack.

Because of the small size of the house, the Kalinina kitchen served as the center of activity. Most discussions were held at the table except when a group was too large for the small kitchen and had to be situated in the study-living room. Aside from meals being eaten at the kitchen table, newspapers were also read there. Likewise, Natalya's babushka, Anna conducted the family finances at the table, collecting Natalya's and Katya's weekly paychecks to draw up the family budget. When calculating budget figures, Anna preferred a wooden abacus and a pencil and paper.

Each week proved to be a greater challenge because of the steep inflation. Almost always it seemed that there was not enough money to cover the family's expenses. Because of this, the Kalininas were grateful to own their apartment that had been given to them through the long drawn-out privatization process in the middle 1990s.

Although larger quarters would have been more desirable, the Kalininas knew that having a place to live in downtown Moscow, a city plagued by severe housing shortages fueled by the exorbitant rents charged by greedy speculators, was a luxury in and of itself.

During the hyperinflationary decade of the 1990s, these speculators gained their holdings by preying on the elderly and infirm. The elderly and infirm, the most vulnerable of people, willingly took anything offered to them. They were desperate for quick cash to pay for their transportation to the countryside to live with relatives or to pay for their next meal and/or vital medicines. They sold at unconscionably low prices. Because of this situation, size and amenities such as air-conditioning mattered little to the Kalininas and most Muscovites fortunate enough to have their own dwellings in the City.

Although owning private property appeared to be a benefit brought about by "Western-style" reforms, many Russians yearned for the day when they had rented from the State for one or two Rubles a month, free of worry about heating, gas, electricity, and repairs and maintenance costs. Yet in spite of their increased hardships, each family took special pride in their humble dwelling and meticulously maintained their abodes.

In sharp contrast, no one took charge of the common areas. Paint peeled in hallways whose floors consisted of small craters, missing tiles, and fallen chunks of plaster. Stairs were missing planks from years of trudging and elevators did not work with any regularity, if at all. Few were willing to chip in for routine repairs and maintenance. They only did so with great reluctance when major emergencies such as a broken pipe or boiler failure occurred. Common areas were basically managed by the severity of the crisis.

In addition, without prior knowledge of a building's outlay, one found it difficult to navigate through the poorly lit hallways, especially at night. Antiquated mailboxes in the small, dark lobby provided no clues as to apartment numbers or family names.

Outside was little better. Unless the elements had not eroded away the original markings, it was next to impossible to read the hastily scrawled apartment numbers in the night's darkness.

Since the days of Western colonialization, Moscow's housing had become polarized. The majority of Muscovites had great difficulty finding affordable housing while the tiny "entrepreneurial class" was presented with unlimited possibilities. They resided in spacious well-maintained modern and/or renovated dwellings that stood out in stark contrast to the abodes of typical Muscovites.

Furthermore, by the end of the twentieth century, nearly all of the country's dachas had been purchased by the "entrepreneurial class" and foreign concerns eager to convert them into luxury hotels that Russians, rats and other riffraff, as the typical natives were viewed by these organizations, could ill afford to stay in. The exorbitant rents charged were as much as ten times the average Russian's monthly salary.

In addition, as a further insult, these foreign concerns refused to accept Russian currency as payment. Top them, the Ruble was not much better than the coarse toilet paper most natives used. Hindered by the high costs of transportation, fuel, and lodging, most Muscovites had long since abandoned their annual summer excursions to the cool, refreshing countryside.

In contrast to their country's bleak state of affairs and the outside dreariness, the Kalinina living room was filled with warmth and brightness. A pleasant aroma of delicious smoked fish permeated through the room.

All helped themselves to generous servings of fresh filet mignon drowned in lemon and cream sauce, baked onions and potatoes, and a verdant salad of green cucumbers, lettuce, red tomatoes and radishes, immersed in imported Greek olive oil and vinegar. Everyone,

14

including young Tatyana, drank numerous sips of ripe imported Italian Vintage 1982 red wine over toasts to family, friendship, health and happiness.

During the course of their meal, the Kalininas and their relatives spoke about everything that came to mind. All shared their sorrows, worries, and joys. Anna reminisced about the past, reliving the Brezhnev Era of 1964-82 when things were simpler and better for Russians. She recounted the days when Russia was able to match the United States in every political and economic facet. Back then the Soviets were able to compete with western industrial output and goods were plentiful and affordable.

Natalya's mother, Katya, Uncle Ivan, and Aunt Sofya were born during the last years of Soviet parity with the United States, in 1971, 1974, and 1975, respectively. They were able to visualize Anna's story, having lived through some of the glory days themselves. However, Natalya and Tatyana found it difficult to imagine. They could not comprehend the time when the Russian Ruble was worth twice as much as the U.S. Dollar.

Everyone laughed at how the United States had once feared the Soviet Union. Out of grudging respect and jealousy, former U.S. President Ronald Reagan even labeled the Soviet Union – "the evil empire." Yet in fact the Americans had engaged in the same activities of espionage and rivalry throughout the world. If the U.S. intervened militarily in Vietnam to defend its interests, it was only natural for the Soviet Union to defend her national interests in Afghanistan.

They all laughed at how the West had visualized Soviet industry as operating with "monopolistic harmony and monolithic discipline" when in fact the opposite was true.1 Anna recounted the days when she worked at a transistor production facility. "Our work was predictable all

15

right. There were many times when we couldn't even do an hour's worth of work because the materials we needed were either in transit or not available. Since everything was 'скоробудет' ["It will be here soon"], we made up our own routines. We never worked seriously until the middle of the month when the necessary materials finally arrived. By the twentieth we had fallen so far behind, we had to work furiously to catch up. We worked 16 hours a day, seven days a week. We worked so fast to meet our quota, we never knew if the gadgets would actually work. All we cared about was meeting the plan's quota. I remember one time when one of the party bosses came for a surprise inspection. He found that only two out of every 10 transistors actually worked!" Anna declared, promptly being interrupted by choruses of laughter. "You should've seen the look on his face!" Anna exclaimed before continuing when the laughter died down. "And by the end of the month we were so exhausted it took us two weeks to recover!" More laughter followed. "But with the lack of necessary materials, we didn't have to work. It was a well-deserved break, I must add. And by the time the middle of the month arrived, the cycle began all over again. Work a little, work feverishly, and then recuperate for two weeks!"

"Maybe our products didn't always work, but the Pentagon (the key U.S. defense organization) bought screws for $70 and toilets that couldn't even flush for $700! So who's to say who was worse off," Uncle Ivan boasted, unable to resist taking a swipe at the West's leader.

"And there was this period of 'launch and fail!' When the U.S. tried to launch a satellite, the rocket exploded. Gone was $500 million. Then they launched a weather satellite that failed shortly afterwards. And then there was this Mars mission. Everything worked well until the Americans shut down communications to save power. Then when the time came to restore communications to guide the craft to its landing site, they couldn't do it. One billion dollars down the drain," Katya added as all laughed. "We had our 'quality' products and they had theirs," she continued sarcastically.

"Tell me about their great quality!" Ivan retorted.

"That reminds me," Aunt Sofya began. "Recently I bought Tatyana American-made sneakers. The sole fell off in one week's time." Everyone laughed. "The other wasn't much better. The stitching was already unraveling when I brought them back."

"It's so hard these days. Every child wants Western goods. You pay a fortune and you can't even expect quality," Katya sympathized.

"That's because they sell us leftovers. If you have dollars they give you the best. If they see Rubles, they say, 'here take our брак [junk]!'" Ivan replied. "Tell them what they said to you, Ivan prodded his wife.

"When I took Tatyana's sneakers back to get a refund they thought it was funny," Sofya spoke with indignation. "As angry as I was, I offered to pay them a couple of Rubles to replace them. And you know what they said?" she asked with incredulity in her voice. "They said, 'with this kind of money, sew them yourself!' So I left them on the counter and walked out. For now on, it's 'Минск' brand only."

Although momentarily taken aback by the clerk's audacity, the Kalininas were not surprised. They had experienced the same Western arrogance.

After reminiscing on the ups and downs of Russian society in the past few decades, the families spoke about recent weddings and tragedies among friends and neighbors. They spoke about the latest gossip and rumors

17

in their respective countries and relayed the latest news about their lives. There were moments of tears, others of laughter and concern, and still others of pure joy. The conversation then shifted to typical Western stereotypes.

"And they say we're unemotional robots!" Ivan declared mocking the West's condescending attitudes towards Russians. "They say we're faceless without feelings. Huh! Nothing could be further from the truth. When we love we know what true love is. When they love they merely express words. Everything is purely a succession of motions for them. All they want is sex and money. True love and devotion have hollow meaning to them," he continued.

"That's because they don't know us," Natalya interjected. "We have the same likes and same desires," she continued.

"That's because they make no effort to know us," Ivan quickly declared. "And even if they did, they're so closed-minded, it wouldn't make a difference."

"We love good music and we love adventure every bit as much as they do," Natalya replied. "We want the same things in life."

"We have true culture. We know how to appreciate culture. For them, unless there's sex, scandal, or violence, they're not interested. Take the Bolshoi for instance. Even if they watched the same performance a hundred times, the fluid artistic beauty of the ballerinas' delicate, graceful moves would pass them by. After watching a few minutes, they would more likely than not lose there concentration and ask, 'when is it going to happen?' when they don't even know what the 'it' is!"

"That's why they have such a broken and confused society, dear," Sofya interrupted her husband. "There's no more loyalty.   Even their presidents can't keep their families together!"

"Fortunately that's the one thing they haven't taken from us yet, not to say they haven't tried.   We still know what family loyalty is. Family still means something. We can bridge the generations while their husband and wife can't even stay together.   And forget about the children," Katya added reflecting on the high Western divorce and child abuse rates, as she pictured the lingering nuclear families, such as her own, in Russia.

Everyone spoke well into the night, helping themselves to numerous servings of Закуски [zakuski -- hors d'oeuvres], ice cream and rum-steeped cake over steaming cups of rich, dark, well-sugared tea after the entire bottle of wine had been exhausted. By the time they retired to bed, brightness began to encroach on the dark sky, revealing scattered flurries that sprinkled the cold, wintry city. All were tired except Tatyana who managed to catch an hour or so of sleep at the table.

---

1 Henrick Smith, "The Russians," (NY: Ballantine Books, 1976), p. 286.

Chapter 3

The KGB (renamed back to Committee for State Security from Federal Security Services [FSB] after widespread corruption plagued the agency during the early 2000s that resulted in a massive reorganization) offices in Лубянка Площадь [Lubyanka Square] buzzed with activity as agents came and went. Typewriters and computer keyboards clanked and clicked in cacophony. A thin haze of cigarette smoke drifted through the complex.

Natalya Kalinina, two years out of St. Petersburg University, ran her hand through her neatly cropped, short, light-brown hair which hung in loose bangs across her forehead as she sifted through a pile of case folders that cluttered her mahogany desk.

"Natalya, I need you to put everything aside," Valentin Makarov, her immediate supervisor interrupted. Although he was three times Natalya's age, the 66 year-old Makarov was one of her closest friends who served as the paternal figure in the young agent's life.

Natalya Kalinina, having lost her father, Vladimir to liver cancer when she was six and never seen her grandfather, openly embraced her gray-haired supervisor as a "father," because of the keen interest he took in her personal life and career. Their relationship involved a strong mutual respect for each other. As a result, both placed considerable value on the other's opinions, ignoring the agency's hierarchical structure.

"I need you to read these telexes on China and come up with an assessment by tonight," Makarov requested. "The U.S. State Department would like to consider our assessments before making a final judgment."

"I'll get to it," Natalya replied taking the thick packet of papers. "So how were your holidays, Valentin?"

"They were nice. It was great to see grandchildren."

"How are they?"

"They're all fine and really getting big. I just hope when my granddaughter grows up, she'll be half as pretty as you," Makarov kidded Natalya.

"You have nothing to worry about. She's such a cute little girl," the young agent warmly replied, briefly placing her hand over Valentin's hand. "I've seen her new portrait in your office. If I was nine, I think I would be a little jealous," she added, playfully hitting her supervisor.

"So how were your holidays? How are your relatives?" Valentin Makarov asked.

"They're all fine. Little Tatyana kept me running all the time. And then there were the drinks. I'm still worn out."

"Sounds like you had a great time," Makarov replied. "I'm glad you got to see them, especially Sofya. How is she?"

"She seems to be taking this winter all right, спасибо [spasibo -- thank you]."

"Glad to hear that," Valentin Makarov answered before growing serious again. "I'm sorry about the short notice, but you know..."

"Valentin, you have no need to apologize. I know how they [the U.S. Government] work, and besides I would do anything for you. You've always been here for me," Natalya warmly interrupted, remembering her first days with the KGB. During her first weeks with the agency, Natalya would have quit, had it not been for Valentin Makarov. Although much of the pain and guilt had since faded from her memory, Natalya could still picture the traumatic events in her mind, as if they had happened only yesterday.

It was a bright sunny day in Moscow. The summer temperature hovered around 75° Fahrenheit. A cool refreshing breeze gently drifted through the crowded metropolis. Natalya Kalinina, fresh out of college, worked closely with two senior KGB agents on her first assignment in the field. Although Natalya was new to the field, she was assigned to perform all of the paperwork and interrogations resulting from the simple criminal case. The two agents were merely present to supervise her activities and assist if the need should arise.

All wore casual clothes -- short-sleeved collared shirts, shorts, and sneakers, as they walked through the maze of stands at Измайловский Парк [Izmailovsky Park]. Although the agents were inconspicuous to the crowd at the bustling market, they were able to recognize each other by the white-color of their footwear.

At first glance, the KGB agents appeared to be three ordinary people viewing the many displayed goods consisting of colorful matroyshki dolls, paintings, t-shirts, icons, and kitchenwares. Each carefully scrutinized the large crowd, searching for criminal activity as they casually walked along.

"Look at this," Natalya spoke to one of her comrades. "I've got a samovar just like this at home and we paid only 32,000 Rubles for it. Here they want 325,000!" she exclaimed displaying the shiny copper teapot.

"Look over there," the third agent declared pointing out a well-dressed Western tourist not much older than Natalya. "He's about to make a transaction with those two over there. They've been caught dealing before. Let's check them out," the agent suggested.

Natalya Kalinina watched as one of the dealers received a handful of dollars, while the other stood behind the Westerner. She quickly replaced the samovar and followed her two companions. Although Natalya's instincts questioned their strategy of pursuing the tourist in lieu of the two dealers, she went along in silence.

As the KGB agents briskly made their way through the masses, the unsuspecting tourist casually browsed at a merchant's значки [znachki -- small colorful badges that made up Russia's most popular hobby] collection. Meanwhile, the two suspected dealers disappeared into the crowd.

"You go up to him," Natalya was instructed as the three neared their target. "We'll back you up if you need us."

Without hesitating, the young KGB agent approached the tourist. Taking him by the arm, she pulled him aside. "Excuse me, but I would like to speak to you for a minute," Natalya declared in English, leading him away from the crowd after flashing her KGB ID at him.

"What for?" the tourist asked, visibly shaken by the agent's appearance, with pictures of "Solzhenitsyn's Gulag" dancing through his mind. "I did nothing," he protested.

"Relax," Natalya tried to calm him. "All I want to do is talk to you. If you've done nothing then you have nothing to fear. You can then go on your way with my apologies."

"I did nothing," he repeated, trembling. He could see the two other agents in close proximity. Their stares heightened his fears. Both wore grim, serious expressions.

ВЕСНА РУССКАЯ

"Relax," Natalya reiterated trying her best to allay his fears. "May I have a look in your bag?"

"Go ahead. You'll find nothing," the Westerner answered, handing it over.

Upon taking the bag, the young agent sifted through its contents. She carefully examined two wooden icons, which had once been illegal to take out of the country. However, after years of continued Western pressure on Russia to lift her export restrictions and the steady doses of propaganda about the country's need to earn "hard currency revenues," the Russian Government had relented, allowing the country to be robbed of countless priceless cultural treasures.

The tourist became filled with concern as Kalinina studied the icons. "It's all right," Natalya warmly smiled upon seeing his petrified look. She then examined a matroyshki set, gradually separating its nine pieces. "So what brings you to Russia?" the agent asked trying to strike a more casual conversation.

"Tourism."

"Where are you from?"

"The U.S.," he replied with great discomfort.

"Relax, this is only a routine check," the Russian agent tried to reassure him. "You look like you could have been one of my classmates. How old are you, if you don't mind?"

"Twenty-five."

"I'm 21. Are you here with your family?" Natalya asked piecing the matroyshki set back together again.

"My father's here on business," the American replied, as his captor sifted deeper into the bag.

"My name is Natalya. You can call me 'Natasha'," she offered. "So what's your name?"

"I would rather not say."

"Now that's not fair," Natalya tried to joke. "I told you my name."

"You're still KGB. I would rather say as little as possible."

"I understand," the Muscovite tried her best to smile, resolving not to press him any further.

As she neared the completion of her search, Natalya Kalinina suddenly came across a tiny plastic packet containing a white, powdery substance. "What is this?" she inquired, growing serious. The two male agents quickly closed in upon catching sight of the suspicious packet.

"I don't know. It's a plant," the American protested in fear before bolting.

"After him," one of the KGB agents shouted as they took off in pursuit.

The tourist was tackled after a brief foot chase. He was then frisked and cuffed as a black Zil quickly pulled up along side them. Before the American could protest any further, he was shoved inside. Natalya quickly followed, seating herself to his right, while one of her partners placed himself to the American's left and the other in the front passenger seat.

"This is a set up! I demand to call the embassy," the cuffed American loudly protested as the vehicle roared off for Лубянка Площадь [Lubyanka Square].

"The American Embassy will be called in due time," Natalya firmly replied. "You should not have run," she then added after a brief pause. "You only made matters worse."

"What were you going to do with this?" the male agent seated to the American's left demanded to know, waving the small packet. His question was met with silence.

Although Natalya was supposed to conduct the questioning, she did not protest the infringement in spite of her instincts telling her to do otherwise. She did not want to countermand her superiors.

"You were going to use this, weren't you?" the senior agent declared with hostility. "Or were you going to sell it?" His question was again met with silence.

"You must answer if I am to help you," Natalya finally spoke up. "But in order to help you, we need your cooperation."

"I swear I know nothing."

"Then why did you run?" she asked.

"Because you set me up."

"No one set you up," the senior agent retorted. "Come clean with us," he then demanded in a threatening tone of voice.

"Let me handle this," Natalya finally suggested. "I think I can get to the bottom of this," she added as the dark vehicle pulled up to KGB headquarters. As it stopped, the doors were simultaneously swung open and the American was hustled through the yellow and gray building's glass doors.

"Listen to me. You have to be open with me. You must tell me everything. That is the only way I can help you," Natalya urged her prisoner, holding him by the arm.

"I told you, I did nothing. I don't know how it got there. Call the Embassy," he pleaded as they reached a small cell beneath the KGB offices.

"Sit down," Natalya firmly instructed as she removed the tourist's handcuffs under the watchful eyes of her two partners.

After taking a seat next to the prisoner, Natalya continued, "I can sympathize with you."

"How could you? You've never been set up before."

"If you believe you've been set up, it's imperative that you cooperate with us."

"Yeah right. You're the ones who set me up and now you want me to cooperate with you?" the American asked with indignation. "You have a hell of a nerve! What do you want me to say? That I'm guilty? What do you want me to do? You won't quit until I confess!" he angrily added growing defiant. "I won't confess to something I didn't do!"

Having heard enough, Natalya Kalinina stood up. Facing her prisoner, she firmly placed a hand on each of his shoulders. "Look at me!" she demanded. "I want to help you."

"Don't give me that fucking crap."

"Listen!" the agent's voice grew sterner. "I want to help you. Personally I want to believe your story, but you must help me do so. That's the only way I can convince my superiors to release you," Natalya spoke in reference to the two senior agents that stood nearby.

"Likely story! You're just some schoolgirl out of college. You have no experience. You have no influence. They're the ones calling the shots. They're the ones who will make the decisions," the tourist angrily insulted his young captor.

"You want us to handle this matter?" one of the senior agents offered.

"No. It's all right. I can handle it," Natalya answered before suggesting that she be left alone with the prisoner. "Perhaps he'll be more cooperative if we're alone."

"Very well. We'll be outside," they obliged stepping out of the cell. "Remember to get his passport and personal articles, they reminded Natalya."

"Yes, I know," she called back.

Once the two agents were out of sight, Natalya Kalinina resumed her interrogation. "I know you did not know how that packet got into your bag, but the fact is we still found it there."

"Yeah because you planted it there."

"I did not," the young agent defended herself.

"If you didn't then one of your partners surely did!" the American angrily declared. "I'll bet you've been following me right from the start. What is it? Are you trying to embarrass my father or something? It can't be me you really want!"

"Just listen to me. Hear me out," Natalya requested, growing impatient.

"Why should I?"

"Because, for one, you have no other choice. Your fate is in my hands."

"It makes you feel powerful to play with other peoples' lives, doesn't it? It..."

Natalya, having grown irritated firmly placed her hand over the prisoner's mouth, smothering his defiant words. "Enough!" she sternly commanded. "You have two choices. Number one, you can cooperate and help us and perhaps be free in a short while or number two, you can continue feeling sorry for yourself, refuse to cooperate, and stay here! Think about it!" Natalya demanded trying to talk reason into him. "And while you're thinking about it, I'll call the U.S. Embassy so they can send someone to represent you. But you had better know that if you don't cooperate with us there is nothing your Embassy, or anyone else for that matter, can do for you! I don't care how much influence or control your country has over us!"

After finishing, Natalya removed her hand from the American's mouth. "In the meantime, I'll take your passport and personal belongings," she declared. Hopefully you'll

28

make it easier for both of us and voluntarily hand them over. Otherwise my colleagues will handle matters."

"Here take them," the American offered, knowing that he had little choice. He did not want to face the other two agents. As he surrendered the items, Natalya recorded them on a manifest. "Michael Levine," Kalinina quietly read her prisoner's name from the American's passport. "Is this everything?"

"It's everything."

"So if you're searched, we won't find anything else, will we?"

"No you won't."

"Very well. This is a list of your belongings and the amount of money we'll be holding for you. Count your money and if you agree, please sign and date it here," Natalya requested pointing to a dotted line.

After the American placed his signature on the paper, Natalya tore off a carbon copy and handed it over to him. "This is your copy. You'll get everything back when you're released."

"When will that be?"

"It all depends on your cooperation. If you help us, you'll be out of here a lot sooner than if you don't," the agent answered, placing Levine's belongings into a large plastic bag. "Let me tell you what is going to happen now," she then offered. "I'm going to leave you alone for a half-hour or so. While I'm gone a doctor will examine you. You'll be required to submit urine, blood and hair samples. Then you'll be searched for additional narcotics that you may have concealed or consumed. We may take an X-ray of your stomach," the Russian agent spoke. "I highly recommend that you voluntarily submit to any and all tests. Don't make things any worse for yourself. If you hadn't run before, I don't think you would be here now," Natalya lectured her prisoner.

29

"I also want you to think about how that packet got into your bag. We'll need a written statement."

"How many times do I have to tell you, I don't know," he answered pausing between the last three words.

"I realize that, but maybe if you retrace all of the steps leading up to your arrest, you might be able to remember something that can be of help to both of us," she continued, ignoring Levine's protests. "And as I said before, I will contact the U.S. Embassy so they can someone to see you."

"Please call my father."

"Sure. What hotel are you two staying in?"

"Izmai... something."

"Izmailova?"

"Yes, that's it."

"Good. I'll notify your father. In the meantime, sit tight and cooperate with our doctor," Natalya instructed the American, before momentarily pausing. She then placed her hand on his shoulder as a gesture of reassurance before leaving, adding, "I want you to know, I don't enjoy this anymore than you do. I believe you're innocent."

"Then get me the hell out of here."

"In due time. We have procedures to follow. Once we know everything... once we have a written statement and know the identity of everyone you've come into contact with and are able to determine who is responsible, you'll be released."

"No one in his right mind would confess, so who are you fooling?" Michael Levine asked with indignation.

"Rest assured we have our methods," Natalya softly declared. "And when we release you, I will be there waiting for an apology for your condescending remark," she added trying to boost the American's sagging spirits, before leaving him to the doctor.

When Natalya Kalinina returned to her desk, she began to go through the paperwork. К18616дл was the number assigned to her first case.

"How's your first case? What do you think?" Natalya's supervisor, Valentin Makarov inquired, noticing that his young agent had returned from the field.

"I think we're holding an innocent person."

"Then you must prove it, which I have no doubt you will."

"Even though he tried to flee from us and was caught with narcotics in his possession, my instincts tell me that he's innocent. I believe the drugs were slipped into his bag without his knowledge," Natalya declared siding with the American's story. "Do you think that's possible?"

"If you say so, I believe it," Makarov replied having the utmost of faith in his young subordinate. "I trust your judgment."

"Then you'll back me if I ask for his release following one more interrogation session, even if I can't obtain the required written statement, да [yes]?" Natalya Kalinina ventured.

"I'll stand behind you."

"Спасибо [Thank you], Mr. Makarov," she replied. During her first few weeks at the agency, Natalya felt a bit uncomfortable addressing her boss on a first-name basis.

"Please call me Valentin. `Mister' reminds me of my advancing age."

"Okay Valentin, but only if you call me `Natasha' instead of `Ms.' or `Agent Kalinina.'"

"You have a deal," Natalya's supervisor agreed.

Following the brief conversation with her supervisor, Natalya Kalinina contacted the American Embassy and left a

31

message for Michael Levine's father at Izmailova Hotel. Afterwards, she sat tight waiting for the American Ambassador's representative to arrive.

Although Natalya was eager to complete her interrogation of the American, she declined to do so out of respect for the Ambassador's wishes. He did not want the prisoner to be questioned any further until someone from the Embassy had spoken to him and advised him of his rights. As the Russian agent thought about her first contact with someone representing the U.S. Government, her mouth became dry. She could not help but wonder if the American representative would try to take advantage of her inexperience.

As the time passed Natalya glanced at her watch. More than an hour had passed since her last contact with the prisoner.

Having little to do but wait, Natalya Kalinina could not help but think about the young American. "What is going through his mind? How would I handle it if I had been in his place, held by the intelligence service of a foreign country? He must be getting increasingly worried. Can he take the pressure?" the Russian agent asked herself. Natalya's heart pounded as images of his incarceration weighed heavily on her mind. She could visualize the small, dimly lit basement cell, and imagine herself a prisoner in its restricted confines. She could imagine its cramped quarters slowly shrink as its drab walls gradually closed in. She could imagine the space becoming more constricted with each passing second. She could see herself slowly suffocating.

"Where is he?" Natalya anxiously asked no one in particular. She glanced at her watch. Nearly two hours had passed. "I'm not going to wait much longer," the KGB agent vowed wanting to ease her prisoner's torment.

As she visualized the American's predicament, the ringing of her desk phone suddenly interrupted Natalya's thoughts. "The American attaché is here to see you," came the receptionist's voice.

"It's about time," Kalinina declared, quickly thanking the receptionist, before making her way to the lobby.

"I'm Robert Salerno. I represent the Ambassador of the United States of America," the tall, six foot, balding attaché proudly introduced himself in a somber tone of voice. He held little respect for Natalya or any other Russian for that matter.

"I'm Agent Kalinina," Natalya returned the introduction, feeling uncomfortable with the attaché's cold, unfriendly demeanor. "Follow me," she then instructed, leading the American representative to a small, well lit, carpeted conference room that consisted of a naked, wooden table and four cushioned chairs. Two guards stood outside its sole door. "Please have a seat while I get the prisoner," Natalya then offered sliding one of the cushioned chairs over to the American attaché.

"What is he being charged with?" Robert Salerno demanded to know with little warmth in his voice. He refused to take the seat.

"Right now nothing. I am..."

Before Natalya could finish, the tall attaché up at her. "Then why the hell are you holding him?"

"It's in the folder," the KGB agent quickly retorted, tossing a manila folder onto the table. Although taken aback by the American's animosity, Kalinina restrained her emotions. She drew in a deep breath and continued, "We caught him in possession of a small quantity of narcotics. We're hoping he can help us. Now if you'll excuse me, I'll go and get him."

ВЕСНА РУССКАЯ

Once Natalya left, the American attaché took a seat and carefully examined the folder's contents. "Stupid kid," Salerno muttered under his breath, concluding that the American prisoner like a lot of young people his age was guilty as charged. He did not feel it was worth his while to serve the American prisoner's best interests. "Don't they know better? Especially here? How can anyone be so stupid?"

"It's about time," Michael Levine declared, more with relief than anger, upon seeing the thick, reinforced steel door open.

"I apologize for the delay, but your embassy was a little slow in sending someone. I would've spoken to you a lot sooner, but they insisted that no one was to speak to you until you had been counseled by one of their representatives," Natalya exclaimed. "I also contacted the hotel but your father was out. He'll be notified by the concierge as soon as he returns."

"I'm still a prisoner aren't I?"

"Listen. I assure you that once you supply us with a statement, you stand a good chance of being released," the agent answered leading Michael Levine into the conference room. "Your representative is in there," Natalya added, motioning for her prisoner to enter. "I'll leave you two alone," she then declared, softly shutting the door.

"Notify me when they're finished," Natalya then instructed the KGB sentry before returning to her desk. Nearly an hour passed before she was alerted to return to the conference room.

"You may question the prisoner now," Robert Salerno grudgingly declared. "But I warn you, we'll be looking into this affair and if anything happens to him, your head will roll."

34

"Are you threatening me?" Natalya demanded to know, stopping in her tracks. "Because if you are, I will not tolerate it," she then added with visible irritation. She refused to restrain herself any further. She resented the attaché's animosity towards her.

"You can call it what you like," Salerno replied with contempt. "My conclusion is that your charges are unwarranted. This is harassment on your part. The Ambassador will not stand for this," he warned full of hypocrisy, before hastily departing from KGB headquarters. Although Salerno could care less about the fate of Robert Levine, he enjoyed the sense of power it gave him to flaunt his American connections. Nothing gave him more satisfaction than threatening and putting down the Russian natives, especially young women like Natalya. To him, all Russians were primitive, simple and naive, especially the women. He harbored great hostility towards women ever since the day his wife left him. She had filed for divorce after only two months of marriage having been unable to tolerate his chauvinistic ways any longer.

Following the attaché's rude departure, Natalya regained her composure and returned to the conference room. She placed a paper pad and a recorder on the table and then took a seat facing her prisoner. "Now we're going to go over everything that has happened to you since you left the hotel this morning. Why don't you start when you left your room?" the Russian agent began.

"I can't help you," Michael Levine answered.

"What do you mean?" Natalya asked placing her hand over his hand. "You must," she softly recommended.

"I've been advised not to answer your questions."

"Don't do this to yourself," Natalya pleaded, growing even more agitated with the U.S. attaché.

"I'm sorry."

"Please don't do this to yourself," she repeated. "If you help me, I promise you that you'll be free by tonight."

"He warned me that you would make promises you had no intention of keeping. So stop pretending to be my friend."

Afterwards both sat in silence for several minutes, carefully studying the other. Each tried to figure out what the other was thinking.

"He advised you incorrectly," the KGB agent finally declared breaking the uncomfortable silence. "I'm your friend," Natalya offered. "But what does he care. He's not here, you are! As long as he can use you as some kind of pawn to further his own personal ambitions, what does he care!" she angrily spoke out, holding the American representative in contempt. "Let me tell you. We don't want you. We want whoever is responsible for setting you up. But we can't go after them without your signed statement. Trust me, we have no interest in you," the Russian agent quietly added.

"Why should I?" the American asked with bitterness in his voice. "I'm tired of being toyed with."

"Come on, please help me. I've tried my best to be your friend, but you've got to meet me half-ways. Will you do that?" Natalya asked, extending her hand half-ways across the table.

After debating the KGB agent's words for several seconds, Michael Levine reluctantly gave in. "Okay, I'll answer your questions."

"Shake on it," Natalya insisted until the American reluctantly took her outstretched hand. "Thank you," she softly exclaimed after they had shaken hands.

"When I left my room, I walked down the street to the back of the hotel complex, to go shopping."

"Did you notice anything peculiar?" the agent asked, hastily scrawling notes.

"No nothing."

"What about those two people whom you were with just prior to your arrest. I saw you give them a handful of dollars. What did you pay them for?"

"Nothing."

"Come on, I saw you give them dollars," Natalya Kalinina insisted. The American fell silent, caught by his lie. Natalya could see beads of perspiration break from his pores as he uncomfortably shifted his legs. "Okay, you know I caught you, so you might as well let it out."

"What'll happen to me now?" he asked slumping a bit forward. He was filled with concern, knowing that the agent had cornered him and that she knew that he knew it.

"Nothing if you help me. I'll overlook it. Believe me, I can understand your fear," Kalinina tried to reassure him. "So tell me, why did you pay them?"

"Okay, okay. I needed Rubles. Having only dollars, I went to exchange them for your money at this kiosk that was offering 16,000 Rubles to the dollar. But as I was about to trade them in, these two people came up to me and offered me 25,000 for each dollar. Their offer was too good to pass up."

"Did you not know that it is illegal to convert currency on the black market?"

"I swear, I did not realize that they were not legit," the American answered with a sense of panic sweeping across his body, realizing that he had just incriminated himself further. His heart pounded as he thought about the attaché's bleak warnings. "He was right, I should've kept my mouth shut," Robert thought to himself. "How could I have fallen for her supposed acts of compassion?" the American tourist further chastised himself feeling that he was doomed.

"Calm down. I assure you I will not hold it against you," Natalya gently answered. She could not help but feel pity for him. "So continue. When you exchanged currency, did you not notice anything unusual?"

"No, I did not."

"Wasn't one of them behind you?" Natalya asked, remembering how the two Russian's had positioned themselves.

"Yes, you're right. One of them stood behind me. He said that he was looking for a companion."

"And that's why you're here now."

"What do you mean?"

"I mean, they spotted us and used you as a decoy. The person behind you dropped the packet into your bag and you never knew it. They are both known drug dealers with links to organized crime. The exchange of money was nothing more than a ruse to distract you. They saw us and panicked. Fearing that we were on to them, they had to find someone to take the fall," Natalya concluded.

"And they found me."

"That is correct."

"So where do we go from here?" Am I going to be released?"

"In short time. But first you'll have to read this and sign it," Natalya instructed, handing him her narrative of the interrogation session.

Upon hearing the agent's words, the prisoner quickly picked up a pen to sign the three-page statement.

"Wait a minute," Natalya demanded, restraining the American's hand. "You must read each line before signing it. Not doing so is a good way to get yourself into further trouble."

"I just want to get the hell out of here. I trust you."

"I know you do. But for your sake, I must insist that you read it. If you do not, I will not allow you to sign it. I will tear it up and we can start over again," the Russian agent warned, confiscating the pen. Kalinina did not return the pen until she was satisfied that the American had read the entire statement and agreed with it.

"Am I going to be released now?" Michael Levine asked after signing the three-page statement.

"In short time. I'll have to file my report and get final authorization."

"So you lied to me. You're not going to release me."

"It's only a formality," Kalinina gently replied, getting up from her seat.   "By the time your father gets our message, you'll be a free man," she declared, taking the American back to his cell.

"So you're not going to release me," Michael Levine repeated as he saw the tiny cell again.

"Listen to me," Kalinina commanded. "I haven't let you down yet. I assure you, you'll be out of here before nightfall. And furthermore, I'll explain everything to your father so that he has no doubts about your innocence. Please trust me," she added before resealing the heavy, steel door.

Once back at her desk, Natalya Kalinina raced through her paperwork. She was determined to make her prisoner's stay as short and painless as possible. "Valentin, I need you to sign off on my report," the young agent requested, stepping into her supervisor's office.

"What are your findings?" Makarov asked taking the folder into his hands.

"He's innocent. He was set up. With your permission I would like to have him released and obtain an arrest warrant for the two real suspects."

"Permission granted," Valentin Makarov quickly answered. "So your first case was not that bad, да [yes]?"

"It was all right. Fortunately everything worked out well."

"Good, I'm glad to hear that," Makarov added, signing off on the authorization.

Following their brief conversation, Natalya returned to her desk and quickly punched in a request for the City Police to arrest the two drug dealers who had framed her prisoner. Satisfied upon seeing the computer confirm retrieval of her request, Kalinina got up and returned to the American's cell to set him free.

"One minute, please," the receptionist interrupted Natalya. "Mr. Levine is here for his son. What should I tell him?"

"I'll handle it," the Russian agent replied. "In the meantime, please get an escort to bring his son up. And see to it that he gets his belongings."

"Right away."

"Спасибо [thank you]."

Upon seeing the approaching agent, Michael Levine's father promptly demanded, "What has my son done?"

"I must apologize. It was a terrible misunderstanding," Natalya Kalinina answered as she tried her best to smile at the American's livid father.

"Then why did you arrest him? In your incompetence, what did you think he had done?"

"I would rather not discuss it. All you have to know is that he is completely innocent and we will not bother you any further," the agent tersely replied as the escort reunited the younger Levine with his father.

Although she had expected to see father and son hug each other in a joyous reunion, the pair merely turned to depart with the elder Levine demanding his son to reveal the reason for his arrest. Aware of the younger Levine's discomfort, Natalya decided to deflect questioning away from the topic of his arrest. "Don't you want to apologize to me?" she asked taking the young American by his wrist, fully conscious of their first moments together when he had insulted her.

"For what?" the younger Levine asked, momentarily caught by surprise.

"Think. What did you say to me a few hours ago," she pressed him.

"Oh that," he exclaimed remembering his condescending words. "Okay, I'm sorry."

"Wait a minute. What the hell is he apologizing for?" the infuriated elder Levine demanded to know, eager to get back to the hotel and interrogate his son.

"I'm sorry, but that's between us," Natalya answered before redirecting her attention back to her former prisoner. "Apology accepted. I'm sorry too," she added, extending her hand in friendship. "By the way, I've told your father all he needs to know about this unfortunate misunderstanding," she added as they shook hands. "Most importantly, I've told him of your innocence, so if he presses you for further details, that is something you'll have to decide to discuss on your own. And please try to put aside this unfortunate incident and enjoy your remaining stay in Russia," Kalinina continued, trying to smile. before the Levines stepped into a chartered limousine and departed.

Throughout the duration of the ride, the elder Levine angrily accused his son of disgracing his reputation and jeopardizing his business dealings. He did not care what the young KGB agent had said. "You keep getting into trouble

41

and I'll have no clients," Michael's father continued thinking of the potential amounts of money he could lose. "I don't need you drawing unfavorable attention to us!" he went on.

Unaware of the senior Levine's tirade, Natalya Kalinina could not help but feel satisfaction that justice had been served when the young American was released and the two drug dealers subsequently arrested. In her satisfaction, the young agent had failed to recognize the strained relationship between father and son that she had witnessed.

The favorable outcome had reinforced her confidence. During this moment of triumph, Natalya Kalinina never suspected that her victory would be very short-lived and that she was about to undergo the most serious crisis of her 21 years of existence.

Chapter 4

A day later when Natalya returned from lunch with her St. Petersburg University classmate and colleague, Elena Potapova, she picked up her first hint of trouble. A feeling of foreboding swept over Natalya as she entered the KGB offices. Despite the bright, radiant sunshine, the office appeared dark and depressing. Thick, dark clouds of restraint hung over the busy headquarters, enveloping thoughts of the cheerful lunch she just had. Each time Natalya tried to brush aside her thoughts, she found that she could not do so. The more she tried to concentrate on her work, the more acute her sense of isolation became. Feeling increasingly uncomfortable with each passing minute, Natalya stepped away from her desk and walked into her boss's office.

"Valentin, do you have a minute," she inquired feeling uneasy about distracting him from his work merely to talk.

"What is it, Natalya?" he asked with concern.

Seeing the concern on Valentin's face, only exasperated the young agent's uneasiness. "I get this feeling that everyone's trying to avoid me. Почему [Why]? Is there something I should know?" Natalya asked, her discomfort heightened by her boss's terse demeanor.

ВЕСНА РУССКАЯ

"No one's trying to avoid you," Makarov answered trying his best to smile. "You had that extended lunch with your friend, Elena, didn't you? She's a person. Just relax and go back to your work and before long you'll realize that your concerns were unfounded."

"No, Valentin, I'm not leaving," Natalya Kalinina replied pulling up a seat. "Not until you tell me what's going on!"

"Everything's fine, Natasha," Valentin reiterated.

"Since when have you called me `Natasha.' You always call me `Natalya!' You're a terrible liar," Kalinina quickly answered knowing that she had trapped him. "Come on, you know me. 'We're friends. As one friend to another, please tell me what's going on."

Knowing that his young subordinate had cornered him, Valentin Makarov took a deep breath. "I was hoping to avoid this, but if you insist..." his voice trailed off in resignation.

"You were hoping to avoid what? I insist that you continue," Natalya commanded.

"It involves the case you just finished."

"What about it?"

"Early this morning, the Police sent a fax to my attention. That's why I made a deal with Miss Potapova's supervisor. I wanted you to have a long lunch so that you could get away from the office."

"So that's what it was about!" Natalya began only to be interrupted by her boss.

"I didn't want to cause you any unnecessary trouble. I didn't want you to suffer any unnecessary grief."

"What exactly happened?" Natalya firmly asked.

"The Police found Michael Levine's body. He hanged himself sometime early this morning," Makarov slowly spoke clasping Natalya's hands.

"It can't be true," Natalya softly muttered taking the fax. As she read it a sense of depression exploded from her unsettled stomach. "Почему [Why]?"

"I don't know. They're investigating right now. As soon as I know something, I'll let you know."

"I'm responsible. I killed him," Natalya declared filled with pain and guilt. "It's my fault."

"Don't talk like that. You had nothing to do with it," Valentin Makarov quickly interrupted. "That's why I didn't want to tell you. I knew you would react like this, putting all blame on yourself even though none of it's your fault. I knew you would take it hard."

"It's my fault," Natalya continued, ignoring her supervisor. "It's all my fault," she quietly repeated covering her face with her hands as Valentin Makarov got up and softly shut his door.

"Listen to me, Natasha. You are not responsible for his death," Makarov spoke gently after retaking his seat.

"You don't understand but I am. If I had spoken up, maybe things could've been different."

"What're you talking about?" Makarov asked with concern.

"If I had listened to my instincts I could've prevented it."

"Are you telling me you knew he was going to kill himself, because if you are, I don't believe you! I'll hear none of it!"

"Нет [Nyet - No]! What I'm saying is that I should've spoken up when the decision was made to go after him. I could've stopped it. I should've insisted that we go after the two known dealers. But knowing that I was the junior agent

ВЕСНА РУССКАЯ

and not wanting to ruffle any feelings, I kept silent," Natalya somberly spoke, taking several deep breaths. "I was such a coward. Don't you see that I allowed us to ruin his life. No, I allowed us to destroy his life!"

"You're not a coward. There was nothing you could've done. Believe me, I've been in your position before. Even if you had said something, your partners would've ignored you."

"How can you be so certain? No one will ever know for sure. I should've at least spoken up and taken my chances."

"Natasha, listen to me. When I was your age... and don't you go telling anyone this. Promise me that."

"I promise," Natalya swore trying to smile.

"I was a rebel. Where there were feathers to be ruffled, I ruffled them. I made waves. I did not like to take orders. I spoke out regardless of how it would go with my supervisors. And you know what?" Valentin Makarov spoke, taking Natalya's young hand into his hand.

"What?" Natalya asked raising her head to look him straight in the eyes.

"Every time I suggested or merely said something, they ignored me. Those SOBs were determined to prove that they and they alone knew best. They were right all the time," he sarcastically remarked. "They could not make a mistake!"

"How did you handle it?"

"Let's just say I got cited for insubordination on several occasions. It took me to the brink of being fired before I decided to play their game. That's how I know your recommendation, regardless of how hard you would've tried to persuade them, would've done nothing to change the outcome. They were in charge and wouldn't have ceded their authority to you.   Believe me, when I speak, I speak from experience."

"Спасибо [Thank you]."

"You know why I've taken an interest in you?   You know why we're not just supervisor and subordinate, but friends?"

"Почему [Why]?"

"Because when I first met you, I could see a bit of myself in you.   You are a lot like me.   You're not afraid to express your views.   You're a very assertive young woman who can break down the toughest of people.   When you believe in something, you have conviction.   That's why I value your judgment.   Let me tell you this -- I trust your instincts as if they were my own.   And if you make a mistake because of inexperience, I know I would've made the same mistake 40 years ago."

"Спасибо [Thank you]."

"That's why I don't want to see you put yourself through this torture.   And besides, I need you.   I respect and admire you for your truthfulness and determination."

"Спасибо [Thank you]," Valentin, but it is I who admire and respect you.   Since day one I've aspired to be like you."

"You're already a lot like me, except much younger and much, much more beautiful," Makarov replied forcing a smile on Natalya's lips.   "You're not responsible for what has happened."

"You know what I like best about you?" Natalya asked feeling a small measure of relief from their conversation.

"No, tell me."

"You treat me like a person.   Not only that, but you're a true Russian at heart.   I can feel the pain you're going through every time you must serve some foreign interest.   I can see your pain when you look at how our great country has been brought to her knees."

"Natasha, if you feel as you say, I need no further proof. You are me 40 years ago. Likewise, you too, are a true Russian. Perhaps your generation will restore Russia to her past greatness."

"We'll do it together," Natalya warmly replied grasping his hand. "It's not too late for your generation. Besides, we'll need all the help we can get."

"I'll help you get started. If you don't mind, between official assignments, I'll give you additional work aimed at liberating our country. You must tell no one, though. Not even your best friends or your family. One small leak and our efforts could be destroyed. The consequences would be grave not only for you and me, but for all of Russia. If our efforts are compromised, I have no doubt that the West will not stop until we have been reduced to ruins."

"No one will know. You have my word."

"I believe you are ready to join the RNR (Russians For a New Revolution) movement consisting of members like yourself whose loyalty and love for Russia is limitless. I must warn you, though, that you will never know who is involved except when absolutely necessary," Makarov spoke. "I'll fill you in on more at another time. In the meantime, this last part of our conversation never took place."

"Agreed," Natalya firmly answered unaware that Valentin Makarov, having given her a new and extremely difficult and dangerous goal to strive for, had lifted her sagging spirits, renewing her confidence.

The brief respite proved most to Natalya especially when she walked the six blocks to Moscow Police Station No. 12. However, before long, her mind was again tormented by reoccurring feelings of guilt. Obtaining and reading the suicide note did not help matters. She sank into deeper depression.

> *My family doesn't believe in my innocence. They insist on my guilt and claim that the only reason I was freed was to satisfy the American Embassy. Nothing I say or do can repair the damage. With my reputation ruined and no family to turn to or anyone to believe in me except for maybe one person, I have no other choice. Life is no longer worth living especially when all your family cares about is their reputation and their income. I hope by my death everyone will realize what they have done and how wrong they were.*
>
> *Michael Levine*

Natalya held the note in her hands for several minutes. She read and re-read its contents, desperately grasping for something that could absolve her troubled conscience. In the blindness of her pain, she found nothing. In frustration, Natalya reluctantly gave up, blinded by her intense feelings of guilt. Then to add further nails to her self-crucifixion, Natalya made a photocopy of the suicide note to present to her supervisor. After carefully folding her copy and placing it in her pocket, the distraught agent headed back to KGB headquarters.

"Valentin, I was right. I didn't do enough. Look here! I am responsible for his death," Natalya broke down, thrusting the copy in front of her supervisor. "Nothing I can ever do will bring him back."

"You did what you had to do," Valentin quickly answered sliding the note back to the young agent. "I don't care what it says. You did not kill him. He killed himself," Makarov declared, refusing to read the copy.

"Maybe there was something more I could've done," Kalinina shot back. "I did a terrible job in convincing his father of his innocence. Now he's dead!"

"You spoke to him. You told him everything you had to. It is not your fault that he refused to take you at your word. If anyone, he must bear the guilt. He's the one who refused to stand by his own son!"

"I don't dispute that. But still I find myself asking if there was something... anything that I could've said or done. Why didn't I see that his father didn't care to believe me. How couldn't I have seen how cold and uncaring he was?"

"You couldn't have read his mind," Makarov retorted, growing increasingly impatient with Natalya's stubbornness.

"Still, I cannot... I guess my instincts and judgment are not so good after all."

"Damn it, stop torturing yourself," Valentin demanded snatching back the note. "If you're going to trouble me with this nonsense, I might as well read that damn thing," he added quickly scanning through the note's contents. What Valentin read made him stop short.

"What is it?"

"In your self-imposed misery you don't even want to or can't even read it right. Look right here!" Makarov demanded sliding the note back holding his finger under five words – 'except for maybe one person' which had been squeezed into the note's text as an afterthought. "You're vindicated! In no uncertain terms he wrote that to clear you, because he damn well knew that you had believed in him."

"Little good that did. It was not enough to deter his suicide. I took away everyone in his life and left him only with me. What good was that? When he would get back to America, he would have no one."

"Natalya, I don't want to hear anything more of it. There are only three guilty parties -- Michael Sr., Michael Jr. and the American attaché, whatever the hell his name is," Valentin Makarov angrily declared crumpling the note. "Girl, if you don't pull yourself together, then you will not only be responsible for destroying the life of a wonderful person, but also of causing undue pain to your mother, myself and everyone else who cares about you," Valentin added tossing the note into his wastebasket.

"Maybe I should resign and look for another line of work," Kalinina reluctantly suggested.

"If you do, I will not accept it. You resign and you betray Russia. And for that I'll never forgive you!" Makarov angrily vowed.

Badly shaken by her supervisor's harsh words, Natalya sat in silence for several minutes. She agonized over her limited options. His anger had hit at the very heart of her identity -- her great love for Russia.

Watching Natalya suffer filled Valentin with sympathy. "I'm sorry for yelling at you. It's just that..." he tried to apologize.

"You have no need to apologize," Kalinina cut him off. "I'm the one who should apologize for wasting your afternoon with my problems."

"Natalya. Natalya, please listen to me. Please answer me -- do you still have respect for me?" Makarov inquired in growing desperation.

"You know I do, Valentin."

51

"Then out of that respect for me I implore you, please don't resign. Please don't be so hard on yourself."

"What choice do I have? I mean, if I don't resign, then how can I get rid of this pain and guilt?"

"First go to Church. The Cathedral of the Annunciation [located within the Kremlin's walls] would be a good place."

"Me? I haven't gone since I was a little girl?" Natalya answered feeling uncomfortable at the prospect. During those years Natalya had merely attended the orthodox services to placate her babushka.

"You're not alone. I haven't gone much either. But deep down... Somehow, somewhere there must be a God," Valentin answered knowing that even agnostics like himself could always go call on God without feeling any guilt. "Sometimes when I find myself in need or in trouble, I stop by to pray for a few minutes. If there is a greater power, it can't hurt asking for His help. And if there isn't – the quiet, the solitude will still help. Also, take some time off and share your feelings with your friends and family. You'll find that talking will help a lot. In time your pain will heal," Makarov assured Natalya, placing his arm on her shoulder. "I'll give you as much time as you need. Don't worry about a thing. I'll make sure that you and your family are taken care of," he offered.

Natalya quietly listened to her boss's words, desperately trying to grasp at anything that might help comfort her heavy heart. "Listen to him. You've always believed in him before. Don't fail now!" she commanded herself, struggling to resist her desire to question Makarov's words.

"Tell me Natalya, when your father died, how did you handle it? What did you do then?"

"I was only six then."

"That's old enough to feel the loss. How did you cope knowing that you would never see him again and that he would never be there again to play with you or to read you a story?"

"My mom and babushka helped me through it."

"Precisely. So when they comforted you, did they not put aside their own feelings of pain?"

"Yes. They put up a strong front whenever I was around," Natalya softly answered recalling that painful chapter in her life when her mother and babushka restrained their own feelings of grief to be there for her in her time of need. Natalya could vividly remember the day when she caught her mother off guard in the privacy of her bedroom. She could still see her mother sobbing uncontrollably, her face buried in a pillow.

"How long did your mother take off from work?"

"Two or three days. I don't quite remember. But you must know, she had no choice. She had to work to support me," Natalya quickly answered.

"Well you also have to work to make life easier for your mother and babushka," Valentin countered. "But as I said, I'll give you as much time as you need. Don't worry about pay. I'll make sure you receive your salary."

"Большое спасибо [Thank you very much]."

"During that time, I don't want you to worry about anything. Take it easy, pray, and be open with your friends and family. You have to get all that pain out of yourself before you'll ever find peace again. And remember, if you need me, I'll always be here for you."

"Большое спасибо [Thank you very much]," Natalya replied with gratitude, getting up from her seat.

53

ВЕСНА РУССКАЯ

"I need you," Makarov added, taking her hand into his. "I need the Natalya Kalinina I know, not some other Natalya."

"Большое спасибо [Thank you very much]," the young agent softly answered, throwing her arms around Valentin. "Большое спасибо [Thank you very much]," Natalya quietly repeated tightly embracing her supervisor who wiped away her tears. "I don't know what I would do without you," she gratefully added before regaining her composure and departing on a leave of absence.

"If there's anything I can do, please do not hesitate to contact me," Valentin Makarov called after Natalya as she departed. "I'll always be here when you need me."

With the time off, Natalya Kalinina gradually recovered. With each passing day, the young agent grew stronger as her feelings pain and guilt slowly subsided. With the time away from the office and a combination of quiet reflection, prayer and talking, the Natalya of old returned. During this healing period, a strong bond of friendship and trust developed between Natalya and her boss. Without his constant comfort and support, it was unlikely that she would have recovered. With this episode, he became the father she had missed for the last 15 years and she became the daughter he had never had.

Chapter 5

Deep in thought about the dreadful events of two years ago, Natalya Kalinina never saw her supervisor, Valentin Makarov depart back to his office nor did she notice the arrival of her former classmate and friend, Elena Potapova, who silently stood next to her for several seconds before interrupting. "Natasha," Elena called out distracting Kalinina from her painful thoughts. "What are you doing? It must be awful important since you didn't notice me. I've been standing here for nearly five minutes!" Elena exaggerated.

"Lena, what are you doing here?" Natalya cried out with surprise, relieved to have the painful thoughts jarred from her mind. "I thought you were in the field," she exclaimed getting up to embrace Elena whom she had not seen for more than a month.

"I was, but we finished our end sooner than we had anticipated," Potapova replied. "Please, sit down. Stay a while. Talk to me," Natalya urged, sliding a chair to her friend.

"Why not." Elena answered taking the seat.

"So how did it turn out? Did you shut down the ring and get the culprits, or did the West no longer need our services?" Kalinina inquired knowing that her friend had

ВЕСНА РУССКАЯ

been part of a KGB team working in "partnership" with American and German intelligence agents on a massive counterfeiting ring that had produced $100 notes and 50 Deutsch Mark notes that were next to impossible to distinguish from the genuine bills, even through the use of optical scanning devices. She knew that KGB agents were only used because the illicit ring operated out of Tblisi, Georgia (a former Soviet Republic) and used Russia as a major storage and transit point. It was more out of desperation, to preserve the seeming invincibility of their currencies that the West had requested KGB assistance.

"They no longer needed us," Elena replied. "It's the usual. We do the legwork for them. We put our lives on the line, and then when we get close to solving the case, they push us aside and take all the credit," she added with bitterness and frustration. "No one ever mentions how much we helped. In fact they don't even acknowledge us."

"Of course. We're Russians after all. All we have to do is keep them happy. It's like with a dog. They make it perform tricks and when it delivers, the masters pride themselves on how good they are. They never think that it was actually the dog that did the hard work."

"I think in their arrogant pride, they congratulate themselves so much, they sometimes even forget the dog exists! I'll bet the poor thing doesn't even get a biscuit," Elena added as both laughed.

"How many of them have even made an effort to learn Russian?" Natalya then ventured, as both laughed, well aware of the answer.

"Well there was this one American agent, who had been here for the last nine years. He was always trying to impress the Germans with his knowledge of our language. Every time one of the German agents asked him a question he would start with 'нет [nyet - no]' or 'я [ja].' He could never get it straight – 'да [da]' was 'yes,' not 'я [ja]!' It was so funny. We had to fight to restrain our laughter while the Germans out of politeness went along with him."

"What a jerk!"

"Even the Germans said so in private!"

Both again laughed before growing serious.

"It's really frustrating. Whenever I work with them, I mean for them, I have to do the grunt work. I never get challenging tasks. Not once have I been able to see one of these cases through from the start to the finish. Just once I would like to see the whole case, not the morsels they throw at us like some kind of bone," Elena Potapova complained, bitter about the Western attitude towards Russians.

"Join the club, товарищ [tovarishch - comrade]," Natalya answered, placing her hand on Elena's shoulder to comfort her. "Or should I say 'друг' [friend], since our colonial masters don't like connotations that remind them of our past greatness," she sarcastically added.

"Please use 'товарищ [comrade],'" Elena quickly answered. "'друг [friend]' just doesn't sound right. It lacks the warmth and meaning of 'товарищ [comrade].'"

"You can say that again, товарищ [comrade]!" Natalya Kalinina replied thinking back to the history books and 1993 when the United States stepped up its quest to colonize Russia, employing the term "joint-cooperation."

The United States, and its Western allies to a lesser degree, began to consolidate their gains over Russia in September 1993, after a year of applying intense pressure to get Russia to conform to their will. They cruelly utilized offers of bribes, which they had no intention of living up to, and when that did not work, they issued oblique threats of dire consequences. After months of constant unrelenting pressure they broke the Russian spirit, adding a new painful chapter to her history.

The first signs of Russia's broken will were revealed when the United States Government announced in the early part of that month that they and Russia had reached an accord of cooperation in the fields of Space and Oil Production. In reality this cooperation agreement marked the beginning of U.S. colonial exploitation.

The space agreement locked Russia into a subservient role of inferiority, despite the fact that Russian space-station technology greatly surpassed that of the United States. Likewise Russia's database on the physiological and psychological effects of long-term space endurance was far superior to America's miniscule records. When the agreement was announced, Russia was still the only country in the world with an inhabitable space station in orbit and the only State that routinely sent crews of cosmonauts to live in space for more than a year at a time.

"Khasbulatov was right when he said that the Russian Government (referring to U.S. backed President Boris Yeltsin who had deposed President Mikhail Gorbachev in an illegal coup two years earlier) was conducting "a foreign policy of national humiliation, the policy of a lackey,"[1] Elena Potapova also reflecting back to September 1993, quoted Ruslan Khasbulatov, leader of the Russian Parliament (1990-93).

"And our humiliation and subservience continue to this day. We're just like the 19th century serfs," Natalya Kalinina declared, backing her friend's statement.

"Only worse off. At least the serfs had ample amounts of food. Today we have ничего [nichevo - nothing]! I don't even know what 'quality of life' means anymore."

"It means we survive another day to serve them," Natalya answered thinking back to the beginning of that fateful September 1993.

Prior to the breakup of the Soviet Union, the Americans, still locked in a cold-war mentality had planned to build their own space station. They mocked the Soviet Mir Space Station as a primitive obsolete outpost, vowing to do better. However, by 1992, the U.S. space station project still had not gotten off the drawing boards. It was severely plagued by huge cost-overruns and chronic mismanagement.

During that year, with hopes of attaining a mutual relationship with their one-time adversary, the Russians in a gesture of goodwill offered to share Mir Space Station with the Americans as "equal partners." The Americans arrogantly rejected. They refused to accept anything that fell short of giving them control.

Despite the lack of gratitude by the United States, Russia made another offer. They offered to cooperate in a joint-venture construction project of a new space station. The Americans again spurned the Russians, and refused to consider any joint-efforts until it became apparent that they could not succeed on their own. By this time, the U.S. and its allies had done considerable damage to Russia's past invincibility. Victimized by the West's gruesome rape of the Ruble, Russia became vulnerable to their deceptive tactics. To further compound matters, the Executive Branch of the Russian Government had become subservient to its colonial backers. Fully aware of this, the United States wasted no time in implementing its program of space exploitation. The U.S. allowed Russia to assist in the construction of an international space station as long as Moscow abided by the following restrictions:

1. Limit its sales of missile technology.
2. Limit the number of satellite launches it conducted for the international community to an American formulated 8 over 7 years and
3. Fix its launch bids within an American-established tolerance range

On the other hand, the United States placed no limits on its own weapons exports and gave the Russians no say over the quantity and price of satellite launches conducted by NASA (the U.S. Space Agency) over this same seven-year period. In short, the Russians did all of the giving and the U.S. did all of the taking. They opened their space station to American astronauts, agreed to confine their space program within American-dictated parameters, and subsidized a portion of the construction costs of building the new space station, reducing the amount the U.S. had to put up!

Furthermore, despite Russian superiority in space station technology and the fact that Russia had already produced an inhabitable station, the U.S. Government arrogantly questioned Russia's "ability to fulfill the deal!"2 In doing so, the United States ignored its own incompetence and failure to deliver!

Consistent with the Space Agreement, the Oil Production Agreement was also created solely to satisfy U.S. interests. Determined to reverse its strategically unsound policy of over-dependence on Middle Eastern oil, the U.S. Government drew up an agreement that enabled America to exploit Siberia's rich oil fields.

To accomplish this, the U.S. established an investment fund and provided Moscow with $2.5 Billion in loans under the pretext that these monies would enable Russia to purchase much needed parts to re-open her dormant wells, thus increasing her export revenues.

In reality the agreement consisted of a two-fold strategy exploit Russia's resources and make her more dependent on the West. American companies were given direct control over Russia's oil fields and the new debt gave Washington greater leverage over Russia's economic viability. The two tools of exploitation worked in the following manner:

1. Monies from the investment fund to encourage "private investment" in the Russian oil-sector enabled U.S. Oil Companies to gain control over the rich Siberian Oil fields. With control over the Siberian oil fields, the U.S. was able to deplete Russian reserves to satisfy its own interests and potentially deprive Moscow of oil supplies from her own fields. At the same time, Russia no longer had any recourse.

2. The loans pushed Russia further into debt, increasing her vulnerability to

> economic war and like such
> attacks (e.g. currency
> manipulation, etc.).

Another even greater series of injustices also began in 1993 when two unscrupulous U.S. joined forces to defraud Ukraine, a neighboring former Soviet Republic. These companies deliberately sold more than 195,000 bags of rotting fungi-covered, moldy corn seeds to Ukraine to enhance their profits despite their prior knowledge that these seeds were incapable of germination. Otherwise the only alternative would have been to market them to ranchers as cattle feed resulting in a 50¢ per bag loss. Also to further exasperate matters, these same companies sold 200 farm combines to Ukraine at $143,000 each, an unconscionable 59% markup over original cost.

To ensure their profits, these American companies concealed their price gouging for the mechanized combines and falsely declared that test samples projected a 92% germination rate (the minimum acceptable tolerance rate for American farmers) when in fact their results showed a 30% rate. They also took upfront payment to limit possible recourse by Kiev.

Although the terms of their sales contract were so unfavorable, Ukrainian officials went along due to bribes of cars and jeeps even though these bribes violated the U.S. Foreign Corrupt Practices Act.

When the seeds were planted only 10% yielded a harvest. Many farms like the Gigant Collective, which had planted 250 acres of the fungi-covered seeds failed to yield a single cornstalk. Furthermore, in spite of the meager yields, the two unapologetic organizations skimmed an extra $10 Million from the bitter harvest. Driven by immoral greed

("We are in business and our goal was to make a profit. We are not a charitable organization")3, they were more concerned about making money than worrying if innocents starved as a result of their faulty products.

To compound this injustice, the U.S. Government refused to prosecute the two criminal organizations since poor harvests would put the former Soviet Republics at their greater mercy. In taking no action, Washington indirectly encouraged additional fraudulent agricultural deals with Russia and the other former Soviet States.

Past deals like these did not bode well with Natalya Kalinina and her friend, Elena Potapova. Both, despite having lived all of their lives in an "Era of Russian Capitulation" could not understand how their leaders could have knowingly sold out their beloved homeland. It was the continuation of these policies through the decades that caused the greatest hurt among most Russians. In response to the growing numbers of capitulations and failed promises of prosperity under "Western-style Capitalism" Russians had become so disillusioned that they lost all faith in their Government. Having lost faith, the majority of Russians imprisoned themselves behind thick walls of apathy, rendering themselves helpless in halting their leaders' West induced dismemberment of their country. These lackeys along with the tiny, unconscionable entrepreneurial class had gained such control over the country that they were able to commit daily acts of treason with impunity.

Constant reminders in the daily lives of Natalya Kalinina and Elena Potapova made them weep for Russia. The warm tears filled their hearts with pain. Each new crime perpetrated against their beloved homeland and heritage made the Russian blood that flowed through their veins boil with rage. As Russia sank deeper into the dark abyss, her identity, the very meaning of her existence, became increasingly threatened.

To accomplish their de-facto conquest, the United States and its Western cohorts had relentlessly attacked the Russian economy with massive doses of psychological warfare. By 1992, the Russian people had been brainwashed into believing in the superiority of Western "hard-currencies" over their once sacred Rubles.

Having gained control over the Russian financial system, the imperialist sharks implemented the second phase of their operations, also in 1993. With the objective of destroying the already vulnerable economy, they urged the Russian government to float the Ruble on the free market, arguing that this was the only remedy for Russia's economic crisis.

Deceived into believing that their currency would suddenly gain the same level of respect as the West's "hard-currencies," the Russian Government relented. Instead of the stability and respect that the West had promised, the Ruble was quickly reduced to 1/2000th of its past value. With the Ruble's disintegration, the West, to the envy of loan sharks everywhere around, legally inflated Russian debt 2000-fold. As a result, the Russian economy fell at the complete mercy of enemies who had routinely extended false facades of friendship to entice them.

Through history, it was no coincidence that the U.S. and its Western allies always maintained their monetary advantage over just about every nation that did not belong to their elite "Group of Seven" (Group of so-called economic powers -- The United States, Canada, England, France, Germany, Japan and Italy). It was the only way they could perpetuate colonialism on much of the world and keep it in a perpetual state of poverty without having to directly take part in spilling the blood of their slaves or risk-taking casualties in quelling periodic revolts.

By 1997, these elite nations had become so emboldened that they attacked and manipulated the currencies of many of their key rivals, focusing primarily on much of Asia and Latin America. Another attack was launched against the Ruble in 1998. Only after fears that these attacks would eventually impair their own economies, evidenced by wide-spread market contractions, did this group relent and offer assistance to favored countries such as Brazil and South Korea, that had inadvertently fallen victim to their evil attacks.

In accordance with this policy, the value of the Ruble was reduced in a series of Western-controlled manipulations (called "trades"), every time the Russian Government tried to stabilize its rapidly deteriorating economy by issuing credits. The West justified this by calculating the credits into "Rubles in circulation" figures. At the same time, the United States, in an effort to maintain the strong value of its Dollar, refused to consider their T-Bills and Bonds (the equivalent of Russian credits) as additional "currency in circulation." In short, the Ruble suffered and the U.S. Dollar went unscathed every time additional debt was issued by their respective governments.

Aleksandr Rutskoi, a 20th century Decembrist hero and Constitutional Russian President for a week before being ousted by Yeltsin accurately described Russia's predicament, which continued to persist after two decades of "reforms" when he declared that "before Yeltstin there were no beggars, no children peddling pornography. This is not freedom or democracy. It's pure colonialism. The [U.S.] dollar is Russia's national currency now. The ruble is just a candy wrapper. We've handed our sword to America..."4

ВЕСНА РУССКАЯ

These Western practices of double-standards and hypocrisy infuriated the two KGB agents the most. Neither could understand why the U.S. with a burgeoning debt of $10.5 Trillion could go unscathed while their once, proud country fell deeper into ruin. "Someday we'll hold them to account," Elena Potapova angrily vowed. "They can't keep us and the rest of the world enslaved forever."

"Don't worry, they too will fall. Look at Rome. Two thousand years ago, who could've imagined her collapse," Natalya Kalinina added.

"No one thought that about the Soviet Union either," Elena replied, trying to lift their sagging spirits.

"Don't start with me," Natalya warned, before growing serious. Then in a hushed tone, she added, "I'm not supposed to tell you this just yet, but since it's only a technicality, I'll go ahead. My boss, being the rebel that he is, has had a group of us conducting secret analyses on the United States, looking for chinks in its armor."

"Are you serious?" Elena whispered.

"Да [Yes], but please be aware that I'm only telling you this because you're my friend, I've gotten a little latitude and most of all, because I trust you. You will not speak to anyone about this, will you?"

"Нет [Nyet]."

"Promise me."

"I promise you. Go on," Elena then urged.

"Through our analyses, we're beginning to see cracks in the American Empire. Personally, if you ask me, I think their increased aggressiveness is a symptomatic of this. They're trying to conceal their growing vulnerability. America's false sense of invincibility is crumbling! They're like a cornered, injured animal, most dangerous yet most vulnerable. They will succumb."

66

"Then we will be free soon?" Elena cautiously ventured.

"Eventually. Maybe not tomorrow, but eventually. Every people, once pushed far enough into a corner, will realize that they have nothing more to lose. We're getting there, and when we do, we'll muster up the courage and throw away our chains!"

"I hope it's sooner than later. I don't know how much more we can take. I want my grandparents to be around to experience this newfound freedom. Tell me, Natasha, how many people are in on this."

"I don't know. Valentin has avoided telling anyone. It is part of a pact, just in case someone betrays us. That way no one will be able to find out the identities of everyone involved. Only Valentin, who is willing to suffer and even die for Russia, can be implicated."

"He is very brave."

"I know and I admire him for it. I don't think there is anyone in the world who can break him. He would rather die with honor than capitulate."

"That's good, because if the United States ever found out, they would ruthlessly interrogate and torture him and demand his execution for treason."

"Treason against whom?" Natalya sarcastically huffed. "They've been planting submarines in our Bering Strait for years without our permission - so why can't we do the same. If being a friend means spying on your friend and stabbing him in the back, then we'll gladly reciprocate in the spirit of friendship!"

"I'm with you one-hundred percent."

"I also want to tell you another secret," Natalya quietly resumed, changing the line of their discussion. "Valentin is looking for more agents who are willing to work for Russia during light periods -- agents who would be willing

to destroy their careers and reputations, and if necessary, give up their lives for Russia. He wants people who can be trusted. I want you to know that I
have recommended you and Valentin has already approved. That is the only reason why I've spoken to you about this. It is only a matter of time before you get transferred under his supervision. Then we'll be together."

"I'm honored. Спасибо [Thank you]. Большое спасибо [Thank you very much], Natasha," Elena whispered with gratitude, getting up and embracing her friend. "You don't know what this means to me."

"I do," Natalya quietly countered. "I'm Russian too. I feel the same pain. But someday it'll all be a nightmare of the past. We'll be able to breathe the fresh country air again. We'll get back our rural cottages and be able to share them like we had in summers of the past," she wishfully sighed.

"The cottages they stole from us!" Elena interjected.

"We'll be able to walk through the cool pine forests and sit lazily by the our country lakes, fishing with none of the urban hassles on our minds. We'll even be able to tend our own gardens again. And when that day comes, you'll be able to take pride in knowing that you helped Russia liberate herself. There will be no more entrepreneurial class to prey on the helpless. There will be no more entrepreneurial class to flaunt their ill-amassed fortunes. Try as they might, they'll never strangle us. They'll never suffocate the breath from Russia, nor stifle her heartbeat. They will not succeed in extinguishing our soul. You agree, да [yes]?"

"Most definitely. History is on our side," Elena Potapova exclaimed, knowing the dark Era of Humiliation and Capitulation could not extend forever.

"Tell me, Lena, what do you have to do this afternoon?" Natalya changed the subject.

"What have you got on your mind?"

"First tell me what you have to do?"

"Ничего [Nothing]," Elena replied willing to cast aside thoughts of returning to her desk and the mundane tasks requested of her by the CIA, should a more palatable opportunity arise.

"Very well. Then you can help me get through this," Natalya answered, handing her friend a packet of papers relating to her China assignment. "I know it's not what you had in mind," she apologized before continuing. "But all you have to do is read though these reports and come up with your own conclusion, for our Western masters. Normally I would put these reports aside, but since I promised Valentin that I would complete them by this evening I cannot do so. I don't want to let him down. Consider it playing along in the name of deception. Tomorrow I will help you," Natalya then added as they laughed.

Both could not count the many times they had promised to help each other only to forget or be too tied up the next morning, causing the Americans to growl with impatience when their imposed deadlines came and went without results. In addition to the delays, the American-assigned tasks sometimes disappeared all together, into "a massive black hole of Russian bureaucracy," as both liked to joke, aware that their supervisors would not hold them accountable, since they had always delivered when it was absolutely necessary. "That way we can go out and celebrate our growing revolution, Natalya declared."

"Sure thing, товарищ [Comrade]," Elena replied between bouts of laughter, knowing they had a reputation to live up to. She knew they had to reinforce the stereotype of their imperial masters that "Russian, Laziness, and Incompetence" were all synonymous with each other. It was

69

an effective way to lure their colonial masters into a false sense of security.

"Talk to you later," Elena added before departing, still chuckling, as she visualized the image of "an aggressive, imperialistic American Eagle angrily glaring down at the double-headed Russian eagle that was lazily looking everywhere but where it should."

1 Newsweek (NY: Newsweek, Inc., October 4, 1993), p. 69.
2 The New York Times (September 3, 1993), p. 1.
3 Raymond bonner et al., "A Bitter Harvest for Ukraine From U.S. Seed Deal," (The New York Times: June 19, 1994), P. 14.
4 Maynard Parker, "Inside the Kremlin: The Man in Charge," (Newsweek: May 2, 1994), p. 49.

Chapter 6

The large crowds, many of them tourists and sightseers, bustled along the well-lit floors, walking over and underneath the majestic, ornate bridges and balconies that decorated GUM Department Store. Many peered into the windows the numerous baroque-style Russian storefronts that lined each of GUM's three floors.

The tourists easily stood out from the natives by the cameras they carried, the colorful imports they wore, and their reluctance to venture into shops above the first and second floors that contained most of the souvenir shops. The Russian-made ties, suits, blouses, lingerie, housewares and hygiene products were only of interest to Muscovites who hunted around for the best bargains, oblivious to the majestic 19th century chandeliers that brightly reflected off the mirrored-stucco walls and glass-vaulted ceiling.

The many voices of Russian, English, Japanese, and German, the sounds of hundreds of footsteps plodding across the hard floors, and the gushing of GUM's majestic fountain blended into a bazaar-like cacophony.

After entering the huge Victorian shopping center (22,680 sq. meters) which had celebrated its 120th anniversary a year earlier in 2013, Natalya Kalinina sighed

71

with disgust as she passed the Western-run first floor shops and came across the small pockets of "entrepreneurs," all dressed in the finest foreign apparel, who were negotiating deals in a modern well-lit shop next to Улица Куйбышева [Kuibysheva Street]. Its large-screen, high-resolution digital TV's, camcorders and state-of-the-art DVD players and flat-screens were all out of the price range of ordinary Russians.

With a bitter taste in her mouth, Natalya proceeded up the stairs to a small shop selling housewares. She then waited on line for nearly five minutes before making her order. After receiving a ticket listing the quantity and price of the detergent, soap, and shampoo she wanted, the Muscovite woman moved to a second line where she waited to pay the middle-aged cashier. The cashier carefully examined each ticket as she rang up the order

Despite the growing availability of calculators, the Cashier, out of custom, added the price of each listed item a two-colored wooden abacus. As a result, this line moved the slowest out of them all. Upon compiling the total, the Cashier shouted instructions to another clerk who gathered and wrapped them. After paying, Natalya had to wait on a third line to receive her items.

Despite the large number of Western-run shops at GUM, that maintained only one queue to pay a cashier who utilized a computerized hand-held bar-code scanner and allowed their customers to physically examine and select their own goods, most Russian-run shops continued to adhere to the same tiring practices that had predated the Bolshevik Revolution in 1917 -- a process which proved too cumbersome and confusing to most foreigners.

As Natalya Kalinina walked towards the staircase, she noticed a young man standing on line at a small Russian clothing shop - "Красная Заря [Krasnaya Zarya]." Although Natalya was sure she knew him, some doubts persisted since she could not see his face. Only when he turned around to move into the final line, did Natalya know for sure.

Carrying her shopping bag in her left hand, Natalya walked up to him and placed her right hand on his shoulder. "Remember me?" she asked, catching him by surprise.

"Aren't you the young woman who attacked me on New Year's Day?" the American asked in fluent Russian referring to the time when the Muscovite had jumped him in Красная Площадь [Red Square].

"Нет [Nyet]! You're the one who attacked me!" Natalya objected.

"It was necessary, because you were taking advantage of your little sister. I felt sorry for her."

"You mean, my cousin. So we meet again! So how are you?" Natalya inquired, taking hold of the coarse, brown paper that the shop clerk was wrapping the American's clothing in. Unlike in Western-run stores where items were placed into bags, it was a tradition for Russian clerks to wrap everything, including such minute items as postcards.

To speed up the process, Natalya firmly held the paper in place while the clerk applied strips of tape.

"I'm fine. What about you?"

"That's good to hear. I'm also fine," Natalya answered as the American took his package. "What is your name?"

"Jim Keating. What about yours?"

"I'm Natalya Kalinina," the Russian introduced herself. "The last time we never got each other's names. Are you American?"

"Да [Yes], I'm American," Jim answered. "I don't have to ask your nationality. I know you're Russian!"

73

ВЕСНА РУССКАЯ

"How?" Natalya asked in a somewhat serious tone of voice, trying to act a little surprised.

"With a name like Natalya, what else could you be? Every woman here is either a Natalya, Tamara, Tatyana, Olga or an Elena." Keating replied in good nature.

"Every man in America is named Jim, Mike, John, or Tom," the Muscovite countered.

"With you I can never win, can I?"

"No you can't," Natalya answered. She then suggested, "Let's go get an ice cream and sit by the fountain," after taking the American by the arm. "You have time, don't you?"

"Do I have a choice?" Jim asked, fully conscious of the Russian's grip on his arm.

"Нет [Nyet]!"

"Okay, then let's go."

For a brief moment, both went in silence, walking down the stairs to the first floor until they came to one of GUM's many ice-cream stands. "Here, I'll take this," Jim offered relieving Natalya of her shopping bag.

"Спасибо [Thank you]. What kind of ice cream would you like?"

"Anything you don't take for yourself," Keating teased his Russian friend.

"For that I order for both of us," Natalya countered, playfully striking the American with her hand. She then ordered the same flavor, "butter-pecan" drowned in rum, for both of them."

"10,000 Rubles," the shop clerk requested, handing Natalya two cones.

"Here, I'll pay," Jim offered momentarily searching for a 10,000-ruble coin. "It's so hard find any coins these days!" He added upon finding a dull coin to pay the cashier.

"Спасибо [Thank you]," Kalinina thanked the clerk, before redirecting her attention at the American's remark as they turned towards the majestic, Victorian fountain. "That's because you Americans destroyed our currency!" she rebutted.

Knowing that Natalya's words had some truth to them, Jim chose not to respond.

"Did I offend you?" Natalya quickly asked, immediately becoming conscious of her friend's discomfort at her remark. "I'm sorry," she apologized.

"No harm done," Jim reassured Kalinina, placing their bags on the floor and taking a seat by the fountain.

"Tell me, since you're American, why were you shopping for Russian goods?" Natalya asked handing Jim his cone. "No offense intended, but don't most Westerners prefer the likes of Estée Lauder and Nike?"

"I can buy their products at home. Besides I don't want to look too conspicuous."

"Like the `entrepreneurial class?'"

"Excuse me?"

Seeing that her friend did not understand the meaning of her remark, Natalya took his hand and pointed to a group of well-dressed young men wearing dark imports, gold cufflinks and sunglasses. "You know, like those people over there."

"Oh, them. I guess you could say that. Besides I have to live here, so I don't want to make any enemies nor be mistaken for some Mafioso."

"I'm impressed. Many of your compatriots are insensitive to our feelings. They openly flaunt their wealth. Don't think I'm referring to you in any way. You understand don't you? Да [Yes]? Natalya asked, again taking hold of her friend. She did not want to unknowingly offend him in anyway.

"Sure I do. I know things are tough here," Jim Keating answered placing his hand over the Russian's hand. "You don't have to worry about offending me. I worry more about offending you," he added before momentarily pausing. "Between the both of us, I get embarrassed every time our embassy uses those large stretch limos."

"You work for the U.S. Government?" the Muscovite ventured. "Which branch?"

"Let's say foreign affairs."

"I understand. I won't press you any further if you won't press me, Natalya offered, aware that she was also in an uncomfortable position. "I'm in the same situation. I work for our Government and also deal with foreign affairs. I hope this won't get in the way of our friendship."

"I don't think it will. It shouldn't," Keating assured her.

"Good. So tell me, where in America are you from?"

"New York City."

"What's it like? I've seen pictures. Are the buildings really as big as they look?"

"Да [Yes]. In New York, 50 stories is nothing. Many are well over 50 floors. Two of them, which I'm sure you've seen pictures of, are taller than 100 stories. Another two used to be, but 9/11 changed all that."

"I know. I'm sorry about that," Natalya gave her condolences well aware of the September 2001 day when terrorists attacked New York City and Washington, D.C. murdering 3000+ people. After pausing for a brief moment, the Muscovite continued. "On the other hand, don't all those tall buildings make it depressing when they block out the sunlight?"

"When you live in New York, you get used to it," Jim answered.

"And the crowds and traffic. How can you live with it?"

"It's accepted, although on some occasions we do lose our tempers. That's life in New York City," Jim continued before both were interrupted by the shouts of an agitated British tourist.

"I insist you sell me a new pair of glasses," the Briton shouted at two clerks who manned a counter in a small nearby shop called, "Открытка [Otkritka]."

"Another typical day," Natalya sighed. "You Westerners come here without knowing a word of Russian and then you get frustrated when you can't read our signs and when no one can understand you," she added playfully hitting her American friend.

"Don't blame me. What language do you think I'm talking?" Jim protested.

"I know. I'm just giving you a hard time."

"Look right here," the Briton demanded pointing at the shop's sign, as a small, curious crowd began to gather. "Your sign says `Optical!' So here's my pair of glasses. Sell me a new pair of frames!"

Both Natalya and Jim laughed at the frustrated tourist's persistence. "How about doing a good deed for your Russian friends. Go over to him and point out his mistake," Natalya suggested.

"Me?"

"Why not? You're the American here. He'll be more receptive to you. Besides, once he hears my Russian accent he'll ignore me. After all, you Westerners don't like listening to Russians!" Natalya teased her friend.

"All right, I'll tell him," Jim reluctantly gave in, seeing that the Muscovite woman was serious.

"Well then they should correct their sign!" Natalya heard the tourist angrily grumble to her American friend upon

ВЕСНА РУССКАЯ

being told the store only sold postcards. "Well it sure as hell looks like 'optical,'" the Briton protested one last time, refusing to recognize the Cyrillic alphabet, as he snatched back his broken pair of glasses and stormed off.

"Спасибо [Thank you] from my heart. Now don't you feel better?" Natalya asked as Keating returned.

"If it makes you feel better."

"It does," Kalinina answered putting her arm around him. "So tell me what was it like growing up in America?"

"I don't know. I guess much the same as growing up here. I had to go to school like you and take the subways like you, although our subways are much less dependable and much dirtier. I guess the only significant differences were that we had plentiful supplies of affordable goods and didn't have to wait on long lines. We didn't have the same turmoil and worries that you Muscovites have, and definitely not the same inflation," he answered as they got up and departed from GUM.

"Because you gave us yours!" Natalya teased Jim, softly hitting him, knowing that the United States had precipitated Russia's hyperinflationary era when they had convinced the Russian Government to raise fuel prices in 1992. During this time, the Western Governments led by the United States had vigorously argued that Russian fuel prices were artificially low and below cost. In reality they only appeared to be, because of the strong value of the Ruble. However, once the Russian Government acquiesced ushering in the new Period of "Capitulation and humiliation," merchants immediately raised the prices of other goods. Before long, the price increases accelerated, spiraling out of control, destroying the confidence that Russians had once placed in their Ruble. With the Western-dominated Russian Government unwilling to reestablish price controls for fear that they would alienate their colonial masters, the Ruble's value plummeted. They did not dare consider anything that could be construed as a Communist instrument.

"What can I say," Keating surrendered.

"An apology for starters, would help," Natalya continued to tease her American friend.

"Okay, I'm sorry."

"Apology accepted," the Russian declared again putting her arm around Jim. "Say, what are you doing tomorrow night? How about coming over to my house for dinner? I would like you to meet my mother and babushka," Kalinina offered.

"I'm sorry, but I can't. I have a reception to attend at the German Embassy. I really wish I could. Maybe some other time," the American apologized.

"But you will come some other day? Да [Yes]?"

"Definitely if you will give me another chance. I'm really sorry."

"Don't apologize. I understand. These things come up and you have no control," Natalya replied knowing there would be times when she would have to put her personal desires aside for her job.

"I feel so bad," Jim continued to apologize as they gathered their belongings, preparing to head for the metro.

"You needn't. Unless you have plans of spurning me in the future," Natalya added, hopeful that her growing feelings for the American were mutual. With each minute they spent together, Natalya could feel her heart falling more and more for Jim Keating. With her growing attraction to him, Kalinina found herself silently praying that he was also falling for her and that their careers would never rise above their growing friendship. Despite her hopes, Natalya knew as Russian resentment, including her own towards Western colonialization of her homeland, increased it might someday

79

chill their relationship. Despite the sobering thoughts that gnawed at the back of her mind and other warnings that future political events which neither could control, might permanently tear them apart, Natalya found herself increasingly ignoring her instincts as she grew closer to the American. Even though she knew deep down that her friend was a CIA agent, Natalya refused to allow her brain to override the emotions of her heart.

"I promise I won't turn you down the next time," Jim pledged to his Russian friend, sharing many of her feelings.

"That's reassuring to know. Then let me give you my phone number," Kalinina found herself offering, momentarily placing her shopping bag onto the snow-covered cobblestones.

"Here let me hold your bag," Jim offered, lifting the Muscovite's bag from the snow.

"If you refuse me the next time, then I'll definitely hold it against you," Natalya teased Keating as she industriously scrawled her number onto a scrap of paper.

"I have no intention of doing so," Jim reiterated his promise.

"Good. This is my number," Natalya exclaimed slipping the piece of paper into the American's shopping bag. "I'll be expecting to hear from you soon," she added before requesting his phone number. "That way if I don't hear from you soon, you'll make it easier for me to track you down," the Russian woman added after Jim had recited his number.

"I promise I'll call you before the weekend."

"Then maybe you can come over this weekend? Да [Yes]?" Natalya ventured.

"I would like to very much."

"Then I'll be looking forward to it," Kalinina replied, retaking her shopping bag as they walked the final steps to

Охотный Ряд Metro Station, a short distance behind the Russian Museum of History and Красная Площадь [Red Square]. "До свидания [Good bye]," Natalya bidded as they prepared to part their ways -- the Russian for Красные Ворота Metro Station and the American for Станция Баррикадная [Barrikadnaya Station].

"До свидания [Good bye]," Keating returned his friend's farewell before both disappeared into the bustling rush-hour crowds.

ВЕСНА РУССКАЯ

Chapter 7

A biting chill cut through the icy Moscow air as a heavy snow fell upon the city, snarling traffic and blinding pedestrians. People hunched over, tightly bundled in thick fur coats, struggling to navigate through the harsh, wind-swept elements. Crowds gathered at the city's kiosks buying steaming cups of rich, black coffee and chocolate to warm themselves.

While the mid January blizzard raged, Natalya Kalinina sat in the comfort of her warm abode. She leafed through contraband intelligence reports relating to U.S. capabilities in the former Soviet Republics and relinquished Russian territories. Because of the sensitive nature of these RNR-generated reports, Natalya found the snowstorm a welcome blessing since it gave her a legitimate excuse to stay in the privacy of her home. The RNR was an underground faction of the KGB and Russian military.

Had she been working in the KGB offices, Natalya would have had to keep up her guard, intently listening for the approach footsteps, fearful that an agent with Western loyalties would discover the contraband intelligence reports.

She did not know who the moles were and could not take a chance of being discovered.

In the safety of her apartment, Natalya found herself able to devote her full attention to the reports. She did not have to concentrate on extraneous factors or have to constantly worry who was around her workspace.

As she carefully sifted through the report's pages, occasionally jotting comments in the side margins, the young agent, reasoned that if there was a Higher Power, He was on Russia's side. How else could the welcome blizzard be explained.

As Natalya read deeper into the reports, her mind drifted back to the heroic attempts of past Russian generations. Two centuries earlier, Russia had suffered under similar circumstances. In 1825, after having endured two decades of corrupt rule, watching their proud country deteriorate, a group of similarly young, aristocratic military officers belonging to several secret societies not unlike the RNR movement (most notably the Northern and Southern Societies based in St. Petersburg and Tulchin, respectively) had formulated their own strategy to free Russia.

During the Decembrists' planning stages, Russia's leader, Czar Alexander I unexpectedly died. The country appeared to be headed towards chaos when Alexander's two brothers, Constantine and Nicholas, engaged in a power struggle for the throne.

With the added turmoil, the young officers accelerated their plans to bring about popular reforms -- the abolition of serfdom, equitable land distribution, and the establishment of a constitutional Republic similar to Europe's new democracies. However, just before they could implement their revolution, Nicholas I took firm control of the Russian Government, eliminating the brief period of chaos.

ВЕСНА РУССКАЯ

Still undaunted by the passing of their best opportunity, the young officers backed by 3000 troops who had refused to swear allegiance to the new Czar, went ahead with their plans. They gathered in Senate Square (in St. Petersburg, then the Russian capital) on December 14th and attempted to overthrow Nicholas. A bloody battle ensued as troops loyal to the Czar defended the imperial palace. During the intense fighting many of the rebels were shot and thrown into the icy Neva River.

Within hours, the Decembrist uprising was crushed, leaving over 60 dead. Its five leaders, including Colonel Paul Pestel and Conrad Ryleev, a well-known poet, were imprisoned and executed at Peter and Paul Fortress across the Neva, a short distance away from the battle scene. 130 of their followers were subsequently exiled to Siberia.

Despite the revolution's failure, the Decembrists, having died trying to help their country, eventually became some of the most revered figures in Russian history. Senate Square was later renamed Площадь Декабристов [Ploshchad Dekabristov - Square of the Decembrists] in their honor.

A second Decembrist uprising, for many of the same reasons, took place in Moscow when Natalya was a little girl of two. Although at the time she was too young to comprehend the significance of the violent events, the young agent could vaguely remember being held by her mother, who along with many other Muscovite parents, had brought their children to watch the tragic events unfold, as pro-Yeltsin tanks mercilessly pounded the Russian White House, the country's symbol of democracy since August 1991.

The bloody events were precipitated in September 1993 when President Boris Yeltsin, a de-facto Western puppet decided to abolish Russia's system of checks and balances, a critical component of democracy. At the time, his heartless Government, blinded by IMF (an international bank operated by the "elite 7" Western nations) monetary offers to impose their policies on his country, ignored the plight of Russia's millions of new poor, who had fallen into their predicament as the very result of these policies.

Frustrated by the failure of his attempts to impose further "Western-style market reforms" on Russia and driven by dreams of ruling as a noveau Czar, Boris Yeltsin decided to take sole control of the Russian Government. Yeltsin was determined to impose the rest of the West's corrupt policies on his country to the detriment of his own people. He had sold his soul for a few humiliating IMF Dollars. Accordingly, on September 21st, Yeltsin issued a decree dissolving the Russian Legislature.

In response, the Parliament, which had prudently urged caution in introducing "reforms" that could decimate the people of Russia, issued its own decree impeaching Yeltsin. Led by Speaker Ruslan Khasbulatov and Afghan war hero, Aleksandr Rutskoi, they were determined to prevent the new Czar from crushing Russia's young, fragile democracy. As a result, the Russian White House, their headquarters, again became the symbol of Russian democracy.

After 11 tense days of talks in which Yeltsin refused to call simultaneous Presidential elections, despite overwhelming popular support for the idea, and his continuous threats to forcibly eject the elected Legislators from their offices, thousands of people staged their own Decembrist uprising on October 3rd. Within minutes, the pro-democracy crowd smashed through lines of police officers deployed by the Yeltsin Government to isolate the White House and repress the democratic resistance movement. As the police lines crumbled, many of the officers, secretly sympathetic to the democratic cause, joined the uprising.

Shortly after the liberation of the Russian White House, the crowds converged on Moscow City Hall and easily captured the office held by the pro-Yeltsin Mayor, Yuri Luzhkov. Within hours, the 20th century Decembrists controlled several blocks of downtown Moscow.

As support for the new Decembrist uprising grew, Yeltsin's desperate officials called in military reinforcements, which arrived early the next morning. Once in place, the Pro-Yeltsin army brutally crushed the revolt. Tanks relentlessly pounded the White House with heavy artillery in a fierce 10-hour battle, leaving nearly 500 dead and another 500 injured, contradicting "official reports" released by the Yeltsin Government that listed the total dead at 149.

When the daylong uprising came to a bloody conclusion, the two 20th Century Decembrist leaders surrendered to a Western diplomat, a representative of the colonial leadership behind the Yeltsin Government. Following their surrender, Khasbulatov and Rutskoi, along with hundreds of their supporters, were shipped to Lefortovo Prison.

As the last remnants of the revolt were subdued, the White House burned, sending thick, billowing clouds of smoke into the sky. With the dark smoke, Russia's faint hopes of preserving her constitutional democracy and extricating herself from colonialism's shackles evaporated.

Following his victory, Yeltsin banned most opposition parties, shut down numerous newspapers including respectable publications such as Pravda, censored others (until the public outcry became too loud to ignore) and ordered all 88 Provincial Legislatures to either submit to his hand-picked Governors or dissolve themselves. Several

Governors, including Yuri Lodkin of Bryansk (who had been elected to office two years after Yeltsin) were also removed from office for merely exercising their democratic right of free speech by supporting constitutional authority over Yeltsin's heavy-handed tactics. The Constitutional Court was also abolished.

While fundamental principles of democracy -- free speech, free press, an effective system of checks and balances and a legitimate opposition were being extinguished, the West openly lauded their lackey. They publicly proclaimed that Yeltsin "was establishing a democratic system!" Yet, if a U.S. President had carried out the same measures, dissolving Congress, shutting down the Supreme Court, and nullifying the Constitution, it is highly unlikely that these same Western leaders would have been so supportive and enthusiastic in their comments.

When Yeltsin called for Parliamentary elections in December, a desecration of the democratic system he had destroyed, the West quickly supported him, ignoring the hollow nature of his "democratic" vote. With the legitimate opposition crushed, scattered, or in hiding and prohibited media exposure and/or outright banned, it was impossible for elections to be free or fair. But in the West's view, fair elections merely consisted of a free vote with a token opposition and enough fairness to guarantee a victory by their stooges.

In spite of Western attempts to guarantee the outcome, the 45+% of Russian citizens that did vote, expressed their lack of approval for Yeltsin's Government. They elected a new parliament that mirrored the one that Yeltsin had destroyed. Out of disgust, the remaining 50+ percent of Russian citizens did not vote at all.

Although the Russian People expressed their desire for a "Russia-First" Policy, pro-Western forces continued to pander to U.S. and West European interests weakening Russian prestige and credibility. As these pro-Western forces maintained their control over the country, ignoring the needs of their people, Russians' hopes for a better future evaporated. The loss of hope then resulted in a demographic catastrophe. The birthrate fell sharply compounded by a steep drop in life expectancy. Russian's lived shorter lives due to lack of necessities such as food, shelter, and healthcare and from drinking in larger amounts to drown out their depression. This ushered in an unprecedented peacetime era of population implosion. With the evaporation of her people and the steady depletion of her resources, Russia became increasingly vulnerable. And as Russian vulnerability grew, Russians' hopes and optimism continued to deteriorate. This further aggravated the vicious cycle.

As Natalya thought back to Russia's only attempt to free herself from the tightening grip of her colonizers, she wondered if the new revolution, that she and many of her brave compatriots were planning, if it was needed, would also go down in failure. Although she was willing to be martyred for her people, Natalya did not want to die in vain.

While thinking about Russia's past failures to take control of her own destiny, Natalya Kalinina wondered how the Russian people could have let down their guard in the first place. She could not understand how they could have allowed their country to fall into the humiliating state she now suffered. "Hadn't they learned anything from history and will we be any different?" she silently asked.

All through the centuries since the first Rus State was established in 862 AD by the Swedish Varangians (Rurik), Russians had been subjected to numerous hostile occupations. In 1223, the Mongols launched their first attack, routing Russian defenders in the Battle of Kalka. They then withdrew shortly after Ghengis Khan's death in 1227.

Ten years later, the Mongol armies under Batu Khan, launched a new attack, easily capturing Moscow. The Mongol occupation was completed in 1240 when the Rus State's capital, Kiev, fell.

Upon sealing their victory, the Mongols ruthlessly exploited the fallen Rus State, establishing the "Golden Horde" which required Russia's citizens to pay hefty taxes to the Mongol thieves.

During this period of brutal Mongol rule, most of Russia's principalities were devastated. Russian Princes, although still allowed to maintain symbolic rule, were subordinated to their occupiers. The dignity of the Russian people was destroyed. In homage, they were required to kiss the hem of the ruling Mongol despot's robes. Women were reduced to second-class citizens. People refusing to pay homage to the foreign occupiers were subjected to torture and other forms of barbaric cruelty.

The first credible strands of resistance did not begin until 1327 when a Russian Prince openly opposed the Mongol taxes. Despite brutal reprisals, the resistance movement continued to grow, aided in part by internal power struggles among the occupiers. With the grip of the Mongol rulers weakening, the Russian people began a war for independence in 1380, and decisively defeated their occupiers in the Battle of Kulikovo. In retaliation, the Mongol despots burned Moscow to the ground before fleeing.

Having regained their independence, Russia became a flourishing, orthodox country until 1555 when she fell victim to new wars -- the Russo-Swedish War (1555-57), the Livonian War (1558-83), and the Crimean-Tatar War (1571). As a result of these wars, Moscow was again ravaged, and

Russia lost much of Siberia and all of her water access to the Baltic.

Poland next took advantage of this 20-year period of economic ruin and famine. Warsaw sent its military forces under the ruse of assisting discontented peasants and Cossacks. They toppled the Russian Government and installed a Polish-national, who claimed to be the son of Ivan IV (the Terrible) -- False Dimitry I (Ivan IV's real son died in 1591) to the throne in 1605.

Despite this new occupation, the Russian people refused to recognize the illegitimate Czar and subsequently executed him eleven months later. Poland then responded by installing False Dimitry II. However as Russian armies recaptured the Kremlin in 1611 and forced the Poles to relinquish power, this new false Czar met the same fate. He was executed, his body was burned and his ashes were fired back at Poland from a cannon atop the Kremlin walls.

Having once again ridded herself of foreign occupiers, Russia experienced a period of unprecedented prosperity (1612-1812). Under the leadership of Czars Peter I (the Great) and Catherine II (the Great) Russia ended her self-imposed state of isolationism and became a major player on the world stage.

During this period of greatness, Russia established its first Navy, successfully resisted foreign invasions by Sweden and Turkey, and acquired major pieces of territory -- Livonia, Estonia, Vyborg, Finland, Ingria, Karelia, water access to the Caspian and Black Seas, Ukraine, the Crimea, and parts of her one-time aggressor, Poland. In addition, the City of St. Petersburg, the new cultural center of the East was established. Spectacular palaces and cathedrals of stone and hundreds of canals were built out of once, desolate swampland.

Despite Russia's revived greatness, a new despot with the objective of conquering all of Europe, Napoleon of France, launched war on Russia in 1812. Before being turned back in the fierce Russian winter, Napoleon's forces sacked much of Moscow, desecrated St. Basil's Cathedral (using it as stables for his troops' horses) and burned much of the Kremlin.

Then in September 1941, German despot, Adolf Hitler, with designs on controlling the world, launched his own attack on Russia. With little advance warning, Russian defenders, despite their heroic efforts, were driven back. As German forces wracked up large chunks of Russian territory, and laid siege on Leningrad (formerly and currently St. Petersburg), the Russian people, despite the overwhelming odds against them, refused to surrender. For 900 days, they valiantly endured the brutal siege on Leningrad (1941-44) in which more than 650,000 died of starvation and sickness. Even when offered a chance for safe evacuation, the residents of Leningrad refused to abandon their beloved city.

Again, like Napoleon 130 years earlier, Hitler had also underestimated the severity of the Russian winter and the determination of the Russian people. By 1943, after months of stalemate, the tide of the war shifted in Russia's favor with the Soviet victory at Stalingrad (the turning point of World War II). Two years later, Russian forces captured the German capital, Berlin and Hitler committed suicide.

Having won the "Great Patriotic War," with memories of past occupations fresh on their minds, Russians vowed never to allow another foreign aggressor to violate their borders. Russian children from their earliest years were taught about the importance of protecting their country's borders from the hostile world. With a siege mentality deeply ingrained in their minds, the average Russian viewed the world with suspicion -- China to the south, France, England

Italy and the former West Germany to the West, and the United States (from Alaska to the mainland) to the East were all bent on boxing them in and destroying them.

Influenced by this "siege-complex", Russia rapidly increased her defensive capabilities, first building her own hydrogen bomb in, and then intercontinental ballistic nuclear missiles [ICBMs] which were targeted at major U.S cities to counter the threat presented by America's own intercontinental missiles.

During this period of heightened competition (the "Cold War") when each side strode to protect its interests and carve out new spheres of influence to offset gains by the other side, Russians warily kept up their guard. Since the United States had used nuclear weapons before (Hiroshima and Nagasaki in 1945), Russians feared that the United States might commit another nuclear attack.

Other statements uttered by Russo-phobes including former U.S. President Ronald Reagan that -- "the Russian military was a monolithic machine run amok and that their nuclear arsenal had been designed with emphasis on launching an offensive first strike by leaders obsessed with ‛fighting and winning a nuclear war 'for total world domination,"**1** did not help. As a result, consistent with their "siege-mentality" Russian leaders designed a defensive system geared to deter and if necessary, to react to a Western attack on their country while former U.S. President Ronald Reagan who promoted the premise of "fighting and winning a nuclear war" when he signed NSC (National Security Council) Directive No. 13 in 1981.

From this era, Natalya's mother, Katya had saved a Russian cartoon that in her opinion depicted America's character under Ronald Reagan. It portrayed a bearded Neanderthal man wielding a large wooden club. When the sunlight cast the Neanderthal's shadow it revealed the silhouette of Uncle Sam (the United States personified) wielding a nuclear missile.

Although Katya did not know why she had saved it at the time, the drawing now provided a powerful reminder to her daughter that the West could not be trusted no matter how friendly they appeared to be.

Less than five years after the cartoon had been drawn, the United States pretended to accept President Mikhail Gorbachev's offer of friendship. Gorbachev had vigorously pursued peace, dreaming of the greater stability and safety a new era of friendship and cooperation would bring. In doing so, he single-handedly ended the Cold War.

In his quixotic quest, the Soviet President willingly put his trust in then U.S. President Ronald Reagan. He did so despite the American's life-long animosity towards his country and his numerous slanderous "evil-empire" diatribes. The Russian people, desperate for a new kind of security through "peace and cooperation" in lieu of "Security through strength," blindly went along. Russians accepted America's empty gestures, willing to forgive and forget. In doing so, they threw aside the painful lessons that they had endured throughout history. They let down their guard.

At the time, when most of the world longed for an end to East-West division, few saw through the American President's transparency, with one exception -- the Nobel Prize Committee. As a result, Gorbachev received the Nobel Peace Prize and Reagan received nothing.

The United States and its Western allies quickly exploited the open wound Gorbachev had offered. They quickly took control over Russia when the Soviet Union disintegrated in 1991.

A year after the Soviet Union had disintegrated, the true picture of U.S. global aspirations emerged when a secret Pentagon Policy statement was leaked to The New York Times. The 46-page statement outlined Pentagon objectives to:

1. Guarantee American dominance over the world through the use of military force if necessary. All potential threats were to be suppressed or destroyed by U.S. military power.
2. Discourage the world's industrialized developed nations from challenging U.S. global leadership. No collection of nations (friends or foes) could be permitted to aspire for leadership or influence over global regions since such enhanced prestige could threaten American superiority.

To prevent the emergence of regional competitors, the Pentagon Policy statement recommended the use of U.S. military force against aspiring nations or groups of nations. Regions where potential competitors to U.S. dominance could emerge were listed as Western Europe (including American allies – the United Kingdom, France, and Germany), Asia (including Japan and China), and the former Soviet and East European states, most notably Russia.

In addition, the Pentagon Policy statement rejected collective action through international bodies such as the United Nations (U.N.) since U.S. influence would be reduced. The Pentagon also viewed the possible establishment of European-only security agreements with suspicion, since Washington would then have little say over European security matters.

When the classified Pentagon Policy statement was leaked it drew immediate worldwide condemnation. In response to the global outcry and as a means to placate the concerns of their allies, the U.S. Government officially killed the Pentagon's policy statement. However despite promises that this document had never represented "official U.S. Policy," Washington quietly pursued its objectives, especially against Russia.

Determined to ensure that Russia remain at its mercy, the U.S. Government consistently pretended to be Moscow's friend, freely dishing out advice and token promises of monetary assistance under the pretext of promoting political stability and economic prosperity. In reality, these promises always had rigid strings attached. They were designed to inflict undue hardship and misery, to ensure that Washington maintained a chokehold on Russia's economic and political jugular. As long as economic chaos existed, Moscow could not aspire to regain her past prestige.

Another cartoon, clipped and framed by Natalya's supervisor, Valentin Makarov, illustrated this relationship – "America's promises amounted to nothing more than a noose designed to strangle and suffocate the life from Russia." The cartoon showed the remains of a broken rocket, the prestige of Russia's space program, St. Basil's cathedral in the distance and a hand made out of rope in the form of a noose. There were U.S. Dollars inside it waiting for Russia to take them and be hung.

As Natalya thought about her country's painful situation, fully conscious of the enormous psychological intimidation U.S. troops in Poland, the Baltic States, Georgia and Turkey presented, she wondered how long it

BECHA PYCCKAЯ

would take before enough Russians gained the courage to drive the colonial government from power.

Despite the American presence in Poland and the near abroad, the KGB agent was certain that if the RNR movement, consisting of disenchanted officials from Russia's weakened intelligence and emasculated military communities, waited for the right moment, the American's would be unable to defend their colonial-backed regime. Each passing day provided further confirmation of Kalinina's convictions, as the U.S. became increasingly paralyzed by the growing weight of sprouting domestic crises.

> *The U.S. Presence on the Kurile Islands is small or nonexistent. Japanese forces have neither the willpower nor capability of defending them. They are vulnerable to seizure with minimal risk and associated costs.*

Upon reading the small caption of the contraband KGB surveillance report that mirrored her own growing optimism, Natalya Kalinina highlighted the three sentences. Afterwards, she neatly printed her recommendation against retaking Russia's former islands, which had been bargained away for cheap promises of Yen. The young agent feared that such a move would provide the United States with a pretext to put aside its domestic concerns. She did not want the United States using military force to re-seize the Kurile Islands and hand them back to Japan. Feeling that U.S. intervention was a realistic possibility, Natalya disagreed with

96

the report's assessment that the risk and associated costs would be minimal. To her they were significant – the Russian military could lose many soldiers, the Kremlin would have to spend unnecessary funds to hold the Kuriles, and Moscow could lose additional territory as punishment. Furthermore, she did not want Russia viewed as an aggressor even though the country by taking the Kuriles would only be liberating her own people and lands. The KGB agent felt that if anything, Russian liberation of the Kurile Islands would likely lead to the country's complete and irreparable decline.

Although she was as determined to end American imperialism as any of the RNR members, Natalya knew that patience was critical. They could not afford to throw caution aside and act recklessly. To do so would seriously compromise the RNR movement and possibly set back future Russian liberation movements for decades to come.

As Russians patiently endured their plight, the United States found itself presented with its most serious crisis since the American Civil War (1860-65). Hawaii, a tiny, prosperous and ethnically unique Island state, which had been unlawfully annexed after the illegal American-backed overthrow of Queen Liliuokalani, was set to hold a referendum for independence within two weeks. Despite heavy pressure from Washington, which had delayed the vote for 21 years, polls favored secession by a narrow margin.

Knowing that Hawaii's secession, if successful, could rupture U.S. unity, Natalya intently followed the latest reports out of America. She knew that once Washington had lost some of its territory, it could no longer sustain its interference in Russian affairs. Then, without the United States and its Western allies to prop it up, the puppet Government in Moscow would collapse and be swept away by an angry

ВЕСНА РУССКАЯ

tidal wave of the masses that had been held down for a quarter century. Then Russia would be free!

Chapter 8

Crowds of people milled around the kiosks outside Красные Ворота Metro station, taking advantage of the unusually mild weekend weather. Children played in the melting snow of the nearby, small park. Bustling traffic splashed increasingly darker-shades of slush across the slippery walkways, as pedestrians carefully navigated around the large puddles of ice and water.

As Muscovites enjoyed the mild Saturday afternoon, Natalya waited just outside the metro's heavy metal doors, intently scanning the crowd of departing commuters for her American friend. Despite promises that he would arrive on the 1:00 PM train, Jim failed to show.

Although it was customary for Russians to be late, Natalya could not help but feel a little disappointed. With each additional second the determined woman waited for the next train, her heart sank a little more. Although her heart remained convinced that the American would not let her down, Natalya's subconscious began to emit louder reservations.

While standing in growing disappointment Natalya watched as the new rush of commuters exited from the station. Her heart sank even lower when she saw no trace of the American. Suddenly, the Muscovite woman was interrupted from behind. She quickly spun around and caught sight of the American.

"Are you going to stand there all day?" Jim teased her, having snuck up from behind.

"How dare you do this to me!" Natalya playfully declared upon seeing her friend, who stood with two bouquets of roses. "Thanks so very much, they're beautiful," the Russian expressed her gratitude. After taking one of the bouquets, she warmly hugged her friend. "So who's the other bouquet for?" she then asked, releasing the American. "I don't see any other women around."

"For your mother and babushka. I don't want to get off on the wrong foot with them," Keating replied.

"There's no such chance. As long as you're in good with me, you're in good with them," Natalya answered. "So tell me, how did you get by without me seeing you?"

"Well, knowing you Russians, I felt it would be a challenge just for you to get here on time."

"Don't start with me."

Ignoring the Muscovite, Jim went on, "And for you to get here early, there was no chance at all. So I took the 12:40 train and got here fifteen minutes early."

"If you ever do that to me again, I'll..."

"You'll do what?" Keating challenged the Russian.

"I don't know yet, but believe me, I'll figure something out," Natalya teased him.

"I have no doubts you will," the American replied as Natalya took his hand.

"What do you mean?"

"Well, the first thing I learned about you Slavic people is that you have long memories. You don't forget, especially those who hurt you."

"That's right, so you better be careful," the Muscovite admonished him as they crossed between the traffic.

"Don't you Russians believe in waiting for the lights to change?" Jim teased, as they became momentarily stranded in the middle of the street along with a small group of people.

"Нет [Nyet]! We learned from you Westerners! Especially New Yorkers!" Kalinina countered, as they got their chance to scramble across the rest of the way.

"I'm a New Yorker and I wait," the American protested.

"I don't believe you," Natalya playfully countered. "If you did, then how come I noticed you at my side when we were caught in the middle?"

"That's because you forced me."

"With a gun, maybe?"

"Нет [Nyet]. You pulled me by the hand."

"I didn't see you offer any resistance."

"Can I ever win with you?" the American finally gave up in frustration.

" Нет [Nyet]!" Natalya quickly replied.

"In spite of your stubborness, I'm really happy to see you again."

"Me too," the Russian replied, as they slowly walked through the slushy park, hand-in-hand. "I'm glad you could make it."

"There was no way I was going to let them give me any work to do this weekend, especially after I promised I wouldn't let you down again," Keating replied. "Have you been busy at your job, lately?"

"It depends on how you want to look at it. If I find something more preferable then I'm not busy. If not, then I have work to do!"

"That's you Russian's."

"Be nice," Natalya responded, playfully pushing the American with his own hand. "So what about you."

"I've had more receptions than work lately, or at least that's the way it seems. I don't know how much more drinks I can handle."

"Well you'll have to make it tonight. No one comes over to a Russian's house without drinking our vodka!" Natalya declared as they casually walked across the street into the narrow driveway of her apartment building. "Watch the ice," she then warned, as a chunk of ice slipped from an upper windowsill and fell into the melting snow.

"Maybe I can drink a little."

"Maybe you can drink a lot. Besides, what does it matter, I'll take good care of you," the Muscovite interjected. "You can stay overnight."

"Oh no..."

"Why not? Don't you trust me?" Natalya quickly interrupted.

"I cannot impose."

"You won't be imposing because I've already told my family you would be staying for the weekend."

"I don't believe you. How could you?" Jim laughed. "You never mentioned anything like that to me!"

"So? I did now, didn't I? And besides, some things are better left unsaid until the right moment," the Russian defended herself. "If you don't stay, you'll be hurting us all," Kalinina added before asking, "You're not mad at me, are you?"

"Нет [Nyet]. I don't think I could ever get mad at you," Jim answered as they stopped in front of an-old, splintered, half-opened wooden door.

"Glad to hear that. I wouldn't want anything to come between us."

"However, there is one small problem. I didn't bring an extra pair of clothes."

"Не проблема [Nyeh problema - No problem], I can loan you some of mine.

"Women's clothes, no thanks!"

"T-Shirts can be worn by anyone. Or if you want, after dinner, we'll go back to your place and you can pick up an extra pair. How long can that take, maybe a half-hour at most? Да [Yes]?" Natalya asked, finally opening the door and motioning for her friend to proceed into the dimly lit lobby.

"No offense, but I would prefer to go back and get a pair of my own," Keating replied.

"Не проблема [No problem], so we'll go back. We Russian's are accommodating," Natalya answered in return, briefly placing her hand on the American's shoulder. "I live on the fifth floor, so we'll have to take the stairs. The elevator isn't working."

"So what's new," Jim teased his friend.

"You better be careful what you say, because how did you say it -- `we Slavic people have long memories.' You could have an accident and fall down the stairs and break your neck. Now we wouldn't want that to happen, would we?" Kalinina playfully countered.

"I don't think I need your help. It might just happen without your help," the American toyed with the Russian woman. "You need a flashlight here!"

"It might not help. Our steps could collapse at any time, don't you think?" Natalya again countered, playing along.

"You're right. I must be crazy going into a building that ought to be condemned!"

"I don't think so."

"Why is that?"

"Because you have no choice. Remember the gun I'm holding to your back? The gun I forced you into the street with? Да [Yes]?"

"Seriously, is there anything I should know about your parents before we go in?"

"What're you so concerned about?" Natalya teased him. "Relax. I didn't say anything bad about you. I assure you, they'll like you."

"That's comforting to hear, especially since I'm American after all."

"An American Russian," Kalinina quickly replied before ringing the doorbell. "Believe me, if there was any reason why they wouldn't approve of you, you would not be here now," she then added, as the door was opened by her babushka, Anna who greeted them with a warm, "Здравствуйте [Zdrastvutye - Hello]." "Oh yes, there is one thing, they only speak Russian. But you should have no problem. Babushka, this is Jim. Jim this is my babushka, Anna," the Russian woman quickly introduced the pair, as they were warmly invited in. Seconds later Natalya introduced the American to her mother, Katya.

Once in the warmth of the Kalinina house, the Muscovite and her guest took off their shoes and slipped on a pair of Russian slippers that were customarily provided for family and guests alike.

"Is there anything we can get you," Anna asked the American as Natalya took his coat and hung it in a closet as he was invited to the kitchen. "A glass of water, anything?"

"No thanks, I'm fine," Jim answered, handing the other bouquet to her.

"He brought it for both of you," Natalya warmly declared.

"Спасибо [Thank you]. That's so thoughtful," Anna replied taking the roses while Katya searched for a glass vase.

"Please, sit down," Natalya beckoned to the American, before helping her mother find two vases. "I also need one for my flowers. You weren't the only ones to get flowers, the young Muscovite playfully teased her mother."

While Natalya and her mother tended to the flowers, Anna took out pan of freshly baked sugar-currant biscuits from the hot oven.

"You didn't have to go through this trouble for me?" Keating protested.

"It's no trouble," Anna replied.

"We may not have what you American's have, but we still know how to treat our guests," Katya added. "We are happy you came. In fact you're the first American to set foot into our house, so we want to treat you well."

"And we want you to come back again," Natalya warmly answered coming up from behind and placing her hands on his shoulders.

"Is there anything I can do to help," Jim offered seeing Katya and Anna feverishly working on the finishing touches of the meal.

"Нет [Nyet]," Natalya quickly answered, setting places for four at the small table. "You're our guest. So just sit back and relax."

ВЕСНА РУССКАЯ

"You didn't eat before coming here, did you?" Anna asked, placing a large, steaming bowl of on the table.

"Нет [Nyet]. Natasha warned me ahead of time."

"Good, then you should be hungry. There's plenty of food," Katya added, setting a platter of roast lamb on the table, followed by a bowl of tomato, lettuce, onion, and cucumber salad, while Anna got a heaping dish of Russian butter, and another plate consisting of some of her freshly baked biscuits.

After Natalya uncorked a new bottle of red wine and poured a glass for each person, the three Russians joined Jim at the table. Each then proposed toasts to friendship, health, and happiness. Following their toasts, everyone dug into the delicious food.

"Let me warn you, this doesn't get you out of drinking our vodka," Natalya whispered to her friend as she refilled everyone's glasses.

"Tell us about your family. Do you have any brothers or sisters?" Anna asked.

"I have a younger sister, Michelle. She'll be 23 later in May."

"Really. Natasha will also be 23 this year, but in April," Katya answered.

"So I guess we have something in common," Natalya added. "So how old are you, if you don't mind."

"I'll be 26 in February."

"When? We have to have a birthday party for you!" Anna offered.

"I'm afraid that won't be possible this year."

"Why not?" Natalya asked.

"Because I was born on the 29th of February."

"That figures," Natalya countered, playfully hitting him with her hand. "You always have to make it difficult, don't you?"

"Don't blame me. Blame my mother."

"No way. I blame you. You should've waited for one more day!" the Natalya quickly retorted, still teasing him.

"So we'll have your party on either the 28th or 1st," Katya compromised. "So when do you want it?"

"On which ever day falls on a weekend."

"No way. There's no way I'm going to let you work on your birthday. We'll celebrate on the 28th. And besides you were born in February not March!" Natalya declared.

"I guess then it's settled. On February 28th it is."

"Good," Natalya replied.

"So tell us, what does your sister do? Does she also work for the Government?" Natalya's mother asked, already aware of Jim's position with the U.S. Embassy in Moscow.

"Нет [Nyet], she's in advertising. She works for a marketing firm in Manhattan. That's the part of New York City you hear about most often."

"That's wonderful. Maybe the next time she's here, she can market some of our products," Katya suggested.

"That's if she'll ever come here. Every year I keep inviting her, and every year she finds some excuse or another why she can't make it."

"Well, she was in school only a short while ago," Natalya exclaimed. "With no income, she couldn't afford to come."

"I offered to pay, but she always found some way to convince me to come to the States. I think she's intimidated by the Russian language. She can't read your strange writing."

"What do you mean our strange writing? You're the ones who use a strange alphabet!" Natalya protested, defending her Cyrillic characters.

"She's kind of afraid she would get lost here and no one would understand her. Heaven knows, she can't speak or understand a single word of Russian."

"Then you've got to teach her," Anna chimed in.

"Well, actually, I did teach her two words," Jim replied.

"Да [Yes] and Нет [Nyet]?" Natalya asked.

"Well, not quite. I taught her to ask a question."

"Which question?" Katya inquired.

"Можно [Mojna - May I]?"

"That's only one word," Natalya quickly interjected.

"I also taught her the only answer she would ever hear – 'Нет [Nyet]!' Nobody is ever allowed to do anything here!" Jim teased.

"You're really asking for it," Natalya warned, refilling Jim's glass.

"That's enough," the American protested.

"Нет [Nyet], it's not! No opened bottle goes unfinished!"

"See, what did I tell you, everything is a 'Нет' here," Jim took advantage of the young Muscovite's answer.

"I'll pretend I didn't hear that," Natalya quickly replied. "How about your parents, what do they do?"

"Before she married my dad, my mother used to be a secretary in his law firm. Now she is, as we like to say, a "home-economist." That means she takes care of the family's needs. And my father is a Senator in the U.S. Congress."

"So that's what got you into Government, да [yes]?"

"It had some influence on me. How about your mother what does she do?"

"I'm an editor for Moskva Publishing House," Katya answered.

"And Anna used to work for a transistor factory before retiring," Natalya added, getting up from the table to assist her parents in clearing the table.

After hastily depositing the dishes in the kitchen sink and running cold water over them, Katya made a samovar of dark, Russian tea while Anna brought out a box of vanilla-fudge ice cream.

Once the table was reset, everyone received portions that Jim, already stuffed, found to be too much. His protests went unheeded.

"Has your father ever come to Russia?" Natalya asked.

"Нет [Nyet]. None of my family has ever been to Russia. My father has little to do with foreign affairs. His main focus is on domestic and financial affairs," Keating answered.

"Well, we hope your family comes and visits us someday," Natalya offered.

"Maybe some day. But realistically, I wouldn't be too optimistic."

"That's a shame. We would like to meet them," Katya answered.

"Well, if not your parents, then your sister had better come. She's young and has nothing to hold her back. Not knowing Russian is not a good enough reason to stay away," Natalya declared.

"I'll tell her that the next time I speak to her," Jim answered. "However, if my family can't come here, maybe it would be possible for you to come to the States."

109

"I don't think so. Our Rubles would never get us to France, much less. But your invitation is taken kindly," Natalya answered.

"I'm sorry. I shouldn't have mentioned it," the American apologized, realizing that he had overlooked the country's financial problems. "I'm really sorry if I offended anyone."

"You have no need to apologize. We know you're sincere and meant no harm," Anna answered on behalf of the Kalinina family.

"So I guess we'll be getting ready to go to Баррикадная [Barrikadnaya]," Natalya suggested as they finished the last of their desserts, referring to the metro station outside the U.S. Embassy.

"Thanks for the really delicious meal and desserts," Jim Keating expressed his gratitude to the young Russian woman's mother and babushka.

"You're welcome," they replied before directing their attention to Natalya who was assisting with the clean up. "Go ahead, go with him. We can take care of it."

"You sure?" Natalya asked not wanting to be rude.

"Positive. Go on now," Anna answered taking Natalya's towel and gently shooing her to the door.

"Very well," the Muscovite answered, drying off her hands and walking into the tiny hallway to retrieve her shoes. After allowing Jim to hold her coat while she slipped her arms into it, and reciprocating, the pair bidded one last farewell before stepping out into the chilly, dark hallway. "We'll see you later," Natalya called out.

Chapter 9

Once back into the hallway, Natalya took the American's hand. "So it wasn't that bad, was it?"

"Not so fast," Jim answered.

"What do you mean? My mom and babushka liked you, didn't they?" Natalya quickly asked as they made their way down the dark staircase.

"The day isn't over yet. By tomorrow they could feel differently about me, especially if I make any more mistakes such as inviting them to America," Keating countered.

"Don't worry, they know you didn't mean it. Besides, if you were like most of your compatriots, you would've never set foot in a Russian's house, in the first place. After all, we Russians are beneath most of you American's, да [yes]?" she stated with a tinge of sarcasm.

"Do you seriously expect me to answer you?" the American asked, taking the door and holding it open for his Russian friend.

"You better not or else you'll be sorry!" Natalya playfully warned. "Besides, for you, the hardest part is already over. When we get back, all we'll do is drink some nice Russian vodka," she toyed.

"For a moment, I was hopeful you forgot! Wasn't the wine enough?"

"Нет, нет, нет [Nyet, nyet, nyet]!" the Muscovite woman quickly emphasized. "There's no way I'm going to let

111

you get out of it," she added as the pair walked back across the street into the park.

As they slowly walked hand-in-hand through the darkening park, Jim became increasingly conscious of the evaporating warmth of the afternoon. "I guess asking for three warm days here is too much to ask for," he declared, as a chilly breeze kicked up, and the puddles began to ice over.

"What did you expect, this is Moscow!"

"Can I ever get any sympathy from you?" Jim teased the Russian.

"Sure you can," Natalya quickly answered him. "Here let me help you keep warm," she added, suddenly embracing and kissing him.

"Here in the cold?" the American asked, as the Muscovite tightly pressed his body into hers.

"Yes, here. I'll keep you warm. Kiss me," Natalya momentarily answered before resuming her tight grip and kissing him. The American quickly reciprocated, embracing and kissing her. As they passionately kissed in the dark park, both lost awareness of the passing pedestrians who occasionally glanced their way.

"I'll keep you warm," she repeated between breaths, when they momentarily parted lips. "And you'll keep me warm."

Afterwards, both held onto each other, kissing in silence, for several minutes. As they did so, the American forgot about the growing the night chill. He enjoyed the subtle warmth the young Muscovite's soft body emitted.

"I've waited for this moment all week," Natalya finally broke the silence, gradually lifting her lips from his and relinquishing her grip. "I almost did this when we were at GUM!" she exclaimed.

112

"I'd be lying if I said I wasn't tempted myself," Jim answered sharing the strong mutual attraction. "I only held off because I didn't want to create an international incident," he then playfully added.

"So? Do you think I really care?" Natalya answered, momentarily switching to English, with a serious-sounding Russian-accent.

"I didn't think so," Jim replied in Russian. "Neither do I!"

"Good, then why waste out breaths over it," Natalya answered, again taking hold of her friend. "Let's do it again."

Without hesitating, the American quickly complied as they took each other in their arms. "You're such a wonderful person," Jim exclaimed as they locked lips and kissed in silence for 20 seconds.

"So are you. I'm really glad we met. Thank you for attacking me at Красная Площадь [Red Square]."

"Thank you for being so good-natured about it. Thank you for being there when I was."

"Maybe you should thank, Tatyana. If she wasn't visiting, I don't know if I would've been there then," Natalya answered before kissing him again. "I'll tell her `thank you' for you."

"I'm serious."

"I know and so am I."

"I can't believe I had to come all the way over here to meet you," Jim grew serious. "All these years I've waited..."

"That's because it's hard finding a Russian woman in New York, and besides I've never been in New York, so how could you find me there?" Natalya quickly interrupted the American before kissing him again. "What you need is a good Russian woman!"

"Did you say a St. Petersburg woman?" Jim teased the Muscovite, fully aware of the historical rivalry between the people of Moscow and St. Petersburg as each viewed their respective city as the center of Russian civilization. The roots of the rivalry dated back to 1710 when Peter the Great named the young city the new capital of Russia, only seven years after its first structures were built onto an empty swampland. During Peter the Great's reign, numerous magnificent stone palaces and cathedrals were erected in St. Petersburg, thrusting the northwestern city to the center of Russian civilization. To ensure the new capital's dominance and prevent the emergence of rival cities, Moscow, once the Constantinople of Russia and every other Russian city were prohibited from building anything out of stone. This ban remained in effect until 1741 when it was repealed.

Despite St. Petersburg's advantage, Peter II renamed Moscow the capital of Russia in 1727, only two years after his grandfather's death. However, like Peter II's brief reign, Moscow's standing as Russia's capital was short-lived. In 1732 St. Petersburg again replaced Moscow as the capital of Russia, and held that distinction until 1918, a year after the Bolshevik Revolution.

"If you ever mention that city again, I'll..." Natalya playfully admonished her friend, grabbing him by the collar of his coat.

"Calm down. I just wanted to get your blood boiling," the American playfully interrupted. "Believe me, no one in St. Petersburg comes close in comparison to you," Jim added taking the Muscovite's hand and kissing it.

"That's better," Natalya answered, pretending to forgive him. "I couldn't let you have the better of me."

"I know," Jim exclaimed, kissing the Muscovite's hand a second time, before they embraced again. Afterwards, they again held onto each other and kissed for several minutes in silence.

"We better get going," Natalya finally interrupted. "If we don't get back soon, my mom and babushka might start worrying about us."

"You're probably right. We shouldn't worry them needlessly," Jim agreed as they kissed another time before slowly releasing each other.

"Besides, the sooner I get you back, the sooner I can get you so drunk you'll say anything and do anything I want," Natalya playfully teased her friend, before putting her arm around him as they walked the final steps into the metro station.

"I can imagine," Jim warmly replied, reciprocating.

"I'm dying to have you completely at my mercy, completely under my control – completely mine," the Russian playfully added.

"That's you Russian's. And you say we're the imperialists!" Keating teased the Muscovite in return, before adding, "But since you're a special woman and I trust you like myself, I don't mind."

"I know. Otherwise I wouldn't have forewarned you until it was too late," Natalya cheerfully replied briefing pulling his body against hers.

"I'm sure of that," he replied as they kissed for one last time, before separating to walk through the metro's turnstiles. "You're the only person I trust enough to let you do it."

"That's nice to hear. I guess that's why we're such good friends," Natalya added before both, upon seeing the subway pulling into the station, ran the rest of the distance.

As they boarded the crowded train, Natalya's heart beat with joy and relief that her strong feelings were mutual. "Спасибо [Thank you]," she quietly whispered to no one in particular, grateful of the way the American revered her. At the same time, Jim also silently whispered his own thanks --

ВЕСНА РУССКАЯ

"Thank you God, for having given me the opportunity to meet her."

    With the bond growing between the two of them, afterthoughts about the possible consequences of future political events retreated further from their minds. Both, rapidly falling in love, found themselves powerless to resist. They were fully conscious of their inability to resist the powerful bond of the growing attraction that was sweeping them into each other's hearts. Knowing this, neither needed to explore the reason or purpose of their earthly existence, a question that philosophers had been grappling with for the last several millennia. They had been born for one reason -- to love, care for, and serve each other. Sharing the same common thoughts, Natalya and Jim held hands for the entire return ride to Красные Ворота Metro Station. Unlike the great thinkers of the past, both had found their soul mate and the meaning of their lives.

Chapter 10

"Доброе утро [Good morning], Natasha," Elena Potapova warmly greeted her Muscovite friend, who hurried into the KGB offices nearly an hour late. As she hurried to her desk, Natalya still showed symptoms of the weekend. Her chestnut hair hung in sharp contrast to its usual, meticulous appearance, her eyes were still a little red and irritated, and her head still felt heavy from the weekend. With her brain still in a vodka-induced stasis, Potapova's greetings did not register. "Did I catch you at a bad time?" Elena hesitated, touching her friend's arm.

"Oh what is it. Oh, Lena, I didn't notice you. I'm sorry," Natalya apologized." Доброе утро [Good morning]," the Muscovite quickly added as Elena's greeting finally registered in her sluggish brain.

"Are you all right?" Elena asked with concern, never having recalled seeing her in such a stupor since their college days when they heralded the end of each semester. "Here, let me help you," Potapova offered, taking her friend by the hand.

"Спасибо [Thank you], but I'll be okay."

"Нет [Nyet], let me help you."

"Нет [Nyet] really, I'm okay," Natalya assured her St. Petersburg friend.

BECHA PYCCKAЯ

"Нет [Nyet], I insist," Elena persisted. Resisting Natalya's efforts, Potapova led her friend to her cubicle, tightly clutching her hand. In spite of being several months Natalya's junior, Elena took responsibility for her friend whenever she felt her friend needed help. "I want to make sure you're all right. That's what friends are for."

"Спасибо [Thank you], Lena."

"Stay right here. Don't move," Elena then commanded when Natalya took her seat. "I'm going to get you a cup of coffee. It'll help you feel better," Potapova declared.

"Thank you."

"Here, drink this," Elena immediately suggested, sliding Natalya a thick, large ceramic mug, after returning from the KGB's small kitchen.

"It's too hot," Kalinina quickly protested upon taking one sip of the steaming, rich black coffee.

"It'll wake you up."

"I'm sure it will," Natalya replied, taking a few more burning sips. "If it doesn't burn my insides first!"

"You must've had a great weekend. Tell me about it," Elena prodded. "What did you do?"

"I think I found my love," the Muscovite answered, trying to maintain a straight business-as-usual face.

"Поздравления [Congratulations]!" Elena quickly cried out. "Tell me about him."

Knowing that there was no way of keeping it secret, Natalya relented after securing a promise from her friend that she would tell no one, not even Valentin Makarov, her immediate boss. Natalya was fearful that word of her relationship with an American might damage her supervisor's confidence in her, and ultimately lead to her expulsion from the RNR movement. "Believe me, I'm as dedicated to our

118

liberation as anyone else," she then exclaimed to Elena, taking her by the hand. "You believe me, don't you?" the Muscovite pleaded for a vote of confidence from her friend.

"Of course I believe you. Let's be serious. I have nothing against the American people or any other Westerner for that matter. I'm only against their imperialist regimes. So I see nothing wrong with your relationship with Jim."

"Спасибо [Thank you]," Natalya replied.

"Since he's not like our colonial masters, or else you wouldn't be stupid enough to go out with him, I say good for you. Russia can use some good Americans. If you ask me, I say go for it!"

"Спасибо [Thank you]. I knew I could count on you. I knew you would be understanding," Kalinina expressed her faith in Potapova.

"Likewise, I know I can always count on your support. I guess that's why we became friends in spite of your Moscow roots," the St. Petersburg native replied.

"You mean, in spite of your St. Petersburg roots," Natalya quickly retorted, her brain having been revitalized by the large cup of steaming black coffee.

"Let's call a truce before things get out of hand," Elena warmly suggested, placing her arm on Kalinina's shoulder.

"Truce," Natalya offered her hand in agreement.

"So did you hear, that Meliacherov (Russian President Igor Meliacherov) has decided to sell the West a 50% stake in St. Basil's Cathedral to finance some of our debts?" Elena Potapova asked, growing serious.

"Нет [Nyet]. He can't do that!" Natalya protested with dismay, knowing that the world-famous edifice with its multi-colored onion-domed spires and humble interior antechambers was part of the heart of Russian heritage.

119

ВЕСНА РУССКАЯ

"I'm serious. Meliacherov already agreed to it," Elena replied. "I...," her voice suddenly broke off, as hot tears welled in her Russian eyes.

"When did this go through?" Natalya asked, feeling the anger welling up in her Russian veins.

"He decided early this morning. I found out through a CNN report," Potapova sobbed.

"I don't believe it. How could he?" Natalya protested, embracing her tearful friend. "Whose idea was it?"

"The Japanese. They say it will bring more revenue in private hands."

"Everything is `private' with them. They can't leave anything alone," Kalinina angrily replied, holding back her own tears.

"What a sacrilege. Pretty soon Russians won't be able to go to their own shrines!
After all we won't be able to afford their prices."

"Not if we stay on this path. But why does everything have to be for a cost. Why can't we just visit our own institutions for free like before," Natalya cried, still tightly holding her friend, as a tear slowly trickled down her cheek. "Do the Russian people know?"

"Нет [Nyet], or at least I doubt it. How many people have access to CNN? Meliacherov made no announcements, that's for sure."

"I'm sorry," Natalya apologized as both mourned Mother Russia's great loss. "Someday we'll reclaim what is ours!"

"I sure hope so. As much as it seems that we're making some progress, it also seems like our ordeal will never end," Elena declared thinking of the RNR's inability to stem Russia's hemorrhaging. "Sometimes when I attend services at Yelokhovsky Cathedral I ask what have we done to deserve this. Why have we been forsaken?" Potapova lamented. "Our opinions don't count. We're no longer respected as a people."

"Cheer up. These dark days will soon end," Natalya tried to lift her friend's sagging spirits. At the same time, while her heart ached, Natalya wondered if she could really believe her own words of encouragement. Trying to reinforce her own weakened faith, Kalinina thought back to another period in history, when Russia had suffered under a similar "Era of humiliation."

The decade was the 1680s, which saw Russia fall under the rule of three different Czars and a regent. During this period, Russia was torn apart by chaos. Shortly after the death of Fedor III (eldest son of Alexis), who had left no heirs during his brief five year reign (most of it from his sickbed), a bitter feud broke out among the two wings of the Romanov dynasty -- the Miloslavskys (whose daughter, Maria bore Fedor III) and the Naryshkinas (whose daughter, Natalya became Alexis's second wife, when he remarried after the death of Maria). Each demanded that their offspring be crowned the next Czar. The Miloslavskys did not want to lose the prestige they presently held, while the Naryshkinas wanted to attain the same level of influence. Such a level of prestige and influence could not be shared.

When the decision was finally made to crown Peter (son of Natalya Naryshkina), instead of his elder stepbrother Ivan (brother of Fedor III and son of Maria Miloslavskaya), Ivan's sister, Sofya Miloslavskaya helped stage a revolt, which was ultimately put down.

During this period of turmoil, foreign imperialists, most notably the Governments of England and the Netherlands sought to carve out their own colonial spheres. Each pursued its own policies of exploitation -- gaining access to unlimited amounts of cheap raw materials. Both

ВЕСНА РУССКАЯ

nations reasoned that their wealth, stability and power would be undermined if they did not impose their own policies. Costly substitute raw materials would impoverish their treasuries, hinder their ability to make war to acquire new colonial territories, compromise their standards of life, and ultimately lead to a breakdown of order and stability. One Dutch 17th century Dutch Legislator wrote, "The wealth of our Netherlands is based upon trade and shipping. ...There is ...a new path, which is just as profitable as the sea trade with New Spain. This is the path to Moscow."1

During this period when the European powers (France, Sweden, as well as England and the Netherlands) exploited Russian territorial integrity at will, they viewed Russian's in the same condescending way as their 21st century Western descendents. Russians were labeled as "inferior, primitive Asiatics, sunk in sloth and vice, and uncivilized by any decent standard."2 This attitude of European superiority was captured in a poem by Holsteiner:

Churches, ikons (sic), crosses, bells,
Painted whores and garlic smells,
Vice and vodka everyplace --
This is Moscow's daily face.

To loiter in the market air,
—To bathe in common, bodies bare,
To sleep by day and gorge by night,
To belch and fart is their delight.

Thieving, murdering, fornication
are so common in this nation,
No one thinks a brow to raise --
Such are Moscow's sordid days.3

122

Also during this period, Russians suffered further injustices at the hands of the Ottomans and their Tatar lackeys. They sold nearly one out of every 35 Russians into slavery.4

As bleak as the situation was then, Russia had managed to liberate herself under the guidance of Peter the Great, (the son of Natalya Naryshkina) when he finally gained full control of the Kremlin in 1689.

Reflecting back on that parallel era and its successful conclusion under strong leadership, Natalya Kalinina felt renewed confidence that the present generation of Russians would also be able to find a strong leader and muster the courage to take decisive action to again liberate their country from the clutches of Western colonialism.

"How many times can Russia resurrect herself?" Elena asked, well aware of her country's past history.

"I don't know. The only thing I can say, is that as long as even the tiniest flicker of hope burns in our hearts and the smallest strand of our heritage remains alive, there is always hope."

"As much as I believe that, I still can't help but sometimes wonder whether our beloved country has died and we refuse to recognize it, deluding ourselves with false hopes and a yearning for the past."

"Sometimes I feel the same way. To answer those doubts, I ask myself one question -- `Am I willing to accept the status-quo?' As long as my answer is `Нет [Nyet]!' I know there's hope. I also know that I'm not alone. So I ask you Lena, are you willing to accept the status-quo?" Natalya softly asked, placing her arm around her friend.

"Нет [Nyet]! Никогда [Never]!" Elena passionately answered.

"Well then, Russia has not died," Natalya replied stressing `not'. What the West hasn't counted on is that we're a persistent and resilient people. We'll never surrender. We'll never allow them to extinguish the flame of our pride. We were born Russians and we will die Russians!"

Following their lengthy conversation of the plight of their country, Natalya Kalinina and Elena Potapova devoted their energies to their KGB assignments. Through their arduous labors, both dreamed of the coming day when they would be free again. They could almost hear the rallying cry to retake St. Basil's Cathedral. If anything, the pro-Western Meliacherov Government had fueled Russian passions by bargaining away one of their most hallowed treasures. Instead of giving the West a firmer grip on their society, they had given the RNR Movement a great, new incentive to live, fight and if necessary, to die for.

1 М.Н. Покровский [M.N. Pokrovskii], "Русская История С Древнишк Времен [Russkaya Istoria C Drevneishkh Vremen]" (Moscow, 1933), Vol. 2, p. 177.

2 W. Bruce Lincoln, "Romanovs - Autocrats of All the Russias," (NY: Doubleday, 1981), p. 307.

3 W. Bruce Lincoln, p. 307.

4 W. Bruce Lincoln, p. 309.

Chapter 11

At the dawn of February, a renewed arctic wave swept over beleaguered Russia, which had already suffered under winter's terrible grip for a week-and-a-half, with no relief in sight. Temperatures in Moscow fell to record lows of -35° Fahrenheit, reinforcing the already foot-thick layer of ice that covered the city's concrete walkways.

With the arctic spell came a new, unprecedented period of suffering. The scant amounts of food sold by Russian stores disappeared. Fuel prices soared beyond reach of most of the nation. Unable to find ample amounts to eat and the needed funds for heat, Russians were mercilessly thrust into death's icy bosom.

Light flurries softly fell from Moscow's leaden sky, as Russians struggled to endure the cold while waiting in the long lines. All hoped and prayed that they would be able to find something for their next meal. Old women and pensioners, who had devoted their lives in service of their country, sobbed in the cold streets as they slowly filed past the well-lit, modern windows of the West's Hard Currency shops. The shops' visible displays of fresh produce and premium cuts of meat only magnified the aching of their hungry stomachs.

ВЕСНА РУССКАЯ

"How am I going to feed my grandchildren?" an elderly babushka wept, as two, thin young girls, huddled close together.

"Please help me," an elderly man begged passing Western tourists who cruelly turned a deaf ear to his pleas.

Another elderly woman, unable to withstand the cold's severity, sat slumped over in the frigid hallway of a metro station, desperately trying to catch the escaping warmth each time someone opened the glass doors. Having not eaten for a week, she sifted with resignation, through the dirt and ice. Her hands were badly swollen from frostbite. Incoherent from the affects of her excruciating ordeal and desperate the quench her unbearable hunger, she struggled to push granules of sand into her severely parched mouth. Others, who could afford it, used vodka to drown their misery, peacefully slipping into unconsciousness and then death.

A small group of pensioners and handicapped, still able to stand, held out empty cups nearby, praying that this day, unlike the day before, and the day before the day-before, would yield some fruits.

A few blocks away, small groups of people desperately tried to sell away their only true companions -- for some a cat and others a dog. They were eager to get a few Rubles for a mere loaf of bread. In the saddest scene of all, several babushkas, with ice-caked cheeks, where their tears had long since froze, begged passing pedestrians to take their grandchildren, desperately hoping that they would be able to give them the warmth, shelter and food they could no longer provide.

This horrendous plight was not limited to the elderly alone. Many of the young, victim's of stream-lining to boost productivity of Western-owned plants found themselves sharing in the same, cold, snaking lines with beggars. Small packs of children, some newly orphaned by the arctic chill, others abandoned by parents unable to provide for them, also scrounged around looking for the tiniest morsel and slightest warmth to sustain their young, vulnerable lives.

As the bitter cold entombed much of the Russian nation, apartments became refrigerated coffins for many who quietly breathed their last; slipping away from the icy-hell they had suffered in. Streets became icy avenues of death.

With each passing minute, another person, left all alone with no one to comfort him or her, passed from their earthly existence. There was no one to mourn them.

Life endured as best as possible, with each person oblivious to the mounting toll and the sufferings of their fellow human beings. Death, in its cold and unfeeling way did not discriminate, taking as many lives as possible. Young and old, men and women alike, fell victim.

As if in mourning, the many cathedrals and monasteries that dotted Moscow and the Russian countryside, concealed their once colorful onion-domed spires under blankets of gray and white. Buildings also had their colors smothered under thick colorless blankets of ice and snow. In addition, sheets of gray and white covered, the once vibrant green of Russia's evergreens and the naked branches of her deciduous trees. Like the vitality of her people, Russia had been drained of all color.

Tightly bundled police officers kept a watchful eye as increasingly impatient crowds stood in long lines and small agitated groups milled around Moscow's Western-run shops, peering at the food, though separated by only a sheet of glass, was far beyond their reach. Already, as the arctic weather maintained its hold for eleven long days, several incidents all targeted at Russian-run kiosks and the rich Russian "entrepreneurial-class" had been reported. Although

127

most Russians held the West and their well dressed, well-fed tourists in contempt, no Western-run entities had come under attack, partly due to the massive police presence that stood nearby. Another reason they had escaped unscathed was that as great as the peoples' anger was towards the West, Russians held their own kind who had willingly betrayed their homeland for a few Dollars -- the kiosk owners who stocked their shelves with expensive Western chocolates, cigarettes, and perfumes, members of the entrepreneurial class who flaunted their excesses, and the Meliacherov Government -- in far greater contempt.

With each additional day of -30° Fahrenheit cold, the explosive situation in and around Moscow became increasingly fluid. Fearing for the safety of her babushka, Natalya Kalinina refused to let her venture out of their tiny apartment. Her friend, Elena Potapova placed similar restrictions on her own grandmother in St. Petersburg.

As they quietly reflected on the brutal cold, Valentin Makarov suddenly interrupted the pair. "I just got this cable from Karelian Governor Sheremetev. Come to my office. I must brief you," he spoke in a hushed tone.

Just prior to the unprecedented cold wave, Valentin Makarov had obtained approval to have Elena Potapova transferred under his command, so she could also assist the underground RNR movement. Elena's former supervisor, also a secret RNR member and designate to Makarov, should the movement be compromised and Makarov's identity be exposed, had obliged unconditionally.

Once the two women were seated in Valentin's office, he quickly shut the door. Valentin then began after taking a seat behind his desk. "More than 250 of Sheremetev's people have died of starvation and the cold in the last two days alone." Everyone silently paid their respects with heads bowed for a few seconds before Valentin resumed. "The situation is getting worse. The State's allocated fuel reserves are virtually exhausted..."

"How many day's of fuel do they have left?" Natalya asked, fearful that the province, plagued by temperatures 10 to 15 degrees colder than Moscow would not be able to hold out.

"Only enough for two more days," Makarov glumly reported. "Worse yet, Karelia's privately-run gas consortium refuses to sell its own supplies at below market prices."

"You mean at amounts less than Western-set levels," Elena interjected.

"That is correct."

"What is he going to do about it?" Natalya asked with concern. "They need the fuel. Without it, they'll die!"

"That's the tragic truth. That's why I summoned you. Others are also being informed of the crisis. Contents of his cable, though, must be guarded with the strictest secrecy. Word must not get out. You understand, да [yes]?"

"Да [Yes], you can depend on us," both Natalya and Elena promised.

"As far as we're all concerned, this cable never existed. The only reason he sent it is because he's sympathetic to our movement," Valentin continued.

"We understand," Natalya and Elena repeated their promise.

"Very good. The Governor sent an appeal 24 hours ago to the Meliacherov Government, pleading for assistance. As of this morning, they have not responded," Valentin declared restraining the anger in his voice. "While we suffer and die, they wait for warm weather, hoping this nightmare will go away by itself."

"They don't want to do anything that might offend their masters," Natalya added, knowing that permission to issue new State credits would infuriate the IMF (international bank operated by the "elite 7" Colonial powers).

"Sheremetev is fully aware of this," Valentin spoke.

"Still he must do something. The Karelians are his people," Elena declared referring to Sheremetev's provincial constituency.

"And he will. If by 9:00 this evening, he's still received no word from the President, he'll declare a state of emergency. With backing from Commander Klisov and his 2000 troops, the Karelian Government will seize control of Finlandia's Gas facilities!" In spite of its name, the privately operated gas consortium had no Finnish connections. It was merely named "Finlandia Gas" by its American and West European stockholders, because of Karelia's close proximity to Finland. "Food supplies will also be seized from Karelia's Western markets and distributed evenly among the people."

"It's about time someone's going to act!," the two agents agreed in unity, in spite of the dangers Sheremetev's plan posed. "What are his chances?" Elena finally asked.

"Not good. He expects Meliacherov to intervene. Realistically, how could he not? The West controls him. They'll certainly want their facilities repatriated."

"Our facilities, you mean!" Natalya angrily interrupted.

"Да [Yes], our facilities. I stand corrected," Makarov apologized for his poor choice of words. "The only thing Governor Sheremetev hopes for before his arrest, is that he'll have bought enough time for his people. If all of the food is distributed, there's little Meliacherov's lackeys can do to recover it."

"It's so sad," Elena Potapova exclaimed. "A good man only looking after his own people will be punished or even executed."

130

"Not for crimes against Russia, but crimes against the West!" Natalya added.

"Let's just hope that Sheremetev has enough time, and that this cold spell breaks soon."

"They'll still need heat, even if it does warm up to let's say 20° or 30° [Fahrenheit]," Elena declared.

"That's true, but all we can do now is wait and see what happens," Valentin Makarov replied with caution. "Because of this, I'll have to ask you to stay here tonight."

"Gladly," both Natalya and Elena answered. "Anything for our country."

"I'll need help. We'll have to monitor all Western news reports, especially since it's unlikely the Russian press will be allowed to report objectively. The Meliacherov Government wouldn't want word of the Karelia uprising to get out for fear that it could spread to other provinces and perhaps even to Moscow proper. People here are already on edge."

"We know."

"In addition, Governor Sheremetev has promised to keep us informed. His administration will be periodically sending cables. To avoid suspicion, they'll be sent to various RNR members in our organization. I can't have my fax machine tied up, just in case Meliacherov dispatches his own requests. But before I ask you to accept this assignment, I must inform the both of you that should you accept, you'll be putting yourselves at risk. If discovered, you'll certainly be executed!"

"We knew of the risks when we joined," Natalya quickly answered. "You needn't remind us. I'm ready to accept. I accept," she added.

"I also accept," Elena firmly replied.

"Very well," Valentin Makarov accepted their willingness, before instructing them further. "When you

131

receive the cables, read them and memorize them. Then destroy them. I'll call you in when it's appropriate, and reveal the contents of the other cables. In return you'll reveal your information, so I can share it with other agents in our movement. Do not share your information with anyone else," their KGB supervisor cautioned. "Those that need know will be informed. You may only share information attained from media reports."

"Very well," Natalya and Elena agreed.

"Since you two are good friends, I'll have you working together. I've broken our members into small teams to avoid suspicion. In the meantime, Natalya, since I know you may need to satisfy some family needs, I'm assigning you and Elena to monitor the situation in Moscow until 6 PM. Walk the streets, go into the shops and watch for signs of disturbances. Then get back to me this evening with your observations," Valentin instructed the two agents, knowing of Natalya's concern for the safety of her family.

"Большое спасибо [Thank you very much]," Natalya gratefully thanked her supervisor, placing her hand over his hand. She was well aware that he was giving them the day off to shop and take care of their personal needs.

After both thanked Valentin, they quickly pursued their new assignment to pass the time. They shopped together and spent most of the afternoon at the Kalinina residence, eating and talking with Natalya's babushka, Anna. Their presence provided her with welcome companionship.

Despite the conviviality of the Kalinina residence, both counted the minutes before they would have to return to the KGB offices. As the hour for their return neared, both showered and changed, with Elena borrowing some of her friend's attire. Butterflies fluttered in their stomachs, as they

entered the metro for their ride back to Лубянка Площадь
[Lubyanka Square].

Chapter 12

A howling gale tore through the Karelian night, as the frigid Siberian cold front made a renewed push into western Russia and Eastern Europe. The mercury offered little resistance, quickly plummeting below -50° Fahrenheit.

Under the cover of darkness, groups of tanks and armored personnel carriers (APCs) stealthily rolled along the deserted streets, silently taking up positions outside Karelia's closed markets. An hour after nightfall, all streetlights in the Karelian Republic had been turned off under the pretext of conserving precious, dwindling fuel supplies.

Other tanks and APCs silently and efficiently closed in on the brightly lit facilities of Finlandia Gas Consortium (FGC). As the noose slowly tightened around FGC, all avenues of escape gradually disappeared.

Far removed from the dark towns and bitter cold of Karelia, Natalya Kalinina and Elena Potapova sipped coffee, viewing CNN on a tiny, portable television set situated in Elena's cubicle. Subsequent to Elena's transfer under the command of Valentin Makarov, her cubicle was conveniently relocated next the Natalya's working space. With their close proximity, both got added space and attracted less attention when they held private conversations.

Despite the ruling Government's claims of running a "democracy," Russia was anything but free. Russia was an economically burdened colony of the West. Only supporters of the West and news organizations sympathetic to the pro-West Meliacherov Government were permitted to use the airwaves. In sharp contrast to Russia's continued deterioration and the growing misery of her people, most stories on the evening news dealt with Moscow's rising stock market and "improving productivity." In the latter, only the elite few, many of them members of organized crime were able to participate, while in the former, production rose at the expense of Russian employment as foreign nationals were brought in to supposedly "manage" and improve "quality." What was not said in these news broadcasts was that most of the revenues generated from these "Russian" products were going overseas. Only a smattering of Kopeks went to Russians.

Because of the bias of the Russian news media, Natalya Kalinina and Elena Potapova found CNN the most reliable source of news. Both knew that when Governor Sheremetev's troops commenced operations to repatriate Russian property, Moscow's news would not issue any reports, fearing that such bulletins could cause further unrest. Reports would only be issued after the fact, if the Kremlin felt they could crush any potential, resulting rebellion.

Once in position, Commander Mikhail Klisov's troops awaited further orders from Karelian Governor Valeri Sheremetev. The 9:00 PM deadline came and went without word from Moscow.

With the deadline having passed without any offers of assistance from the Meliacherov Government, Governor Sheremetev urgently summoned his Republic's Duma into emergency session.

ВЕСНА РУССКАЯ

When the Duma convened at 9:30 PM, Governor Sheremetev outlined his plans, passionately pleading for the legislature's backing:

> As you all know, Karelia is faced with grave fuel and food shortages. The FGC refuses to supply us if we don't meet their exorbitant demands. Our kiosks have been depleted days ago. Western-run markets refuse to make their hordes available. Faced with the prospect of a massive human catastrophe reminiscent to the famine of the 1930s, I appealed to President Meliacherov for assistance. My pleas have gone unanswered.
>
> As Governor of Karelia, I cannot allow the Karelian people to perish. To do so would be a gross failure on my part to uphold the duties of my office. I was elected to serve the Karelian people, and will not forsake my sworn duty. Although some of you will object to what I am about to propose and will most certainly call for my impeachment and notify Moscow, I have decided to call this Duma into session to give us an opportunity to stand in unity. This is an historic chance for us to stand up for our people, for Karelia and for Russia. Furthermore, since Moscow will find out about my intentions, the prospect of some of you contacting them is irrelevant.
>
> When I appealed to President Meliacherov to require the FGC to make their fuel available to

us and compel the Western-run markets to share their food with our people, he chose not to act. Because of the urgency of our situation, with no relief in sight, and no prospect of receiving assistance of any kind from Moscow, we must look to ourselves for action. The Karelian people must be saved by Petrozavodsk [capital of Karelia]. *All necessary action must come from Petrozavodsk. It is our moral duty to save our 800,000 people from otherwise inevitable deaths of freezing and starvation if we do not act.*

Accordingly I and the Karelian people appeal for your support in using military force to obtain the necessary supplies of food and fuel…

"Please don't let us… please don't let your families down," Governor Sheremetev concluded his speech in front of the convened Duma."

Within minutes of the speech, after a few dissenters warning of grave consequences were rebutted by Sheremetev's supporters who warned of equally grave consequences if the Duma failed to support the Governor's pleas, the legislators held a voice vote, backing Sheremetev's plans by a 90-6 margin with 4 abstentions.

Having obtained backing, Valeri Sheremetev issued orders to Commander Klisov to begin operations. Shortly after 10:00 PM when most had retired for the night, trying their best to shield themselves from the bitter arctic cold, the Karelian military began their mission. Soldiers rushed from APCs, as tanks rolled through FGC's barbed wire fence. Upon breaching the plant's perimeter barriers, the soldiers

ВЕСНА РУССКАЯ

rushed towards the brightly lit facilities meeting little resistance.

As the soldiers backed by tanks and helicopters rushed towards FGC's buildings, the vast majority of the consortium's private security force, all of Russian nationality, switched sides, leaving it up to their poorly-armed foreign supervisors to defend the plant.

Within an hour, Klisov's troops secured the last parts of the FGC complex and took its few foreign resisters and managers into custody. At the same time other soldiers consolidated their hold over the Karelian Republic's towns and cities, setting up heavily armed checkpoints on major streets. Armed guards were posted outside the Republic's posh Western markets, in preparation for the next day's food and clothing distribution.

> *23:45 Karelian Russians have successfully regained control over the Karelian Republic, Russia. First phase of operations have been completed. The Republic's economic facilities have been secured.*
>
> *—Valeri*

Upon receiving the telex from his friend and comrade, Valentin Makarov informed members of the RNR Movement of the successful completion of Governor Sheremetev's objectives to liberate his people from winter's harsh grip. "We have a lot to be thankful for tonight," he told each RNR member in private sessions. "The liberation of Russia has finally begun!" his words echoed in the heads of Natalya Kalinina and Elena Potapova, as they silently stood next to each other on the desolate platform at Станция

Метро Лубянка [Lubyanka Metro Station]. Each knew that the Karelian victory was only one battle won, a victory whose outcome could be reversed within hours pending Moscow's response when pro-Western President Meliacherov learned of the news.

Tired from the long day, filled with hours of tension and anticipation from the moment that the Karelian Governor's plans had been revealed to them, both agents shivered on the icy platform. Feeling the effects of the unprecedented cold, Natalya pulled up the collar of her jacket and tightened the woolen scarf that she had tied around her hair and ears. As they waited on the empty platform, a sobering silence enveloped the station. It was only broken by the howling Siberian winds rushing through the dark tunnels. Both quietly hoped for the best, praying for their country.

ВЕСНА РУССКАЯ

Chapter 13

Clusters of flurries quietly drifted down to Moscow's snow-covered streets sprinkling groups of tightly bundled Muscovites who struggled to make progress against the vicious 70+ MPH Siberian gales. With temperatures sitting around −30° Fahrenheit, the Russian Capital's streets became congested parking lots of stalled cars and trucks. Overcrowded trolleys battled to stay on course as the fierce winter winds violently tore at their overhanging wires, some of which had been supplying these electric vehicles since the days of the former Soviet Union. Metro stations were packed with shivering commuters and large groups of beggars seeking refuge from the harsh elements.

As Muscovites made their way through the crowded platforms, their lines slowed into a crawl. Having grown disillusioned and apathetic with the loss of hope after years of watching their country ravaged by Western and organized crime interests and their lives deteriorate into an abyss of a mere day-to-day existence, they could not believe the headlines that greeted them. In defiance of Kremlin censors, Pravda, Izvestia, and the Moscow Times reported the night's events:

Petrozavodsk: Russian troops backed by tanks and helicopter gunship took control of this city's huge gas consortium (Finlandia Gas Consortium) and Western-owned shops under orders from Karelian Governor Valeri Sheremetev to alleviate the Republic's food and energy crisis.

Although coverage was scant, many for the first time in two decades felt a glimmer of hope. As word of Karelia's repatriation of her facilities spread, many forgot the bone-numbing cold. They were too eager to pass the news on to others who had not yet heard. People began debating the Kremlin's response with total strangers. For the first time since the destruction of the Soviet Union, Muscovites gained an interest in their country. They cast aside the hardened layers of apathy that had accumulated over the years of corruption and disappointments. A sort of spring thaw filled their veins as they celebrated each update on the Karelian revolt. As Muscovites watched their fellow citizens taking control of their own region with the Kremlin failing to respond, their hopes were further buoyed. Some even dared to dream of Russia's liberation!

As Russians celebrated, United States Ambassador Stephen Norcross called an emergency meeting of senior diplomats and Central Intelligence Agency (CIA) operatives. "How could this happen?" the aging ambassador, a career nationalist out of Washington's military establishment, angrily demanded to know. "Why didn't you foresee this?" he questioned the embassy's CIA staff.

No one answered.

141

"This revolt could set us back for years. Democracy could be doomed. Worse yet, others who sympathize with these criminals may decide to overrun our embassy," Norcross continued.

"This is an isolated incident," one of the CIA officers tried to reassure the ambassador.

"How can you be sure? I'm taking no chances. I want the marine guard on orange alert. If the Meliacherov Government doesn't act soon, things could get worse," the American ambassador warned.

"Meliacherov won't stand by," Robert Salerno, a career diplomat who had recently been promoted to Deputy Ambassador, reassured Stephen Norcross. "Politically he can't afford to do nothing. Otherwise Russian relations with the United States and all of Europe will be severely harmed. With damaged relations there'll be no more IMF loans and without these funds, Russia will collapse."

"Maybe so, but with every passing hour they wring their hands trying to figure out a plan, the situation deteriorates. They must act immediately! In the meantime," Ambassador Norcross continued, turning to the embassy's CIA staff, "I want to hear of any further disturbances as soon as you learn of them."

"At the present, the uprising remains confined to the Karelian Republic," Jim Keating answered on behalf of the CIA intelligence staff.

"Very good," Norcross answered relieved that the revolt had not spread. "I e-mailed the President of the United States and informed him of the urgency of this situation. He'll get back to us as soon as he speaks to Meliacherov and makes it clear what must be done."

"He better act quickly. The lines are jammed with hundreds of irate executives calling in demanding we protect their investments!" Salerno declared.

"Quickly and decisively!" Norcross agreed before concluding the brief meeting to await a reply from the President of the United States.

"While the U.S. Embassy held their meeting, thousands of jubilant Karelians flocked into the Republic's icy streets, wildly cheering Mikhail Klisov's troops. Some waved the white, blue, and red tri-color Russian flag while others lofted banners saluting Klisov and the Republic's Governor.

Schools and businesses remained closed to allow families to pick up food and clothing that were being distributed from the Karelia's occupied, overstocked Western-run stores. Many after receiving their handouts, joyfully showered Klisov's soldiers with flowers and kisses. In gratitude, soldiers kissed babies and took young children on tank rides through the Republic's festive snow-covered streets.

Large crowds eagerly carried their newfound goods in sackcloth and paper bags, stopping along the way to assist their neighbors and elderly strangers, in a spirit of cooperation that had not been seen for years. With food and their first heat in a week, most put aside their pent-up misery.

In their euphoria, few in Karelia cared about the Kremlin's response. Not wanting to spoil their celebration, Karelians planned to worry about the repercussions when the time came and the Russian President had acted.

As Karelians celebrated, Natalya Kalinina and Elena Potapova along with most of the KGB, closely monitored the unfolding developments from their headquarters. Both awaited news on the outcome of the Kremlin's emergency session, which at first, when Russian President Igor

Meliacherov had called it, had caused rampant speculation that military action to crush the rebellion was imminent.

While awaiting word from the Kremlin, Natalya and Elena also scanned CNN reports, repeatedly hearing of the "West's resolve" – as leaders across Europe and North America denounced Karelian Governor Sheremetev's actions, calling for his arrest and the immediate return of the West's property. With constant, united condemnations and demands for the use of force from Western leaders, the agonizing wait for the Kremlin's response did little to assuage their fears that a massive spilling of Russian blood was possible.

During this waiting period, both Natalya and Elena were filled with tension, knowing that their organization would be asked to assist Meliacherov in putting down Sheremetev's rebellion. With butterflies fluttering in their stomachs, nightmare visions tormented their uneasy minds. They visualized receiving orders from Meliacherov to assist the Russian Government in uncovering their friends' activities, ultimately exposing the RNR movement. When not being tormented by fears of the Russian President's demands for assistance, they were concerned about being exposed by other agents assigned to cooperate with their pro-West leader.

"It won't happen," Natalya whispered placing her hands on Elena's shoulders. Although unwilling to watch her friend silently endure their shared agony, Kalinina could not help but wonder if her words were not also meant to ease her own fears. "It'll be all right," she quietly added.

"Да [Yes], I know. I'm all right," Elena Potapova whispered back knowing her friend was just as nervous.

"Good," Natalya quietly replied before returning back to her work to suffer in silence. She desperately wanted to know who in the KGB would be assigned the unenviable task of investigating the Karelian revolt. Without knowing whom the investigating agents were, she could not be sure how deep they would delve into the matter. She knew that pro-Western agents were likely to delve deeper into the rebellion than those who didn't share their sympathies. She knew that an in-depth investigation could pose a serious threat to herself, her friend Elena, and her immediate supervisor Valentin Makarov.

While Natalya Kalinina agonized over the depth and scope of the investigation and its resulting fallout, Elena Potapova tried to reassure herself that all communications between the RNR movement and Karelian Government had been destroyed. Despite their fears, both agents had no regrets about joining the secret, revolutionary movement.

As Natalya and Elena along with the rest of the KGB and Russia waited for the drama to unfold, the Kremlin was locked in a bitter debate over the course of action to be taken. On one hand, President Meliacherov's team of Western-educated ministers demanded swift action to appease their masters' impatient demands, while on the other hand, Defense Minister Yuri Likhovtsev resisted their calls, passionately warning that he could not guarantee his army's loyalty. He could still remember, as a young lieutenant, being forced to participate in Yeltsin's October 1993 Massacre when the democratically elected parliament was blasted from their headquarters. He could still remember the mixed feelings it had caused within the Russian military, with most like him, coming to regret the spilling of Russian blood.

With the army's morale already dangerously low from the West's two decades of disarming Russia through the conversion of her vital defense industries into consumer-oriented business owned and operated by foreigners,

Likhovtsev did not want to have to ask his soldiers to fire on their own people and repeat the mistake made two decades earlier.

With the conversion of Russia's defense industries into pots and pans outlets, the country lost much of her power and prestige. With her diminished standing, Russia was repeatedly denied regular NATO membership. Instead she was relegated to a perpetual, humiliating "observer status" in the defense organization.

"We can't just stand by," Russian Foreign Minister Sergei Kruchkov, a young pro-Western, former diplomat to Washington, declared. "If we allow them to get away with impunity, other rogue units will follow in their footsteps."

"They are not rogue units," Likhovtsev angrily defended his soldiers.

"Then how do you explain this criminal rebellion!" Kruchkov shot back pointing an accusing finger at the Defense Minister.

"I don't have to take that. My soldiers are all good people. What they have done falls far short of a revolt. The last time I looked, every elected official was still in power," Yuri Likhovtsev responded, making no effort to conceal his dislike for the 42-year-old, well-coiffered Foreign Minister who had become a popular member in Western circles.

During his tenure in the Foreign Ministry, dating back to his Washington days, Sergei Kruchkov had become a fixture at Western socials. He constantly delighted his Western hosts and friends with his pro-Western ideology and demeanor. He was also an especially popular attraction in the homes of many Western women to the dismay of his country's embassy. "That doesn't matter. The fact is they've looted stores and taken businessmen hostage!" Kruchkov declared.

"No one is a hostage!" Likhovtsev angrily countered before conceding that some prisoners were being held. "In spite of all, their motives are sincere," the Defense Minister tried to justify the acts of his soldiers, knowing that he could only count on their cooperation if he had their trust.

"I don't care how sincere their motives are. The fact remains – they've defiled everything we stand for. Theft and kidnapping are unacceptable and must not be tolerated!" Kruchkov retorted.

"What do you want me to do? Tell my soldiers to fire on their fellow soldiers?" Likhovtsev sarcastically asked.

"If necessary, да [yes]! We must restore law and order. We cannot allow chaos and anarchy to prevail."

"You give them the order and see how fast they'll obey!"

"I don't have to. They're your problem. You're the Defense Minister, and besides, my department is in order!" Kruchkov spoke with sarcasm.

"Okay, that's enough," the President finally intervened. "We have important business to discuss. Arguing will solve nothing. The way I see it is that we have a serious crisis that must be addressed immediately."

"That's what I've been saying while he's arguing that their motives are sincere and all that other bullshit," Foreign Minister Kruchkov took another shot at Likhovtsev. "I've been on the phone all morning. Everyone's concerned with what's happened in Karelia. Every ambassador I've spoken to demands prompt action. If we do nothing, they're threatening to pull out their investments. That's the last thing Russia needs!"

"We all agree on that," Defense Minister Likhovtsev concurred, ignoring his adversary's latest swipe. "But we must act with caution and give diplomacy a chance."

147

ВЕСНА РУССКАЯ

"Diplomacy for what and with whom? It's pure and simple – all property must be returned to its rightful owners and all hostages must be released. The renegade forces must either surrender or be suppressed by force. There can be no compromises," Kruchkov interrupted.

"Sergei is right," President Igor Meliacherov agreed. "If we give in now, the world will perceive us as impotent."

"Furthermore, if we cave in now, everyone will know they can take advantage of us. Our Government will be badly weakened. To do nothing or to compromise will give others ideas that they can defy us and get away with it because the Kremlin is soft. Before long, some ambitious son-of-a-bitch will plot a coup!" the Foreign Minister warned.

"No matter what, we can't give new life to the putsch movements of twenty years ago," President Meliacherov somberly spoke. "If we do, I'm afraid they'll be emboldened and our own blood will be spilled!" he added fully conscious of the Kremlin's ghosts. "I do not intend to be another victim on the long list of leaders murdered in the confines of these walls!" Meliacherov declared, fully aware of the Kremlin's violent history of betrayal and murder and the blood of fallen Czars, their families and supporters, and rebel forces who had died violent deaths through the ages. "We will take decisive action! That is the only way we can defend ourselves, our country and her interests."

"Which include continued Western investments and stability," the Foreign Minister interjected.

"I've spoken to the President of the United States and the leaders of the United Kingdom and Germany and assured them that order will be restored. The only question is how to proceed. How to proceed in a way that'll deter any such future activities," President Meliacherov continued, trying to present an atmosphere of calm. "But before we begin, I need to know who, in addition to the Karelian Governor and Klisov are involved. I must know how many people are involved and who they are so that each and every one of them is brought to account. Did anyone get the KGB reports I've requested?"

"I have them here," the Russian Prime Minister, Pavel Romanov, who despite his surname, was no relation to the Romanovs that had ruled Russia for nearly for centuries prior to the 1917 Revolution.

"How can we be sure their information is reliable?" Sergei Kruchkov inquired, concerned about KGB sympathizers for the rebel cause. "I recommend we get info from an outside source. Until we know for sure how many and who in the defense and security establishments are involved, I don't feel comfortable placing sole reliance on their reports."

"Very well, you may request outside assistance," Meliacherov reluctantly agreed knowing that his Foreign Minister's concerns were valid. "You may request CIA assistance, but in the meantime we'll have to rely on our own intelligence reports. We cannot rule with paralysis."

Hearing no objections, the Russian President continued. "I'll send orders to Klisov that he immediately return all seized property, release all captives, and order his men back to the barracks. That should buy us some time until we can obtain more facts."

"And then what?" Sergei Kruchkov asked.

"Then we'll arrest the Karelian Governor and dissolve the Karelian Duma. Only those opposed to the revolt will be allowed to retain their seats when a replacement government is chosen," the President declared. "We'll also send in replacement forces to restore order."

"And what about Klisov and his group?" Kruchkov ventured further.

"They'll be dealt with in due time. Rest assured, they'll be prosecuted for treason," Meliacherov vowed.

"The military won't go for it," Defense Minister Yuri Likhovtsev warned. "It is my duty, Mr. President, to implore you to use prudence. I believe we can convince Klisov and his troops to withdraw to their barracks, but to demand anything more won't be possible."

"It must be. We can't allow a single rebel to go unpunished!" Foreign Minister Kruchkov demanded.

"Sergei is right. I won't allow them to go free and undermine Russia's well-being. If necessary, we'll use force to bring them to justice," Meliacherov answered.

"I'll do as you say," Likhovtsev reluctantly agreed, "but I must warn you, the army won't like the idea of going after their own."

"They don't have to like it. The only thing they have to do is obey. That's what they should've been trained to do! And if they refuse, it's treason no matter how you look at it and traitors must be punished!" Kruchkov interjected.

"Igor, I urge you to reconsider," the Defense Minister pleaded with his long-time friend. "Please, in this case be satisfied with an unconditional withdrawal and don't press the situation any further."

"Нет [Nyet]! You mustn't cave in," Kruchkov protested.

I know it's a very difficult situation and all of your concerns are warranted. Having listened to everyone's arguments, I must admit that I now lean towards diplomacy," the Russian President suddenly softened his stance. "Pavel, what do you recommend?" Meliacherov turned to his Prime Minister, whom he trusted a lot.

"That we exercise prudence. I believe we must follow Yuri's advice and settle for a mere withdrawal and the voluntary resignations of Sheremetev and his supporters. The way I see it is, we have two choices: We can either order Klisov's troops to withdraw and avoid bloodshed, even if it means granting them immunity this one time and only this one time, or we can see vengeance and risk civil war," Prime Minister Romanov answered.

"Our allies will never accept such a timid solution," Sergei Kruchkov warned, referring to the West's leaders, all of whom called for swift, decisive action.

"It'll have to do. As hard as it is for me to accept such a course of action, I must go along with Pavel and Yuri and settle for a peaceful solution. Besides, one favor from the West shouldn't be too much to ask for," Meliacherov somberly declared. "Believe me, in my heart, I'm with you Sergei, but this one time I cannot risk destabilizing our country for the sake of punishing a few. As for you Yuri, I insist that you immediately order Klisov to withdraw his troops and release their prisoners. Furthermore, I want you to make it very clear to him and the rest of the military establishment that any future rebellions will be severely punished. And if Klisov refuses to meet our demands, then we'll use force."

"Да [Yes], Igor. I'll call him right away," Yuri Likhovtsev agreed, promising to notify the Russian President about Klisov's response. Wanting to avoid violence, the Defense Minister desperately hoped that the Karelian Commander would comply.

"Спасибо [Thank you]. Afterwards, if he complies, I'll address the nation to ensure there are no repeats. If he refuses," Meliacherov paused, "then we'll take appropriate measures. As for Sheremetev, I'll deal with him later. In the meantime, I'm going to call Washington to inform the President of the United States of my decision and to address any of the concerns that he and the rest of our allies might have. Their investments are safe and will be kept safe. And Sergei, when you get outside corroboration, I want to see the reports. If further action is warranted, we'll take it," President Meliacherov declared before dismissing his ministers.

Two hours later, Natalya Kalinina and Elena Potapova, along with the rest of their brethren breathed a collective sigh of relief when President Meliacherov addressed the nation announcing that Klisov and his soldiers had agreed to withdraw to their barracks in return for a one-time grant of amnesty. Violence and bloodshed had been averted for that day, at least.

Chapter 14

As the days passed, the bitter Siberian front gradually relinquished its deadly grip over Western Russia. With the warming temperatures life gradually returned to as normal as the country's increasingly desperate situation allowed. Lines of people again snaked through Moscow's ice-covered streets hours before the city's markets opened.

While most Muscovites searched for fresh vegetables and meat to replenish their dwindling supplies of bottled goods, groups of youths peered into the city's "Союз [Soyuz]" kiosks looking for the latest Western albums. Music blared loudly as pedestrians shuffled past rows of brightly lit kiosks stocked with the latest imports. Some were filled with resentment as they glanced at the displayed prices -- all of which were well beyond their means. Others were insulted by large hand-written signs that read "only E (Euros) and US$ accepted."

Although the average citizen could only view the displayed imports with envy and bitterness, lines of people, many with mafia and black market connections, flashed wads of bills, snapping up the stylish goods with ease. Others filed in and out of the many storefronts displaying conspicuous "Обмень Балюты [Currency Exchange]" signs that filled Moscow's blocks to exchange their ill-begotten Rubles for U.S. dollars or Euros. As these leeches -- many of whom extorted from the elderly and infirm and/or preyed on the working class by eliminating their jobs -- conducted their transactions at the exchange bureaus, they attacked Russia's economic vitality by harming the value of her precious Rubles. However, since they were conscienceless and destroyed countless families in their maniacal greed, adding treason to their long list of crimes meant little. God, Russians and country were expendable to them. Their countries were their modern, spacious mansions, their temples of worship were themselves, and their gods were the West's Hard Currencies.

At the same time to reinforce the entrepreneurial class's behavior of conversion in the name of "profit," the West continued to manipulate the Ruble's value. Every few days the Dollar's value was increased by 10 or 15 Rubles. Then the Ruble was held steady for three or four days before it fell again.

Knowledge of this predictable pattern of manipulations encouraged "the entrepreneurial class" to quickly convert their blood Rubles into U.S. Dollars and Euros. This gave the money lords the sufficient cover for their currency crimes -- "the forces of supply and demand" were solely responsible for the Ruble's continued slide.

At the same time, humiliating IMF handouts, each with newer and more restrictive strings attached, created the illusion of sparing the Russian economy from total collapse. The Meliacherov Government refused to recognize the West's plan of transforming Russia into a collection of disunified welfare states devoid of global influence and free-will. As a result, each additional IMF check and the Kremlin's expressions of gratitude moved the Meliacherov Government further from its people.

Despite Russia's de facto surrender, President Meliacherov found it increasingly difficult to satisfy Western demands. While he had been able to restore Karelia's property to its hated kulaks, the West refused to be satisfied. They ignored President Meliacherov's pleas that further humiliations could throw his country into civil war. They refused to compromise and continued to pressure Moscow to seek vengeance against Karelian Governor Valeri Sheremetev, and Commander Mikhail Klisov and his men. They also demanded compensation for their lost goods warning of a possible cutoff of IMF "loans" if the Kremlin failed to obey.

While President Meliacherov struggled to create an illusory balance of a mutually beneficial Russian-Western partnership, trying to placate his disillusioned and humiliated people, the United States faced its most serious domestic crisis since the Civil War (1860-65). A secession vote in Hawaii was only hours away. After decades of suppressing the Island State's simmering independence movement with false promises of greater rewards, the Hawaiian people resolved to decide their own destiny.

Prior to 2014, Washington had treated Hawaiians like Pavlov's dogs. Each time they brought up the "secession option," the U.S. President unveiled new initiatives that promised greater economic opportunities.

Initially, the United States Government believed the island's nationalist desires could be extinguished with token aid packages. They reasoned that once Hawaiians were "conditioned," the Island State would remain firmly in the union. Washington basically made empty promises, not realizing that at some point, its psychological hold over the islanders would be relinquished.

Originally when the first seeds of the Hawaiian Secession Movement began to take root in the 1990s, the

ВЕСНА РУССКАЯ

American President at the time, Bill Clinton mistakenly believed that a "Policy of Honesty" would reconcile the island's differences with Washington. Instead of the new unity he had hoped for, Clinton's apologies for the wrongful aggression of 1882 and the illegal overthrow of Hawaiian Queen Liliuokalani, only strengthened the island's resolve. Upon accepting Clinton's apology, Hawaiians demanded, "Now give us back our country!"

Later, as Hawaii's secessionist movement grew, with many institutions refusing to fly the American flag, Washington began its program of Pavlov's conditioning and in doing so, failed to address the Island's real problems. Even when the Island prospered, many native Hawaiians found themselves relegated to second-class status while transplanted mainlanders grew richer and enhanced their majority control of the Island's economy. Faced with continued high unemployment and few genuine opportunities, native Hawaiians refused to accept further promises from the U.S. President.

When it became evident to Washington that after 20 years of efforts, they were powerless to extinguish Hawaii's growing nationalist sentiments, the U.S. President resorted to threats – "all federal spending for Hawaii would be withheld unless the State's leaders renounced the Island's secessionist demands. Instead of extinguishing the secessionist movement, Washington's threats fueled it into a raging inferno. Nationalist leaders repeatedly reminded their constituents that their state was better off without Washington's money. Already, as was the case with several other major American states, Hawaii received less from Washington for every dollar they paid in federal taxes (80¢ for every dollar paid). With little economic incentive to remain a part of the mainland and backing from his

156

constituents, Hawaii's Governor obtained approval from the State's legislature to hold a referendum vote.

As the Hawaiian vote neared, the U.S. President sent his Secretary of State to Beijing, China in search of better relations. The move filled Natalya Kalinina and most of her RNR colleagues with concern. All knew that a U.S.-Chinese alliance would strengthen Washington's chokehold over their beloved country.

157

ВЕСНА РУССКАЯ

Chapter 15

While tensions between Moscow and Washington increased, the relationship between Natalya Kalinina and Jim Keating warmed. Both spent more time with each other. Occasional weekend visits evolved into regular weekend-long reunions that neither politics nor the weather could hamper. As they grew closer, even Valentin Makarov learned of the relationship from his young agent. Before long Natalya and her American friend began seeing each other two and three times each week.

As both dined at Sadko Restaurant, the impending Hawaiian Secession vote and Moscow's shortages were distant from their minds. The growing attraction between their hearts prevailed. Both knew that their relationship had crossed beyond friendship.

Following their dinner, Natalya and Jim walked through the dark streets of Moscow. They held hands as they made their weekend plans.

Despite her knowledge that the CIA was assisting President Meliacherov and his Foreign Minister, Sergei Kruchkov investigate the Karelian uprising, a grave threat to her personal safety, the Russian woman's subliminal fears went ignored. She talked freely and felt a sense of reassurance as she held the American's hand. At the same time Jim ignored his embassy's memorandum that was issued to CIA agents recommending caution when associating with Russians because of concerns that they were KGB agents. In this case, Jim did not have to wonder, he knew that his girlfriend was with the Russian intelligence service, and he did not care.

"Soon it'll be warm and we won't have to wear these heavy clothes," Natalya spoke awaiting the day when they could discard their thick coats, as they stopped in front of a cluster of darkened, antiquated shops.

"It'll be much better. Then I'll be able to hold you closer," the American quietly replied, taking Natalya in his arms and hugging her.

"And I'll be able to hold you closer," Natalya softly added, before they locked lips and kissed each other, ignoring the night chill. Their lips only came apart for air. "What're we going to do?" the Muscovite quietly asked, feeling the weight of the political tensions suddenly crash upon her slender shoulders.

"What do you mean?" Jim asked in return as they kissed.

"The way things are going, pretty soon we may be prohibited from seeing each other. I'm worried."

"About what?" Jim inquired. "We'll always be able to see each other," he added trying to reassure Natalya, as Stephen Norcross's Memo came to his mind.

"Tell me, do you still want to see me?" the Russian asked, still wanting to be reassured.

"You know I do," Jim answered kissing Natalya. "What about you? Do you want to continue seeing me?"

"Да [Yes], that's why I'm so worried. It seems like everything is going wrong. I'm just worried that someday you won't be allowed to have contact with Russians -- a security measure, you know."

159

ВЕСНА РУССКАЯ

"That won't happen. We're a democratic society. In America people can still come and go as they please and see whom ever they choose to," Jim tried to reassure the Muscovite, clasping her exposed hand in his hand. As Keating spoke, guilt rained down on his conscience. Although wanting to be honest, he feared the truth would only make matters worse. Not wanting to upset the young Russian woman, Jim chose to conceal his embassy's growing restrictions.

"But what if you're not? Things can change," Natalya continued feeling a sense of panic settling in her heart. For the first time in their relationship the worsening political situation between Washington and Moscow, conducted by leaders whom they had no control over, burdened her troubled mind.

"I know," the American reluctantly admitted, as they held hands and kissed each other again. "But no matter what, we'll find some way."

"How can you be sure?"

"Because I promise you," Jim Keating vowed. He continued after reluctantly taking a deep breath. "I didn't want to tell you, but since you must know; our Ambassador has already tried to restrict us."

"How? What has he done?" Natalya asked feeling a resurgence of apprehension.

"He's recommended that we limit our contacts with Russians until the investigation of..."

"The Karelian revolt is completed," Natalya completed the sentence.

"You know he's just worried that in some way someone might inadvertently compromise the investigation," Jim finished before they embraced each other again. "You don't have to worry. I think we both know each other well enough now. You don't have to admit it, but I know you're with the KGB and I don't care. And I'm sure you know that I'm with the CIA. If you don't, then I'm telling you now."

"Спасибо [Thank you] for your honesty," Natalya replied pulling him into her body. "Now that you've told me you're with the CIA, I might as well make it official too. I'm with the KGB."

"Like I said, I don't care. All I know is that I love you," the American declared kissing the Muscovite woman.

"And I love you too," Natalya concurred, feeling her first sense of reassurance since the troubling situation had escaped from her subconscious. "Why don't you come to my house this weekend," Kalinina then suggested as they kissed again. "All I want is to be alone with you."

"Me too."

"We'll have my house to ourselves. My mom and babushka are going to Minsk to visit my Aunt Sofya. She's not feeling too well."

"I'm sorry to hear that."

"She'll be okay, I'm sure," Natalya answered, her voice trailing off. "She needs medicine for her asthma which right now only Moscow has. Unfortunately, with the harsh winter, Belarus has run out. With their Government unable to pay the bills, their stores may not be restocked for who knows how long. But she'll be okay. I'm sure of it," the Russian added, fully aware that her aunt was suffering her usual winter relapse which always saw her recover when the spring warmth arrived. "She's already getting better now that it's warming up."

"I'm glad to hear that, but if there's anything I can do, please let me know," Jim offered, again taking Natalya's hand.

"Спасибо [Thank you]," Natalya expressed her gratitude with a kiss. "In the meantime, since I'll have my

161

house to myself, promise me you'll come. I don't want to be alone."

"You know I'll come," the American promised before both decided to call it a night and returned to the metro station, walking hand in hand.

"I'm looking forward to our weekend," Natalya spoke one last time before they kissed and bidded farewell.

"Me too. До свидания [Good bye]," the American repeated before Natalya stepped onto the subway and waved good-bye before the train pulled away from the station. As she watched her friend disappear, Natalya quietly whispered, "Я ты люблю [I love you]."

Chapter 16

As Muscovites awoke early the next morning to prepare for another day of trials, they were greeted by a bright sun and clearing skies. The intermittent drizzle and leaden skies that had plagued the Russian capital for most of the week had lifted giving way to clear blue skies and a warm, southwesterly breeze.

Preparing for their day's chores, few Muscovites were aware of the significant events that had been unfolding since they had gone to sleep the night before. As they again made their way to work, rushing in human waves through the congested metro stations and bustling streets, grabbing newspapers and something to eat, none were alerted of the explosive drama that had unfolded thousands of miles away. Russian newspapers, rushed to print the night before, in anticipation of the impending secession vote, merely reported, "Hawaiian Secession Vote begins" in a tiny, inconspicuous caption. In addition to the lack of coverage, the Meliacherov Government, at the request of the U.S. President, remained silent.

Despite the information blackout, Natalya Kalinina and most of the members of the Russian defense and intelligence communities were aware that something of significance had occurred during the night. They had been tipped off by the severance of their access to CNN and BBC broadcasts.

Fearful that his own administration would face renewed opposition when news of the U.S. instability got out, President Igor Meliacherov was more than happy to accommodate his counterpart's request to withhold the news. Meliacherov reasoned that it was better this way until things had quieted down and the United States had gotten over its worst domestic crisis in 150 years.

Unbeknownst to Natalya, the turmoil had begun at around the same time she was spending the evening with her American friend. While they had dined at Sadko Restaurant, the U.S. President with Congressional backing had called the U.S. Supreme Court into emergency session to seek legal recourse to thwart Hawaii's independence ambitions. Within an hour, the nine justices had provided their President with the ruling he sought -- the approaching secession vote was "unconstitutional." The decision immediately set off a chain of violent events.

Upon hearing of the Supreme Court's ruling, the Hawaiian Governor called his own Legislature into emergency session, where without much debate, they voted overwhelmingly to defy Washington and proceed with the referendum. As they voted, each legislator angrily refused to acquiesce to the U.S. President's threats. The polls opened at precisely 6:00 AM Pacific Standard Time.

When news of Hawaii's defiance reached Washington, the U.S. President became filled with anger and took prompt action. Within minutes, even before the press became aware of his resolve, unconfirmed reports began flooding in of a dramatic increase in military activity across California and in the Pacific. As television stations began preempting their regularly scheduled shows to report on the dramatic events, the American President called a hastily arranged press conference where he termed Hawaii's refusal to abide by the Supreme Court's ruling "an act of treason."

"We will take whatever measures are necessary to crush this illegal insurrection led by officials whose gross abuse of power violates every covenant of our constitution which we as a people hold sacred. Their acts make them unfit to continue to hold office," the American President read a brief statement on national television. "Because of their refusal to abide by the Supreme Court's decision, a ruling by the Highest Court of the land -- the final ruling, when as you all know that in our democratic society Federal law takes precedence over all state ordinances and legislation, I have been left with little choice -- this criminal act of treason must be punished! But to do so, like our great President of the past, Abraham Lincoln had done 150 years ago, I must make hard decisions and take difficult steps, which I'm sure many of you may not agree with or may deem as too harsh -- effective immediately I am suspending Habeas Corpus for all of Hawaii until order can be restored. I am also dissolving the Hawaiian State Government until the traitors can be separated from the patriots and new elections can be held. The Union, the United States of America must be preserved at all costs. Later, history can be my judge," the U.S. President concluded his brief speech, catching most Americans off-guard.

While the American President made his brief remarks, amphibious assault crafts stormed Hawaii's sandy beaches, scattering the early morning sunbathers and surfers that were gathering to enjoy the Island's white sands and pristine waters. Helicopter gun ships buzzed repeatedly over Honolulu, the Island State's capital as tanks from nearby military bases rolled into the streets tearing up

165

chunks of concrete. They pushed aside vehicles that failed to yield in time.

As the U.S. military closed in on the State's Government buildings, they were met by scattered resistance from the Island's National Guard Reserves, who in spite of their remote chances of victory, chose to defend their sovereign rights. Scattered gunfire echoed through the modern metropolis as nationalist snipers fired into the streets from Honolulu's skyscrapers, taking aim at the invading forces.

"Under the State of Emergency ordered by the President of the United States all people are to remain indoors," a mainland general read over the air from a captured TV station. "Because of the gravity of the situation, all violators will be shot on sight," he tersely warned in an effort to dissuade further civilian resistance.

Despite the general's warnings, groups of people remained in Honolulu's streets -- some caught by surprise, others out of curiosity, and still others out of sheer determination to defend their homes. While some fled for cover as bullets rained down, others watched in silent disbelief. Some shouted angry denunciations and spat at the invaders who consolidated their hold over the capital. Buildings were seized, intersections were blocked and armed checkpoints were erected.

The established checkpoints and soldiers, some taking cover behind APCs and parked vehicles and others running through the downtown business district dressed in full combat gear sent an eerie pall over Honolulu. Echoes of automatic gunfire followed by occasional, thunderous explosions filled many of the capital's residents with terror. Others were gripped by an indescribable fear of future reprisals as they watched soldiers load seized ballot boxes into army jeeps. What had once promised to be a joyous day of celebration became a dark nightmare.

Once firm control was established over most of the capital, the invading forces rushed the Governor's mansion and Legislative building from all directions. As they watched the soldiers and tanks descend upon their headquarters, the Island's leaders were filled with defeat. Knowing that they were beaten, the legislators, many of them still too stunned to believe what was happening, dejectedly waved white flags of surrender from their office windows.

As the legislators were rounded up, the Island's Senate majority leader swallowed a bottle of cyanide while the Governor, his wife and few of his close aides fled into a waiting helicopter.

"Where's Aimee? She's not here!" the Governor's wife hysterically shouted as the helicopter's metal doors were hastily secured. "We can't leave!"

"Forget her! We got no time. We'll have to find her later," the Governor shouted back. "Get going," he then ordered the pilot. The metal bird immediately took to flight.

Seeing the ground peel away, the Governor's wife immediately began sobbing uncontrollably, repeatedly calling out their daughter's name.

"I'm sorry," the Governor quietly apologized to his wife. His eyes watered as he visualized their 16 year-old daughter left alone to fend for herself against the invading forces. He did not know how they would get her back or if they would.

Upon seeing the rising helicopter, army rangers hovering nearby took immediate pursuit. As they chased after the fleeing bird, they demanded the chopper pilot to land.

ВЕСНА РУССКАЯ

"Don't listen to them! Keep flying," the Governor commanded his terrified pilot. "We have to get to international waters."

"We don't have enough fuel!"

"I don't care! We'll worry about it when we come to that. Right now, the only thing you should worry about is getting away from here!" the Governor declared staring down at the once, tranquil paradise they were fleeing.

When it became apparent to the army rangers that the Hawaiian Governor's helicopter was not going to comply with their demands, a squadron of fighter jets was summoned. Within minutes of their takeoff, the much faster, more agile, aerodynamic monsters made their appearance, quickly closing in.

With the fighter jets closing in, the Governor ordered his pilot to drop close to the sea in a futile attempt to elude them. "This is your last warning. "Turn around or be destroyed," one of the fighter pilots warned.

"Go to hell," the Hawaiian Governor angrily, shouted back, grabbing his frightened pilot's intercom. Filled with anger and defiance, the Governor who had originally fled to avoid being killed suddenly found embracing death more palatable than surrender.

Infuriated by the response, the lead dragon belched fire from its nostrils. A second later, the defenseless bird in front exploded into a brilliant red and orange ball of flame. For a brief moment, the mortally wounded bird, pushed by the force of the belching dragon's fire lurched blindly forward. It then fell into the dark blue ocean with a loud and violent hiss and quickly sank to its watery grave.

As the day progressed in Moscow, reports of the Hawaiian crisis began to trickle in. ITA-TASS became the first station to hint of trouble, announcing that the "Hawaiian vote had been cancelled." Later, as Russians continued to seek additional information, despite the Kremlin's attempts to gloss over the situation, other stations began their own reports.

Within a day, most Russians had learned about the invasion and the death of Hawaii's Governor. However, by that time, President Meliacherov breathed a sigh of relief, believing that the U.S. crisis was over. Although the soil across Russia remained fertile with discontent, the Russian President rested easier. He was confident that his Government had been spared because of Washington's victory.

ВЕСНА РУССКАЯ

Chapter 17

Stability had been restored with the incarceration of Hawaii's legislators, nationalist leaders and pro-secessionist remnants of the Island State's National Guard. All awaited trial for treason and murder, in retaliation for the dozen invading soldiers that had died during the fighting.

Despite the invasion's success, U.S.-Russian relations continued to sour. Washington failed to express gratitude to the Russian leader for obediently heeding the American President's request. Although Meliacherov did not ask for additional IMF funds or other financial and economic rewards for his loyalty, he had expected the U.S. President, at the very least, to offer his understanding and allow the Kremlin to close the Karelian chapter. Instead, U.S. President Clint Stoker, buoyed by Washington's military success against an under-armed, defenseless people, hardened his earlier position that Karelian Governor Sheremetev and his rebels be arrested.

Hurt by the new embarrassments to his Government, President Meliacherov finally began to question the price of his loyalty to Washington. "I can't believe that he won't give us a break. I bend over backwards to support him in his time of need and the only thanks I get is to get humiliated in front

170

of the world," the Russian leader bitterly complained during an informal conference of his ministers.

"He has a point," Foreign Minister Sergei Kruchkov replied.

"I guess I shouldn't have expected you to sympathize with me," Meliacherov interrupted in a pained voice.

"I'll be frank with you. The Americans acted out of strength. They crushed their traitors. Meanwhile ours are still walking free, unrepentant for their crimes, and worse yet, those bastards are still getting paid by us!" Kruchkov angrily swore. He resented their escape from retribution. "This thing will never be put to rest until we act like a Government and bring those bastards before a firing squad!"

"I know how you feel, but this one time I cannot do that."

"Sooner or later you'll have to. Otherwise, this thing will never go away," the Foreign Minister answered, softening his voice while trying to restrain his hatred for the Karelian rebels. He took it personally that they had attacked Russia's Western-run capitalist institutions.

"I know that I and President Stoker may not always agree on everything, but just once he should see our way and stop attacking us. He doesn't realize the consequences that could result if we do as he demands. He just doesn't understand. After all, this isn't his country. So why should he care? After all he doesn't have to govern here!" Meliacherov lamented in frustration having momentarily lost patience with U.S. foreign policy.

"He's just trying to help," the Foreign Minister defended U.S. policy. "When he demands us to take decisive action, it's for our own good. He doesn't want investors to get scared off and pull out their money. God knows, Russia would collapse. To tell you the truth, sometimes I'm fearful of even going to bed knowing that those criminals are still loose and possibly plotting another attack," Kruchkov added, staring directly at the Defense Minister.

"They're not criminals! Not everyone who doesn't see your way is a traitor and a criminal!" Yuri Likhovtsev broke his silence, refusing to endure the Foreign Minister's attack. He resented Kruchkov's patronizing. "Let me tell you this. If you and your brainless allies who call themselves `economists' of all things, were not constantly drawing up blueprints for failure, we wouldn't be in this mess today!"

"Нет [Nyet], if you were able to control your army we wouldn't be in this mess today!" Kruchkov angrily shot back. "All you want to do is obstruct our progress. Well I've had enough! Why don't we get this over with for once and for all," the Foreign Minister angrily challenged his ideological adversary, getting up from his seat.

"Sit down! Everything's going to be okay in time," the Russian President intervened motioning for his Foreign Minister to take his seat. "I know things haven't been easy lately, but if we don't work together, we're all going to destroy ourselves. I don't want to hear you two arguing anymore. If you want to fight do it among yourselves and away from here," Meliacherov sternly commanded, frustrated by the repeated displays of enmity between his two ministers. Furthermore, let me make it clear. We have made progress. There's no civil war so like it or not, you're just going to have to accept my decision," Meliacherov lectured Sergei Kruchkov. "And you, Yuri, you're just going to have to accept our economic policies. We're not going to turn away from capitalism for some unproven system or failed system of the past. Our stores have a greater variety of better quality goods than they've ever had before. Maybe there are some shortages, but that's not Sergei's fault. The harsh winter is the cause. And the Karelian rebellion is not Yuri's fault. Again the harsh winter is responsible," Meliacherov declared with a sigh. "I assure you things will get better soon."

"If investors aren't scared off," Sergei Kruchkov interjected.

"That's precisely the reason I've decided to send you to Washington," the Russian President declared. "It's imperative that you convince the American President to see our way so that the world maintains its faith in us. I know it's not going to be easy for you, especially since you don't agree with how I've handled the Karelian revolt, but you must put aside your opinions for the good of Russia. You know as well as I do that foreign investment is critical. You said it yourself. That's why I need you to convince President Stoker of our commitment to protecting investor interests. I've already made arrangements. The tickets will be waiting for you at the airport," the Russian President added. "But before you go, let me assure you, I promise that there will be no forgiveness for any future Sheremetevs and Klisovs," Meliacherov swore, trying to provide his staunchly pro-Western Foreign Minister with a greater incentive to defend the Kremlin's Karelian policy.

Following Sergei Kruchkov's departure for Sheremetevo Airport, President Meliacherov, having resolved to play both sides, summoned his Defense Minister for private consultations. Once they were alone, the Russian President handed Likhovtsev a sealed packet. "These are instructions that I want you to deliver to the KGB. As I'm sure you know, Aimee Kualani, the daughter of Hawaii's fallen Governor, is in hiding and desperate to escape from the Island. I want the KGB to assist her in finding a safe haven."

ВЕСНА РУССКАЯ

"Igor, do you realize the damage it'll cause to U.S.-Russian relations if Washington finds out?" Yuri Likhovtsev inquired with concern.

"Да [Yes], but if I've learned anything from these last few unpleasant weeks, I must keep all options open."

"Whatever you say."

"I think we both know that U.S. policy hasn't been very kind to us lately. What they're asking me to do is impossible. I cannot and will not destroy our country for the sake of punishing a few and satisfying the American President's lust for revenge. And besides, with his Secretary of State in Beijing, I can't help but wonder if they're planning to abandon us for China."

"It's possible. They have much more business opportunities there than here," Defense Minister Yuri Likhovtsev agreed. "Also, I don't like their hush-hush handling of the talks. They could be up to something."

"That's why we must hedge our bets. If we don't, we may be left with little or no options should they abandon us. Hopefully it won't happen, but I can't do nothing and allow us to lose control of our country," President Meliacherov declared. "Make sure these instructions get to the KGB."

"I'll see to it right away," Likhovtsev promised.

"One last thing. Between you and me, I never gave you this packet, which never existed, and you never paid the KGB a visit," the Russian President somberly instructed.

"I understand," the Defense Minister promised before hastily leaving for Лубянка Площадь [Lubyanka Square] on his secret mission.

Once the sealed packet was received by the Russian intelligence agency, it was handed to Valentin Makarov, who after reading the contents summoned Agent Kalinina to his office.

"This is the girl you must find," Makarov instructed Natalya, handing her a dossier of photographs, biographical data and a listing of Aimee Kualani's.

Despite the disappointment of having to cancel her weekend plans, Natalya readily accepted the assignment and the chance to go overseas. Although her heart sagged, Kalinina's nationalist spirit compensated for it. For once, during her two years with the KGB, the young agent had received an assignment from her country's President that actually pursued Russian interests in lieu of Western goals!

"Just be careful," Valentin Makarov cautioned. "I don't want to lose you."

"I'll try my best, I promise," Natalya thanked her supervisor and friend. "Believe me, you'll have many more years of putting up with me," she added, teasing the paternal Makarov who handed her an envelope with a VISA and plane tickets.

"You'll go to Vancouver first. There, someone from the Russian embassy will meet you and give you a Canadian passport. Give him your Russian passport. Until you get back to Moscow, you're going to be a Canadian national," Valentin Makarov instructed, taking precautions to protect his agent and the intelligence agency. "You'll be okay. You'll be able to handle it, won't you?"

"I'll be fine," Natalya reassured him.

"Good. Well then I might as well wish you well," Makarov exclaimed extending Natalya his hand. "Удачи [Good Luck]."

Upon receiving her assignment, Natalya hugged her good friend, Elena Potapova as she said her good-byes. She then left for her house where she quickly packed a suitcase, retrieved her passport and dressed in casual, Western-style clothes.

ВЕСНА РУССКАЯ

After canceling her date, Natalya left for the airport. During the entire taxi ride, Natalya hardly spoke. Instead, she absorbed every site of the city she had grown up in and learned to love. She subconsciously wondered if she would ever see Russia again.

Once at Sheremetevo Airport, Natalya headed for the Aeroflot gate. Ironically, as she made her way, she walked directly past her country's pro-Western Foreign Minister. Although Natalya recognized Kruchkov, having seen him on television defending the Meliacherov Government's capitalist reforms, she said nothing, fearful that it might arouse his suspicions. On the other hand, in a rush to make his Finn air flight, Kruchkov took little notice of the KGB agent. He had greater things on his mind than concerning himself with what appeared to him an ordinary Russian woman.

Chapter 18

When her plane finally landed in Vancouver fourteen hours later, Natalya Kalinina was relieved to escape from its stuffy confines. After being cramped in a small space for half-a-day, the long walk to Passport Control proved refreshing. Natalya's relief, though, was short-lived. Before long, she found herself waiting in a slow moving line.

Although going through the VIP section for diplomats would have been preferable to standing on her aching feet, Natalya knew that it was necessary for her to endure the barely crawling line if she was to preserve her cover as an ordinary tourist.

After clearing passport control, Natalya quickly made her way to the luggage conveyor belt where much to her relief; she did not have to wait too long. Upon retrieving her luggage, the Russian agent, rushed over to the Customs Check area, eager to make her next flight and be on her way to the besieged tropical Islands.

"Purpose of your visit?" the Canadian customs agent asked, glancing through the Muscovite's papers.

"Tourism."

"How long will you be staying in Canada?"

"Three weeks."

"Are you bringing anything to declare?"

"No, nothing."

"Have you any firearms, explosives or drugs in your possession," the customs agent inquired, handing Natalya back her papers.

ВЕСНА РУССКАЯ

"No."

"Do you mind if I take a quick look?"

"Go right ahead," Kalinina obliged, opening her suitcase and allowing the Canadian agent to sift through her contents.

"Thank you. That'll be all," he declared, satisfied with the findings of his examination. "Enjoy your stay in Canada."

"Thank you. Have a good day," the Russian bidded him, taking her suitcase and heading for the exit. Once outside, Natalya boarded a passenger bus and rode over to the Air Canada terminal where she was to meet her contact.

As Natalya walked through the glass doors, a tall, dark-haired, mustached man wearing gold-rimmed spectacles examined her from a nearby seat. Once satisfied that the woman matched the photograph he had memorized earlier in the day, he approached her. "Are you well?" he asked.

"Yes, and how are you?" Natalya answered, following her script.

"I am lost."

"Maybe I can help. Where are you going?"

"Downtown," the contact answered, handing Natalya a thick envelope.

As she took the envelope in her hands, Natalya continued the discussion. "You must go back outside. There's a taxi stand to the left." While she spoke, the young KGB agent casually handed the contact her Russian passport and visa. "He'll take you where you want," she added as he expressed his gratitude and departed.

With her new passport, plane tickets and supply of Canadian currency, Natalya walked up to the Air Canada desk to retrieve her boarding pass to Honolulu. Then she found a seat near the gate and read a newspaper to pass

178

the time. Under the effects of jet lag, Natalya found it increasingly difficult to keep her eyes focused on its text. Fearful that her dry eyes would succumb to sleep, the Russian agent reluctantly closed the newspaper and patiently watched the milling crowd until boarding time.

Once aboard the plane, Natalya took her seat and closed her eyes. Thoroughly exhausted from having gone 26 hours without sleep, she quickly nodded off and did not awaken until the plane had touched down at Honolulu International Airport.

As Natalya disembarked from the plane, she again prepared herself to go through customs and passport checks. Knowing that the stakes in Honolulu were far greater than those in Vancouver, the Russian agent silently tried to comfort her tense nerves. She knew that any visible sign of anxiety could lead to suspicion. It was already bad enough that the American agents had increased their scrutiny of each incoming tourist because of the state of emergency that remained in effect on the Hawaiian Islands.

"One down, one to go," the Russian sighed with relief as the passport control agent waved her through. Despite her relative ease in clearing passport control, Natalya felt her heart pounding as she approached the customs check area. "Calm down, it's going to be all right," she tried to comfort herself. "This is what you've been trained for. Don't fail now," she firmly commanded her tense nerves and queasy stomach as she placed her suitcase on the X-ray machine.

When she finally had to talk to the U.S. Customs agent, Natalya, much to her relief, found herself able to answer in a calm voice. Fortunately, the American could not distinguish her best attempts to imitate the British accent spoken by Anglophone Canadians from the genuine thing.

BECHA РУССКАЯ

"Спасибо, спасибо [Thank you, thank you]," the Muscovite silently expressed her thoughts upon being cleared.

Although she had slept on her flight from Vancouver, Natalya found it a great relief to finally lie down in a real bed when she stepped into her room at the Royal Hawaiian Hotel. After stretching her arms and legs for a few minutes, the Russian got back up and pulled the drapes open. For a few minutes she merely soaked in the sights -- the beautiful sandy beaches, the turquoise blue surf, and the magnificent palm trees. She found the mild 80°-Fahrenheit air, a most pleasant luxury compared to the bitter arctic winter she had left behind.

After basking in the window's warmth, Natalya, still suffering from the effects of her long trip, decided to go to bed. She quickly showered in a well-lit, modern bathroom, a far cry from the tiny double rooms she had known all of her life, and changed into a nightgown.

Once prepared for bed, Natalya pushed her suitcase to the side, requested a 6:00 AM wakeup call, and turned on the radio. Though a decade-and-a-half old, Aaliyah's "I Care 4 U" remained as soothing as ever. As Natalya listened to Aaliyah's comforting words – "I care for you... take my hand... I love you [yes, I do]..." she envisioned an angel standing by her side.[1] It was an angel she hoped to be to Aimee Kualani, the deposed Hawaiian Governor's daughter. Ignoring the light emanating from the setting sun, she closed her eyes and relaxed. Within a few minutes the KGB agent fell into a deep, comforting sleep.

---

1 Missy Elliott/T. Mosley, "Aaliyah" – "I Care 4 U" (Blackground Records, LLC, New York, NY 2001).

180

Chapter 19

A bright sun rose in the eastern sky, spreading an orange river of luminescence ahead of it. The coconut palms gently swayed in the mild, refreshing Hawaiian breeze while the clear, turquoise surf gently rolled up the white sands of Waikiki Beach as Natalya Kalinina, dressed in a short-sleeved shirt and neatly pressed jeans, casually walked along the shore, silently taking in Oahu's beautiful scenery.

With her hair rustling in the pleasant sea breeze, the Russian agent, deeply immersed in an atmosphere of serenity, found it hard to imagine that hostile military forces manned positions less than a mile away. As she slowly walked along the shores of Waikiki before the onslaught of daytime sunbathers and surfers packed its sands under a colorful array of towels and umbrellas, Natalya tried to imagine what it would be like to live in such a paradise. A deep breath of the sea air filled Kalinina's lungs with an ineffable feeling of solace. After a few minutes of fantasizing, Natalya sighed with dismay at the false illusion of tranquility that the quiet shores of Oahu provided. With her mind jolted back to reality -- that paradise had been invaded, the Russian agent thought about the girl in need of her assistance.

ВЕСНА РУССКАЯ

As she slowly took her eyes from the ocean waters and viewed the beautiful panorama of modern skyscrapers that lined Waikiki's shores and the silhouetted background profile of Diamond Head, Oahu's most famous volcano, it became easy for Natalya to understand why the U.S. mainland was determined to hold on to Hawaii -- the mainland wanted paradise all for themselves. To the Russian agent, who walked up to the ocean surf and allowed the waves to roll up to the tips of her sneakers, such greed was inexcusable and unforgivable. Her heart mourned for Hawaii.

"I could really live here," Natalya told herself, dipping her hand into the Pacific's mild waters. "It's so nice here. No bitter cold to endure," she dreamed, again spellbound under the Island's trance. She was embraced by its refreshing warmth. "But I better get going," Natalya cautioned herself reverting back to reality.

As she turned back towards the Royal Hawaiian Hotel, the Russian became acutely aware that unseen forces were drawing her closer to the Island. She knew that for every minute she lingered on the beach, watching the smooth, placid waves roll up to the white sandy shore with the most precise regularity and greatest perfection, her desire to stay was growing stronger.

Natalya's heart ached as she returned to the confines of her hotel -- an historic, architectural landmark of the past that stood among clusters of coconut trees, all descendents of the trees growing in the old royal grove. Despite its Spanish-Moorish facade, the pastel-colored edifice, built in the 1920s, blended perfectly with the palm trees, white sands, and surrounding modern glass and concrete skyscrapers.

182

Once back at the Royal Hawaiian Hotel, Natalya had several Danishes and a cup of coffee. She foresaked her desire to try more extravagant Hawaiian delicacies, eager to begin her mission as early as possible, while the names of Aimee Kualani's friends were still fresh in her mind. Earlier in the morning at 4:00 AM, unable to fall back to sleep, after having gotten nine hours of solid sleep, Natalya had memorized all of the vital information pertaining to her mission.

After finishing her light breakfast, Natalya set out for Iolani School, which the fallen Governor's daughter had attended as an 11th grader until being forced into hiding. With its location being within a mile of the Royal Hawaiian Hotel, the Russian agent elected to make the trip by foot.

As she walked Honolulu's balmy streets, an atmosphere of relative calm hung over the Island State's capital. Only the numerous military checkpoints impeded the tranquility. Even then, despite their unwelcome presence, the occupying forces, having met no armed resistance over the last 48 hours, paid little attention to the passing traffic. The invaders merely manned their checkpoints as a formality. Only occasional passersby were stopped and for a brief search at most, usually because of some package they carried. Wearing the casual attire of mainland tourists, Natalya found it easy to remain inconspicuous among the many pedestrians that walked along the capital's sidewalks.

Natalya walked for twenty minutes, periodically stopping to view the colorful window displays of Honolulu's shops, before arriving to the sprawling 25-acre grounds of Iolani School, a private institution for children ranging from kindergarten to the 12th grade. The diverse school, dedicated to preparing its students for college consisted of 25 buildings, the first of which was built in 1863, years before the first mainland invasion. Annual tuition of $6000 greatly exceeded the combined salaries of Natalya and her mother.

After receiving directions from a group of students, Natalya made her way to the school's large library. Once in the library, she went to the main desk. "Excuse me, but can you tell me if you have any copies of the 2013 yearbook available?" she inquired, preparing to match its photographs with the names she had memorized.

"Yes we do," the Librarian, an elderly, dark-skinned native Hawaiian answered with a smile. "Would you like me to get it for you?"

"Yes, please."

"Just wait one minute while I go and get it."

"Thank you," the Russian agent politely replied, glancing around at her surroundings. Small groups of students were quietly clustered at the library's many tables and cubicles -- some studying and others quietly socializing and teasing each other, as if the occupation of their land had never happened.

"Here you go," the Librarian exclaimed, handing Natalya the book.

"Thank you," Natalya replied, turning towards a group of cubicles where she could be alone.

"I'll need your library card," the Librarian exclaimed.

"Excuse me?" the Russian agent asked with surprise knowing that her contact in Vancouver had neglected to obtain one for her. Suddenly, Natalya found herself confronted with her first obstacle. Although it was a minor one because of a simple oversight, she was well aware that it could impede her entire mission. "Just stay calm," Natalya cautioned herself as she returned to the desk.

"I'll need your library card," the Librarian repeated her request with a smile.

"I'm sorry, ma'am, but I don't have one," Natalya politely answered, feeling her heart accelerating. She hoped that her truthfulness would win over the Librarian. "But if you'll please, I'll sit right here in front of you. It'll only take a few minutes."

"I'm not supposed to," the elderly Hawaiian began, before reversing herself. "Well, all right. You look like an honest person," she answered allowing Natalya to take the book.

"Thank you so much," the Muscovite replied before taking her seat at an unoccupied cubicle to the left of the main desk. She sat directly in view of the Librarian. After breathing a sigh of relief, Natalya opened the yearbook and began searching out the names.

As she delved into her task, four men abruptly rushed through the library's double doors. "FBI," one of them loudly declared flashing his badge in front of the stunned librarian. Upon hearing the words, Natalya shrunk deeper into the tiny cubicle, partially out of fear of being discovered.

"Have you seen any of these girls?" one of the agents demanded of the elderly Hawaiian.

"Why? What've they done?" the Librarian asked with hesitation.

"I can't say. This is an official investigation," the agent tersely replied. "Just answer the question."

"We... we get a lot of students here," the Librarian answered, not wanting to betray any of the students whom she loved as her own children. As the elderly Hawaiian answered her hands trembled.

"I'll repeat one last time and if you don't answer me, I'll have you locked up for obstruction," the impatient agent warned, his voice growing menacing. "Have you seen any of these girls? Yes or no?"

ВЕСНА РУССКАЯ

"I can't say. Please..." the Librarian answered, her voice breaking in fear of the consequences she might suffer for not cooperating with the invading agents.

"Frank, I see one here," another agent suddenly interjected, pointing to a long rectangular table where a group of four girls with open books, quietly talked among themselves. "Forget her," he added as the four agents immediately left from the front desk and headed for the table.

"FBI," the lead agent again identified his team.

Upon hearing the menacing letters, the four girls grew silent. While they sat in silence, filled with fear, the FBI agents mentally studied each one. After a few seconds of unnerving silence, the lead agent finally spoke. "You, you, and you all can go," he declared singling out the three who did not match the bureau's profiles.

Despite being dismissed, the three girls, feeling sick to their stomachs about the impending affair and fearful for their friend's safety, lingered around.

"I said go. Now get out of here," the agent repeated, his voice growing threatening.

"Out of this library," another agent commanded upon seeing the girls head for the back of the library.

Once the three had reluctantly left, the FBI agents took seats at each side of and in front of the isolated girl. "Your name is Erica Lew, is it not?" the lead agent began interrogating her.

As the agent mentioned the teenager's name, Natalya who silently observed from her nearby cubicle, immediately recognized it as one of the names she had memorized.

"Yes," Erica, a slender-shouldered, neatly dressed, dark-haired girl, quietly answered.

186

"We know everything about you and your family -- where your father works, where you live, so let me advise you, it's in your interest to cooperate with us," the agent spoke. "So let me start by asking you, where is Aimee Kualani?"

"I don't know," Erica firmly answered in spite of her trepidation.

"I think that you do," the lead agent retorted. "Tell me where she is!" he demanded.

"I really don't know where she is," Erica reiterated her answer.

"Let me repeat. I think you've seen her. I think you know where she is," the agent continued, while the trapped girl remained silent. "If you do not begin cooperating with us, your father's career will be over," the agent threatened, his voice again growing menacing. "And without his salary, he won't be able to make payments on the house, and God knows he won't be able to pay for the care of your invalid mother. A shame it would be if you and your family suddenly became destitute and homeless!" he added with a slight chuckle and false sympathy.

Despite the agent's harsh threats, Erica Lew refused to speak.

"Think now, what would Mommy and Daddy do if perhaps their precious little daughter did not come home tonight or perhaps ever again, for that matter," he sarcastically warned, momentarily clasping the trapped girl's hand.

"Please," Erica quietly begged, quickly withdrawing her hand from the coarse hands of her interrogator. "I really don't know where Aimee is."

"You still lie!" the agent exploded. "You think we're here for fun and games. Well let me tell you, we're here for serious business and if you don't start..."

187

"Let me handle this," another agent suddenly interrupted, playing the "good guy." "There is no need to threaten the girl," he added in a gentle, reassuring tone, before turning to face Erica. "Erica, I know you are scared and I can understand. But let me assure you, we won't hurt you. You're not a suspect."

"Then please, let me go."

"You must understand," the agent softly spoke. "It's important that you help us. It's not only important to us, but to Aimee. It's not healthy for her to be living in the streets when she should be here with her friends," he continued trying to win Erica's trust. "For Aimee's sake, please tell me where she is. All we want to do is prove to her that her fears are unfounded so that she can get on with her life."

"I wish I knew where she was, but I don't," Erica Lew steadfastly stuck to her story. "I'm sorry."

"Very well, but if you find anything out... If you hear from her, you must let us know immediately," the "good guy" agent urged the cornered girl, handing her his card.

"I tell you, she's lying," the lead agent again took over, as Erica silently accepted the card. "How could she not know where Aimee is? She and Aimee are best friends!"

"Let it go," the "kinder and gentler" agent recommended to his colleague. "Maybe she really doesn't know anything, but if she does, I'm sure she'll come around when she realizes we're here to help."

As the agents debated the matter for several more minutes, Erica felt greatly uncomfortable. She closed her books and got up from her seat to depart.

"No, please. Please sit down," the "kinder and gentler" agent softly urged her. "We'll go now so you may study in peace," he promised, as the three others got up from their seats. "We're sorry for the inconvenience we may have caused you," he apologized before they exited the library in search of their next subject.

Chapter 20

A few minutes after the FBI agents had left, Erica Lew, though shaken by her encounter with them, quietly collected her books and exited from the library. Upon seeing Erica leave, Natalya got up and immediately returned the yearbook. "Thank you," she quickly expressed her gratitude before leaving in pursuit of Erica. She was eager to catch up to Aimee Kualani's friend before she lost sight of her.

"You're with them too," the elderly Hawaiian Librarian dejectedly declared just before Natalya exited.

"I assure you I'm not with them," the Russian agent having heard the Librarian's barely audible response, quickly replied, before going through the double doors into the hallway. Once out of the library, Kalinina broke into a light run to catch up with Aimee Kualani's friend. "Wait!" she called out to Erica, who momentarily quickened her pace. After thinking the better of it, Erica Lew abruptly obeyed. Upon seeing the Muscovite, whom she did not recognize, the High School Junior quickly glanced around the empty hallway. Realizing that she was isolated and remembering the lead agent's ominous words "what would Mommy and Daddy do if perhaps their precious little daughter did not come home tonight..." Erica was over swept by fear. Knowing that escape was out of the question, since her pursuer could easily shoot her with no one knowing, she reluctantly waited for the Russian agent to catch up.

"I just want to talk to you," Natalya declared, relieved that she did not have to chase after Erica any longer.

"I thought you were finished," Erica Lew quickly protested.

"If you think I'm with the FBI, I'm not," Natalya quickly answered, wanting to calm the girl's unfounded fears.

"Then who are you with? The CIA? The Military?"

"Neither of them. Please relax. I have nothing to do with the United States Government."

"Then why do you want to talk to me?" Erica tensely asked.

"I need to find Aimee."

"I don't know where she is," Erica quickly declared, fearful that the invader's agents were playing with her mind in an attempt to trick her.

"Listen to me. We both know she needs to get off this island," Natalya resumed, wanting to gain Erica's trust.

"I don't know where she is," Lew repeated, feeling increasingly uncomfortable at the Russian's persistence. Although terrified at having to lie, knowing that her family could face severe reprisals, Erica also feared the alternative, knowing that the truth would jeopardize her friend's life.

"Please. How can I get you to trust me?" Natalya pleaded, seeing that her efforts were frustratingly futile.

"What do you mean?" the 16 year-old asked, caught off guard by the question.

"I need you to trust me so that I can help Aimee. But for me to help her, I need your help," Natalya spoke. "I know they've made promises to you, but no matter what they've told you, the only way Aimee is really going to be safe is when she's away from here and far away from the United States," Kalinina continued.

ВЕСНА РУССКАЯ

"You said that, not me," Erica, unconvinced of Natalya's sincerity and motives, declared fearing that she would be entrapped if she expressed agreement.

"I know you're scared, but so is Aimee. Every minute she's here, she's in greater danger. You must trust me. I'm not with them. I'm on your side and most of all I'm on Aimee's side," the Russian agent spoke.

"How do I know? How can I be sure? Anyone can say anything they want until they get what they want?" Erica cautiously replied, before stopping herself and reiterating her earlier stand, "No, really, I don't know where she is."

"Please. I really am on your side," Natalya persisted.

"Then let me go. I've told you everything I can. I don't know where she is," Erica requested.

"But maybe you know of a friend who can help me?"

"I know nothing."

"Please, just hear me out," Natalya implored, grabbing Erica by the wrist as she turned to leave.

"As if I have a choice," the High School junior declared with resignation.

"You do have a choice," Kalinina sighed, releasing Erica's wrist. "If you don't want to help me, I can't force you to. If you want to go, I won't keep you. Just remember one thing, as long as Aimee remains here, neither her, you, nor your family will be safe."

"First you say you're on my side and now you threaten me!" Erica blurted out.

"I'm not threatening you. I'm sorry if you took it as..."

"You just said `I'll never be safe!' If that's not a threat, then what is it?" Erica cut the Russian agent off in mid sentence.

"From them not me!" Natalya protested, again taking the girl by her wrist. "Just take a look," Kalinina ordered, leading Aimee's friend to a nearby window. "You see those parked cars out there. Well, there are FBI agents in them. They've got the school staked out. They're going to keep following you until they find Aimee. And with them around, you'll never be able to help Aimee." As the Russian agent spoke, Erica Lew silently stared at the manned vehicles. "As long as Aimee is in hiding and they believe you're harboring her, they'll never leave your family alone!" Natalya continued. "That's why I want to help you. I can get Aimee off this island and to real safety. But for me to do that, you're going to have to trust me and help me," Kalinina added, leading Erica away from the window.

"Then let me go!" Erica demanded.

"Very well. You may go," Natalya reluctantly surrendered, releasing the girl's wrist. Although disappointed, the Muscovite knew that she was not going to gain Erica's trust through coercion. "I'm sorry. I won't bother you any further," Kalinina then apologized before leaving.

For a moment, Erica Lew, not knowing how to respond, merely stood in silence and watched the Russian leave. With Kalinina's words weighing heavily on her mind, Erica succumbed to her instincts and suddenly cried out, "No wait. Don't go!"

Natalya, upon hearing the girl's request immediately turned back.

"If you want to help Aimee, tell me who you are?"

"Into the staircase. I don't want anyone to hear," Natalya urged the High School Junior fearful that the FBI surveillance teams might overhear them. "Officially I'm a Canadian National. You're to call me Michelle," Kalinina continued after assuring herself that they were alone in the staircase and that it was free of electronic bugs. "My real name is Natalya Kalinina. I'm a Russian agent," she whispered.

193

"So! Your Government's on their side," Erica quietly declared, refusing to equate herself with the American invaders.

"Not all of us. Some of us know better," Natalya answered.

"Why?"

"We've lived through two decades of misery. We've had enough. We've seen what they've done to our country. Now they're doing the same to your country. That's why it's important that key witnesses like Aimee be protected so that the truth can be revealed."

"You say you're a Russian agent," Erica Lew continued.

"That's right, but please whisper. I don't want them coming after me," Natalya cautioned the girl.

"Then if you're a Russian agent," Erica consciously lowered her voice, "and I say something that I learned in Russian, you will be able to understand me?"

"Yes."

"And you'll be able to answer me in Russian!"

"Yes, that is correct."

"Okay," Erica replied, trying to think back to some phrases she had learned, before beginning, "Где ты живёшь [Where do you live]?"

"Я живу в Москве [I live in Moscow]," Natalya answered. For several minutes afterwards, both spoke in Russian before reverting back to English, which Erica Lew felt more at ease with. "Now you know that I'm Russian," Kalinina declared with relief.

"Yes, thank God."

"So you'll help me?" Natalya then asked.

"Yes, but first tell me, what will you do with Aimee once you have her? What if she doesn't want to go to Russia?" Erica asked with growing reservations.

"First, if she doesn't want to go to Russia, she doesn't have to. The only thing I want to do is get her out of here and once she's safe, then she can decide where she wants to go. As long as she is alive and able to share her experiences with the world, we'll all benefit. Then Washington will be held accountable and maybe our two countries can be free again. But until then, we both know that Aimee won't be allowed to live."

"I'll talk to her... That's if I can find her," Erica relented. "I hope I can get to her before they do."

"I don't think that's a good idea. The moment you leave this school, they're going to follow you. All you'll do is lead them to her, and if you do, I'll be powerless to stop them. I don't have any weapons to stop them," Kalinina warned.

"Then how will you get her out of here?"

"I have a Canadian Passport for her."

"It won't work. She looks nothing like a Canadian," Erica protested, fearing that U.S. Customs agents would immediately recognize her friend's dark features.

"That's okay, because we've given her an Indian name -- Surya Ramesh," Natalya answered.

"I hope it'll work," Erica tentatively replied.

"Everything will be all right, I promise you," Natalya tried to ease Erica's doubts.

"Very well. I can't do nothing," Erica sighed and then, drawing her lips close to Natalya's ear, whispered her friend's location. "The password is 'kapu.'"

"Kapu?" the Muscovite quietly asked. "What's that?"

"It's 'forbidden in Hawaiian,'" Erica answered. "Without it you won't be able to see Aimee."

195

"Kapu," Natalya quietly reiterated.

"Good luck and please be careful and promise me you won't let anything happen to her," Erica pleaded.

"I promise you everything will be all right," Natalya quietly whispered to Aimee Kualani's friend. "Thank you and good bye," Kalinina added, embracing the teenager before leaving. "You just take care of yourself."

"I guess we'll never see each other again," Erica replied, overcome by a strong feeling of gratitude for the Russian, having become completely convinced that Natalya's motives were sincere.

"I wouldn't say that. I do like it here. Maybe someday when our countries are free, I'll come visit you. In Russia we do not forget our friends."

"I'm sorry I gave you a hard time," Erica quickly apologized, feeling guilty for having questioned the Muscovite's intentions.

"It's perfectly okay. I understand," Natalya answered embracing the Hawaiian girl for one last time. "Good bye."

"Maholo aloha," Erica quietly whispered before they parted. Although Natalya had no knowledge of the Hawaiian language, she fully understood the young girl's words as if Lew's thoughts had been telepathically transmitted to her.

Chapter 21

While Natalya Kalinina nervously walked through Honolulu's besieged streets trying her best to remain inconspicuous, she took constant measures to elude possible tails. Knowing that Aimee Kualani's life was at stake as well as the trust that the wanted girl's best friend had placed in her, Natalya periodically walked into the various shops that lined the sidewalks, casually browsing at articles of clothing. While browsing, the Russian agent cautiously monitored the doors checking to see if any of the same people had entered for a second time. She could ill afford even a mere coincidence.

As Natalya cautiously made her way to Aimee Kualani's hiding place, her country's Foreign Minister, Sergei Kruchkov was sipping coffee with the President of the United States, whom he had first met when he was stationed at the Russian Embassy in Washington, D.C. At that time the American leader was a Senator from Virginia.

"I'll bet you miss this place," U.S. President Clint Stoker spoke.

"Who wouldn't. The cherry blossoms, the bright sunshine, the warmth, and the beautiful women," Kruchkov reminisced. "Those were the days."

"And now you've been exiled to colorless Moscow," Stoker replied, remembering how he had hated the miserable Moscow drizzles that had plagued his state visit to Russia.

"You can say that again. And don't forget our nine months of cold."

"Without the cold, you wouldn't be Russian," the U.S. President spoke.

"I can do without it," the Russian Foreign Minister added, before growing serious. "I know I come at a bad time, but Igor has insisted that I pay you a visit," Kruchkov apologized, knowing that the American President had his own domestic affairs to deal with.

"Yes, how true," President Stoker somberly answered. "And they get worse. Like for instance, take a look at this newspaper. The economy's still jittery from the turmoil in Hawaii and what does the Fed Chairman do? He raises interest rates by half-a-percent! He can't stomach a tenth-of-a-percent inflation! The hell with growth and employment! Zero percent inflation at all costs!"

"He'd jump out of a window in our country! We're lucky if we have 5% in a month!" the Russian Foreign Minister exclaimed, shaking his head in disbelief, as he read the newspaper caption.

"I've got enough problems without having to worry about our economy too!"

"Not only you, but us too. There are many insurrectionists dying for the chance to say `capitalism is a failure' and reverse our reforms," Kruchkov declared.

"There would be less if Igor would follow our advice."

"That's why he sent me here. He wants me to persuade you to support his hideous policy of inaction. I've repeatedly tried to point out the grave consequences of his errors, but he won't listen. Instead, with the Prime Minister and Yuri [the Russian Defense Minister], God how I hate that man, dead set against resolute action, Igor is afraid to act. I can't understand how he can keep such men around -- they know shit about policy!"

"And he sent you to persuade me?"

"He thinks that if I come, because we know each other, and because I and the rest my allies are the only ones with common sense, you will listen. To tell you the truth, I think Igor's getting cold feet."

"Which is very dangerous. If reforms fail in Russia, world stability which we've worked so hard for, will be destroyed."

"You and I both understand that, but he doesn't. His mind is being poisoned by those bastards," Sergei Kruchkov made little effort to conceal his displeasure with Meliacherov's policies. "Sometimes I wonder if he's still committed to reform."

"We've known each other for a long time," President Stoker began speaking. "And because of our friendship, I'll be frank with you. I don't trust Igor and I never have. He allows himself to be influenced by the wrong people."

"You can say that again. That's why I find it so hard to come here and ask you to refrain from any further criticism of his handling of the Karelian crisis."

"I will do so, only because we are friends. But I must ask you, you could say a very delicate question. Do you trust your President?" the American Leader tersely inquired with a look of grave concern on his face.

"I don't know," Foreign Minister Kruchkov slowly answered after silently pondering his friend's query.

"Perhaps would a change be better?" Stoker resumed as a gravity of seriousness hung over the Oval Office.

"In what way? I'm not sure I understand what you mean?" Kruchkov asked, unsure how to answer.

199

"We are friends. That's why I'm asking you this, off the record," President Stoker began.

"Off the record, of course," the Russian Foreign Minister agreed.

"Very good," the U.S. leader replied before resuming his serious questioning. "Perhaps, if, hypothetically speaking, Igor should suddenly die of a heart attack -- You know how these things are in Russia -- and an individual more receptive towards democracy and reform came into power, your country would be better off, wouldn't it?"

"Definitely," Sergei Kruchkov quickly answered.

"And with such an individual in power, there would be no need to doubt his sincerity. Yes?"

"Yes, but there is one problem. If Igor should die, let's say today, Pavel [Romanov, the Russian Prime Minister] would take over. With him in power, Russia would be much worse off. He would replace every progressive like myself with stale, apparatchiks of the past."

"Maybe not. I understand Mr. Romanov is not well," U.S. President Stoker spoke, as Sergei Kruchkov listened in silence, knowing what he meant. "If he should also die, then you will be the next President of Russia."

"Temporarily."

"Maybe not. Under your Constitution, the President may declare martial law during times of emergency. Since your country is already facing a major internal threat, martial law is necessary to prevent anarchy."

"True."

"Therefore with your country under martial law, you will not have to face elections for a while. By the time you run, Russia having finally gotten a chance to implement full-hearted reform measures, will be much better off. And with prosperity you will have no problem winning office."

200

"That is the only way I stand a chance. Without martial law, I'll lose. Although we both know my objectives are the only cure for Russia's ailments, most of my people don't. Some are lazy, others are afraid of competition, and many are ignorant. When they'll suffer through the short-term pain that true reforms will bring, they'll only agonize in their misery. They won't look to the future and see how much gain is in store for them."

"I know that. That is why I will support you. When you declare martial law, you can count on my support and the support of our allies all across Europe," the American President promised.

"Still, Igor and Pavel must both die."

"And they will, since we both know that we must not have leaders that we cannot trust!" U.S. President Stoker declared. "However, in order to proceed, I must know if you would be willing to pursue the Russian Presidency, in the event of Igor's and Pavel's tragic misfortunes."

"Yes, but only if I can count on your support."

"Consider it done. I'll speak to Brian [McClosky, CIA Director] and see what he can do. In the meantime, you can go back to Moscow and inform Igor that you have won my support. I'll keep silent on Karelia," the U.S. President promised.

"Very good."

"Thank you for coming here. I think Igor, by sending you here, has helped all of us," Stoker exclaimed getting up and filling two glasses with vintage red wine. "Let us have a toast to democracy, my fellow President, Sergei," the U.S. President added, emphasizing the latter four words.

"And a toast to your good health and our success," Kruchkov chimed in, clanking glasses with the American President. As they sipped the red wine, an appropriate

201

symbol of the blood their conspiracy might spill, their evil pact was sealed.

Convinced that he was the future President of Russia, Sergei Kruchkov eagerly departed back for Moscow, enthusiastically awaiting the opportunity to deceive his own President into believing that he had secured an unconditional promise from Washington. As he slept during the long flight home, Sergei Kruchkov dreamed of the day he would call the Kremlin his home.

Chapter 22

The Hawaiian sun shone brightly over Honolulu's streets as Natalya entered St. Francis Medical Center carrying a translucent shopping bag of miscellaneous items she had purchased on her way. "I would like a visitor's pass for `B101,'" Natalya requested upon walking up to the reception desk where an Asian-Indian intern sat.

"I'm sorry but you must be mistaken. There's no room `B101,'" he politely apologized to the Russian agent. "But if you tell me the patient's name I might be able to help you."

"That won't be necessary," Kalinina quickly answered. "Her room number is `B101.' I know that for a fact."

"You're mistaken."

"Listen," Natalya commanded, lowering her voice. "I got the room number from a friend whose friend is hospitalized in that room. But if you won't help me, I'll go there without a pass," she threatened. "It's urgent I see her!"

"You won't be able to proceed. Where you want to go is in the basement. The elevators won't take you there without an authorized badge," the intern warned. "But, if there's a legitimate reason why you must go there, I'll give you a badge. Which law enforcement agency are you with?"

"None."

ВЕСНА РУССКАЯ

"Then you won't mind showing me some ID."

"I don't mind. All I have is my Canadian passport," Natalya answered after retrieving it from her pocket.

The intern then carefully studied the passport for several minutes until he was sure it belonged to the young woman standing in front of him. "Very well..." the intern began as he returned the passport. "What is the password?" he then asked, satisfied that the visitor had not come on behalf of the invaders.

"Kapu," Natalya quietly answered.

"This is the pass and this is the authorization badge. Slide the badge through the magnetic reader when you get into the elevator and it'll take you where you want to go. Just be sure you're alone when you use the badge," the intern cautioned the Russian agent.

"Thank you. You can count on that," Natalya quickly answered before heading for the hospital's basement where the deposed Governor's daughter had been in hiding since the invasion. Within a few minutes, the Russian agent found herself standing in a desolate, but well lit hallway.

After briefly acquainting herself with the numerical order of the rooms, Natalya walked over to a large steel door that read "Authorized Personnel only – Sterilization Area." Upon trying the knob and finding the door to be locked, the Russian knocked on the door. She was greeted by silence.

"Kapu," Natalya called out as she knocked a second time. This time the door was opened.

"Who are you?" Aimee Kualani cried out in shock at seeing the stranger.

"Don't be scared. I'm a Russian agent," Natalya answered, quickly stepping into the large, windowless room that held a bed, two chests and a color TV. She quickly entered to thwart the Hawaiian girl's attempt to lock her out.

"A Russian agent?" Aimee Kualani asked upon realizing that she was too late and could not keep Natalya out.

"I'm here to help you. Erica told me I could find you here."

"Erica? I don't believe she betrayed me," Aimee replied, gently closing the thick, reinforced door.

"She didn't. You must understand her family is under a lot of pressure from the FBI. They know that you and Erica are best friends."

"How do you know?" Aimee asked, motioning for Natalya to take a seat on the bed.

"I overheard them questioning her at the school this morning, and unless you're away from here and out of their reach, they'll continue to harass Erica and her family, especially since they're convinced, despite her denials, that as your best friend, she knows your whereabouts."

"What makes you so sure the FBI will leave them alone when I'm away from here? And where will I go? This is the only place where I can stay without worrying about how I'm going to live," Aimee Kualani answered, brushing back her dark hair.

"You'll live far away from here where -- someplace you won't have to worry about being chased and followed," Natalya soothingly answered. "And once you're safely out of their reach, they'll be notified when you speak to media about your plight."

"Then they'll find me."

"I assure you they won't. I'll make sure the press doesn't reveal your location."

"Am I going to Russia?"

"You could if you want. I know the language may be difficult at first, but you'll adapt."

"Don't worry. I already know some Russian. Me and Erica have been taking Russian classes together."

"Good. Then it will be much easier for you."

"Still, how do you expect to get me off the Islands. By now every Federal agent has my picture. I've heard that they've issued `shoot to kill' orders for me and anyone trying to help me."

"That's the risk we're going to have to take. However, I assure you, no one will be shot. It'll be easy escaping," Natalya answered with optimism. She did not want to reinforce Aimee's insecurities. "Here's your passport," she then added, handing the olive-skinned Hawaiian girl a Canadian Passport.

"Surya Ramesh?" Kualani quietly asked.

"Yes. You're a New Delhi immigrant who lives in Vancouver.

"That girl looks nothing like me!" Aimee protested in horror.

"If she did, you'd never get past passport control. I'm going to have to cut your hair and dye it black like hers," Natalya declared, pulling out a package of dye from her shopping bag. After requesting a pair of scissors from Aimee Kualani, the Russian agent set about her task. Within 45 minutes a new Aimee emerged.

"How does it look?" Kualani asked.

"Great, Surya. Now nobody will know the difference."

"You think so?" the Hawaiian asked, harboring a tinge of pessimism.

"I know so," Kalinina answered, assisting the Hawaiian girl in cleaning up the bathroom. Once sure that all traces of Kualani's presence had been washed away, the two at Aimee's insistence recited a short prayer. Afterwards,

Aimee quickly tucked a packet of papers into her pocket. They then set out on their dangerous journey to safety.

"What are those?" Kalinina quickly inquired upon seeing the papers.

"They're my birth certificate and other personal papers," Aimee replied as they headed up the elevator. "I don't want to lose who I am, unless you think it'll be a problem."

"I don't think it'll be a problem. For them to search you, they'll already have to know who you are," the Russian answered understanding Aimee's reason for wanting to keep her personal papers. "There's no turning back," Natalya she then quietly whispered as they hailed a cab in front of the hospital and headed for the Royal Hawaiian Hotel.

"Please God, look over us and protect us from harm as we make our escape," the deposed Governor's daughter silently prayed as she watched the safe confines of the hospital disappear behind them. As they rode to the hotel, Aimee Kualani's heart ached as she thought about leaving the paradise of her home behind, possibly forever, as they headed for an uncertain future.

Chapter 23

When the pair reached the Royal Hawaiian Hotel, they casually walked past the reception desk and took the elevator. Natalya and Aimee were relieved that it was not occupied. Without anyone on the elevator such as a mainland visitor that might recognize Aimee from televised photos and report her whereabouts, they stood a better chance of escaping.

Once in the privacy of Natalya's room, the two began preparations for their departure. As the Russian agent made reservations for the 7:00 PM flight to Vancouver, Aimee at Natalya's request, drew up a list of provisions she needed. When the flight plans were complete, Natalya took Aimee's list and left the hotel to pickup the items.

As Natalya selected articles of clothing including "Hawaiian tourist T-shirts" and personal necessities, Aimee Kualani watched TV. The 16-year-old Hawaiian native found it difficult to concentrate and eagerly awaited the Russian's return. She was fearful that someone at the reception desk might have recognized her and notified the invaders.

Aimee's discomfort grew worse with each passing minute of solitude she was forced to endure. As the minutes passed, Aimee's urge to take flight grew. She began to fear that something happened to Natalya. Yet, despite her growing anxieties, Aimee resisted her urge and remained in the hotel room quietly listening for suspicious sounds. At other times she nervously paced the room or occasionally peered out the window to see if there was any unusual activity.

After completing Aimee's list, Natalya Kalinina bought an extra suitcase and picked up several postcards and souvenir items. She knew that their possession of souvenirs would provide stronger proof that they were foreign tourists who had merely come to visit the Hawaiian Islands at a bad time. One of these souvenirs was a silver medallion commemorating the 120th anniversary of the proclamation of Princess Victoria Kaiulani as heir to the Hawaiian throne. Upon examining one of the medallions, the Russian agent, out of curiosity, could not help but read the black-and-silver cardboard pamphlet that accompanied it:

2011
Princess Victoria
Hawaii's Most Beloved Princess

Princess Kaiulani's grace was said to be pure Aloha as she spread joy throughout the Kingdom of Hawaii. From her birth she appeared to live a storybook life and on March 9, 1891, was proclaimed Heir Apparent.

Unfortunately, Princess Kaiulani lived a tragic life as predicted from her mother's deathbed. Kaiulani left Hawaii at an early age, lived abroad for most of her adult life, and died at the age of only 23.

Upon reading the narrative, Natalya Kalinina took a deep breath and closed the medallion's plush case. Yet, even as she proceeded to pick out a few more souvenirs – some for herself and others for Aimee, Natalya could not clear her mind of the painful thoughts of the young Hawaiian Princess's tragic life. As she thought about the deposed Governor's daughter, she could not help but wonder if Aimee was destined for a similarly tragic future. Even Aimee's last name resembled that of the young Hawaiian Princess – Kaulani versus Kaiulani.

When Natalya returned to the hotel and re-entered her room, both felt a sense of relief. The Russian was relieved to see that Aimee had remained safe; Aimee was happy to have the heavy fears weighing down on her lifted.

Conversation was minimized as Natalya divided the merchandise and both hurriedly packed their suitcases. Aimee felt an especially acute case of sadness as she quietly thought about being forced against her will from the Islands she loved.

Once everything was in order, Natalya and Aimee began their nerve-racking journey to safety. Natalya quietly whispered, "good luck" to Aimee as they disembarked from the cab at the airport and quickly proceeded to the confirmation desk.

"Good luck," Aimee returned Natalya's wish.

After obtaining their boarding passes, Natalya quickly handed one to her Hawaiian teen-aged companion.

As Aimee Kualani took the pass, she was enveloped by a shroud of terror she had never experienced before. Her thoughts focused on their approaching ordeal with the U.S. agents stationed at the airport. Her stomach tightened and her heart raced. She did not think they were going to get past the next obstacle.

"Don't be nervous," Natalya quickly whispered to the Hawaiian girl since she was edgy. "Everything's going to be okay," she added trying to calm Aimee's nerves. "Let's go!" the Russian then beckoned wanting to get through customs control as quickly as possible. She did not want to delay to give the Hawaiian girl more time to ponder potential setbacks.

After a harrowing 15-minute wait, it was their turn. Natalya cooperatively answered the well-built American inquisitor as another agent searched their luggage. While the search proceeded, Aimee could not help but nervously glance at the agents' holsters.

"Let's go," Natalya broke Aimee's stasis. Following customs and passport checks, both were relieved to finally walk through the metal detector, cleared to board. They still had an hour-an-a-half before boarding call. Since they had so much time, Natalya took Aimee to one of the airport's restaurants. She was eager to finally try Hawaiian food which Aimee helped select from the menu.

As they dined on Mahi-mahi, a popular Hawaiian "dolphin-fish" delicacy and a tropical salad followed by dessert of mochi crunch, they quietly listened to Polynesian music that softly played over the restaurant's speakers. For a moment their nerves relaxed.

Following their meal, Natalya and Aimee purchased a few magazines from a nearby bookstore. They then walked over to the Air Canada terminal and took a seat. Both occasionally talked quietly among themselves and glanced through the magazines as they passed the time.

After what seemed like an eternity, the 6:30 PM boarding call began. Both were happy to be finally on the plane. They placed their luggage in the upper compartments and took their seats on the medium-sized Air Canada jet. Aimee even breathed a sigh of relief thinking their ordeal was finally over, but before they could have a chance to relax, several U.S. agents toting automatic weapons boarded the plane.

"I guess this is it for me," Aimee whispered in dismay. "Thank you anyway for trying."

"Don't panic," Natalya quickly replied. "Just sit still and act like they're not here!" Yet, despite her instructions, Natalya was concerned that the Hawaiian teen-ager was going to panic and attract the attention of the unwelcome heavily armed agents.

"Oh please God..." Aimee Kualani whispered inaudibly as the U.S. agents proceeded from seat to seat, carefully examining each passenger's documents. "They know..." echoed from the Hawaiian's mouth.

"They don't!" Natalya quickly interrupted her companion before she could proceed, desperately hoping that her words would prove correct. "Otherwise they'd be here and wouldn't be checking everyone's papers!"

"I know you're trying to make me feel better," Aimee whispered back, all but conceding her capture. "Thank you anyway," she repeated. "Another six seats and they'll have me," she dejectedly concluded.

"They'll have to go through me first!" Natalya vowed, consciously aware that Aimee was seated next to the window.

"Forget it. Don't get in trouble for my sake," the Hawaiian replied not wanting her friend to get hurt or worse.

"It's my job. And besides friends look after each other and stand up for each other. If they're going to get you, they'll have to get me too! Now calm down and try and act natural," Natalya then urged Aimee seeing that the U.S. agents were drawing closer. "Don't say another word and whatever you do – don't panic!"

For another two minutes, Natalya and Aimee watched in silence as the agents conducted their examinations and drew closer. Even though Natalya had spoken firmly to the Hawaiian girl, she was also gripped by fear and fighting to maintain her composure. "You've been trained for this," the Russian silently reminded herself.

"What happened? What're you looking for?" They heard a nearby passenger ask.

"National security," was all the agent said as he proceeded with his task. He refused to divulge the purpose of their visit and Natalya did not care to find out.

"Passports!" Another agent suddenly demanded of Natalya and Aimee in a rough voice without pleasantries. Both immediately surrendered them.

The armed agent slowly scrutinized their documents, repeatedly studying their features. Aware that they were being watched, both sat still and tried to act as calm as possible. Aimee, fully conscious of her ringing nerves and pounding heart, silently prayed that they would persevere. She desperately wanted the examination to end.

"No, please don't!" Aimee silently commanded her pores as she felt hot beads of perspiration begin emerging on her forehead and under her armpits. Fearful that her perspiration would draw the agent's attention, Aimee Kualani felt her heart accelerate. Her head began to throb as her blood pressure soared. Her stomach tightened into an ever more uncomfortable knot. A sickening feeling of nausea crept up her esophagus. Aimee swallowed hard as she struggled to repress her growing urge to vomit. "I knew I shouldn't have eaten!" the Hawaiian girl silently scolded herself.

"Surya? Surya!" Natalya broke in on Aimee's silent agony. "Here's your passport," she then added returning the passport after one of the U.S. agents shoved both into her hands.

Without saying a word, the relieved Hawaiian felt the incredible pressure on her stomach, heart, and head immediately evaporate. Still, despite having averted the serious threat, Aimee could not relax all the way knowing that the armed agents were still on the plane. She remained wary until they finally disembarked, the plane's doors were sealed, and they were cleared for takeoff.

Only after seeing the blue waters of the Pacific did Aimee Kualani finally relax. "We're safe!" she quietly exclaimed with joy, briefly hugging and kissing Natalya.

Sixteen hours later, both arrived at Moscow's Sheremetevo Airport. Aimee again hugged her Russian companion after they stepped off the Aeroflot. "Thank you," she softly expressed her gratitude already loving the gray Moscow atmosphere. Even though the Russian guards dressed in neatly pressed gray uniforms intently studied each disembarking passenger, they provided welcome relief to Aimee. They were like her protectors and Natalya was her guardian angel.

"You're welcome dear," Natalya quietly replied as she gently steered her companion to a worn red-and-silver bus that waited to take them and the other passengers to the airport's terminal.

Once Aimee Kualani had been settled at the residence of an English-speaking Russian family who had a boy and a girl around her age, Natalya began to feel a tinge of sadness. Her part was about to be over and she was going to miss the Hawaiian teen-ager. "I hope you'll like it here," Natalya ventured knowing that Skhodnya on the outskirts of Moscow was anything the tropical paradise of Hawaii.

"I will!" Aimee reassured the Russian agent. "Believe me, anything's better than being locked away in a windowless room always wondering who might be coming to the door!"

"I know, but still..." Natalya's voice trailed off. "I just hope you remember that when winter comes. It'll be real cold! Nothing like you're accustomed to!" Natalya sighed.

"Don't worry. I'll be fine," the Hawaiian answered feeling her eyes grow moist.

Natalya then briefed Aimee on the press conference the KGB would set up so that the international media could confirm that she was safely off the Hawaiian Islands. It was Kalinina's hope that once the media verified that Aimee was out of their reach, the invading agents would leave Erica's family and other Hawaiian families alone.

"If there's anything I can do for you -- anything at all -- please call me," the Muscovite pleaded, quickly writing down her home address and work and home telephone numbers.

"Thank you so much for everything," Aimee gratefully answered taking the sheet of paper. She then embraced the Russian agent. "Please stay in touch."

"I will. I promise," Natalya answered tightly holding the Hawaiian teen-ager.

"I'm going to miss you," Kualani added.

"I'm going to miss you too," Natalya replied as both cried. "Just remember, I don't live too far away. You're always welcome to visit and I hope you do. You're a friend and a comrade."

ВЕСНА РУССКАЯ

"Thank you. You're a friend too!" Aimee replied.

After saying their last good-byes and hugging each other for a final time, Natalya headed for the train station and boarded a train back to Moscow. As she rode the train, Natalya constantly thought of the paradise her friend had been forced to abandon. She knew that starting over in a new country, which included making new friends, and adapting to a new culture was not an easy thing. She vowed to keep in touch with the Hawaiian girl so that she knew she had a caring friend and someone to talk to.

As the diesel train slowly made its way back to Moscow, Natalya hoped for the best. She knew Aimee was going through a lot and had gone through a lot when she had lost her parents. "Please God, give her strength and fortitude" the Russian agent found herself silently praying to a God she hadn't spoken to too often in her adult life. At the same time, Natalya could not help but feel the sorrow and pain the Hawaiian girl was going through. While things would never be the same for Aimee, she prayed they would get better. A depressing silence filled the train as it cut through a misty rain and dreary fog. Tears came to Natalya's eyes as she watched the what scenery was visible through the misty fog pass her by and waited to get back to Moscow. While the mission had not been without its heart-wrenching moments, the ending, though successful, left Natalya with a heavy heart. She was going to miss the Hawaiian teen-ager for despite her professionalism, Natalya's mission had become personal and a special bond had been formed between the two.

Chapter 24

The July sun shone brightly over Petrozavodsk, the Capital of Karelia. A mild breeze gently wafted through the city as white, feathery cirrus clouds slowly floated across the azure sky. With temperatures hovering in the 70s [Fahrenheit], a far cry from the arctic freeze of only months ago, the city's streets were filled with people.

As the weekend crowds enjoyed the balmy weather, Karelian Governor Valeri Sheremetev sat at an open-air café with his fair-haired wife of Finnish descent and two sons, 11 and 8, respectively. They quietly talked among themselves enjoying the day.

With an atmosphere of serenity brought by the summer warmth, the winter's turmoil that had threatened to plunge Russia into a civil war appeared to be a distant thing of the past. Mikhail Klisov's troops had long since returned to the barracks. Karelia's businesses and streets were again left to civilians. In addition, the explosive mortality rate of only months earlier had eased considerably. Karelian residents were again able to find ample supplies of food and clothing. Heat was no longer an issue. Children again laughed and played in the streets.

A semblance of normalcy had returned. The Kremlin even directed greater quantities of goods to the

ВЕСНА РУССКАЯ

Karelian Republic so that there would not be repeats of the winter unrest. Despite the Kremlin's accommodation and general amnesty, Governor Sheremetev, his family, his supporters, and other participants in the winter revolt remained apprehensive. The West with the agreement of Russian Foreign Minister Sergei Kruchkov, remained persistent in calling for the arrests of the revolt's participants. At any time, Governor Sheremetev and his wife expected President Meliacherov to withdraw his pardon to appease foreign interests. At times they found themselves waiting for the proverbial knock on the door from the KGB.

With the strain taking a toll on his wife's health, Governor Sheremetev found himself having second thoughts about remaining in office. Since the uprising, his wife had been hospitalized twice for bleeding ulcers.

Only the continued outpouring of support from his constituents made the job appealing. Without his constituents' gratitude, Valeri Sheremetev would have resigned. To Karelians, the Governor and Commander Mikhail Klisov were heroes. They had stood up to the West and won.

As the Sheremetevs enjoyed the summer warmth, a well-dressed man stood under a nearby tree. He took out a wallet-sized photograph of the Karelian Governor and compared it to the man seated 30 meters away. When he saw there was a match, the man casually took a seat to the rear of the Governor and pretended to scan the menu.

Once sure that no one was paying him any attention, the man got back to his feet. He whipped out an automatic weapon and before anyone could as much as scream, he opened fire on the unsuspecting Governor.

218

The first bullet tore into Valeri Sheremetev's back. His wife immediately screamed in horror as she protectively pushed her two boys to the ground.

Upon being struck by the first bullet, the Karelian Governor, in stunned disbelief, tried to get up from his seat. Sheremetev wanted to face his attacker. As he feebly attempted to get to his feet, Sheremetev was hit by several more rounds. Bullets tore through his back and punctured his heart. Blood sprayed across the table onto food, plates, and his screaming wife.

As the Governor lurched forward from the bullets' velocity, an explosion ripped into the back of his head. A fusillade of flesh and blood tore free. The Governor immediately ceased his attempts to get up and slumped over the wood table. A horrible silence followed as people stared in shock and disbelief.

With his evil deed done, the assassin fled into a waiting car. A group of enraged onlookers, having overcome their initial shock, took pursuit. The angry mob rapidly closed in on the vehicle. The engine stalled as the driver turned his key.

The terrified assassin opened fire on the approaching mob. Despite felling several people, the growing angry sea of people kept up their advance, undeterred by threats to their safety.

Only after what seemed like an eternity to the assassin did the driver finally get the engine started and pull away from the curb. The angry mob soon receded into the distance and then disappeared as they drove down Karelia's streets.

Once safely away from the angry mob, the assassin pulled out a cellular phone and placed a call to Robert Salerno, the Deputy American Ambassador. "It's done," he methodically spoke into the phone.

219

ВЕСНА РУССКАЯ

"Very good," Salerno tersely replied. "I'll wire the money to your account. You should have it in an hour," he then added, ending the brief conversation. "One threat eliminated!" Robert Salerno quietly declared as he filled a glass with champagne to celebrate the occasion in the solitude of his office.

As the car headed out of Petrozavodsk, the assassin reached into his pocket for a cigarette. Though his pack was missing, he thought nothing of it. He then asked his driver for a cigarette.

Without saying a word, the driver pulled a pack from his pocket and offered a cigarette to his passenger. The assassin hastily put the cigarette in his mouth and lit it. He did so partly out of relief for having successfully completed his hit and to calm his nerves. He inhaled deeply. Immediately upon inhaling, the assassin's body stiffened and his eyes bulged. Almost simultaneously afterwards, he slumped forward without muttering a single word. He had been poisoned by cyanide.

After several minutes of riding with the assassin's corpse, the driver met up with another vehicle at a pre-determined rendezvous site. He parked the car and turned off the engine.

Upon being joined by the others sent by the Deputy American Ambassador, the driver put on gloves and carefully lifted the gun from the dead assassin's vest pocket. It was to be smuggled out of the country.

The group then poured corrosives capable of melting steel over the assassin's face and body so that they could destroy his flesh and render identification impossible. Once they had completed this step, they poured gasoline throughout the parked vehicle and set it on fire. With the original getaway car in flames, the group left for the American Embassy in Moscow.

As the group of killers headed back to Moscow, the Governor's wife sobbed uncontrollably crying out, "Почему? Почему? [Why? Why?]" over and over again. She clung tightly to the remains of her fallen husband as her two sons stared in shocked silence not knowing how to express their emotions.

With an outpouring of sympathy, several people tried to comfort the sobbing widow. They gradually separated her from her husband's remains while another passerby, out of respect, took off his suit jacket and covered the murdered Governor's face. A young woman put her arms around the Governor's two sons and gently turned them away from the horrific scene.

Before long, news spread about Valeri Sheremetev's assassination. The Karelian Republic went into mourning for their fallen hero. Many sobbed upon hearing the terrible news. Some wanted to avenge the murder of the leader who had died because he had chosen to save them from almost certain death just months earlier.

Chapter 25

While Karelians went into mourning, Muscovites, unaware of the shooting, went about their business. Some shopped, others held small group reunions, and still others stayed home to get a few extra hours of sleep or take care of neglected household chores. Among those unaware of Governor Sheremetev's assassination were Natalya Kalinina and her American boyfriend, Jim Keating as they walked hand-in-hand in Expo Park.

Since returning from Hawaii, Natalya had seen him only a handful of times. The mounting differences between the Kremlin and White House were the primary cause of this. However, Natalya also spent some of her weekends in Skhodnya with the Hawaiian girl she had successfully rescued. Each visit brought the Russian agent more assurance that Aimee had successfully adapted to her new home and new family. For that, she was happy especially since it gave her closure from the tragedy of her first year with the KGB. That was the year when the American subject of her interrogation, Michael Levine, had committed suicide sending her into shocked depression. To Natalya, Aimee had been her second chance to make right. She was grateful that she did not botch up this time and things turned out well.

The press conference featuring Aimee Kualani further dampened relations between Washington and Moscow when the CIA determined she was living in Russia, that she had been spirited off the Hawaiian Islands by the Russian intelligence agency, and the Kremlin refused to return her to the United States. In retaliation for Moscow's disobedience, American Ambassador Stephen Norcross initially restricted his entire staff from having contact with Russians. Only after vigorous complaints from the Embassy's CIA staff who vehemently argued that they needed these contacts to effectively gather intelligence did he partially relent. However purely social contacts that could not be justified for intelligence gathering purposes remained prohibited.

Despite the restriction, Natalya and Jim still managed to occasionally find time to spend with each other. Unknown to the American Ambassador, the relationship between Jim and Natalya grew stronger because his actions. Their commitment to each other took precedence over politically motivated directives aimed at stopping relationships like the one they enjoyed. To them, the risks were worth it and threats of reprisals did not deter them. When necessary, Jim always found a way to account for his activities away from the Embassy and to justify his phone calls.

Both enjoyed Russian ice cream as they strolled through Moscow's Expo Park soaking in the bright sunshine. They came to a stop in front of Friendship Fountain. It was a magnificent fountain surrounded by dazzling gold statuettes of young women offering bouquets of flowers in the name of friendship.

"Isn't it beautiful?" Natalya asked her boyfriend as they took a seat on the fountain's granite ridge, pointing to the four layers of streaming water that arched their way down into separate, descending pools of crystal-clear water that surrounded the intricate gold figures.

"Да [Yes] and so are you," the American slowly answered, as if momentarily distracted. For much of their walk, Jim found himself pre-occupied by the dilemma that was tearing at his heart. Hours earlier, Jim had received an intelligence report documenting the Karelian uprising. He had instructions to hand it over to the American Ambassador who in turn would forward a copy to Russia's pro-Western Foreign Minister, Sergei Kruchkov. He was heartbroken to see that his girlfriend's name was among those listed. He was troubled and could not decide if he should hand it over as required or alter or destroy it. Betrayal against country and girlfriend were two equally unpalatable choices.

"Спасибо [Thank you]," the Muscovite warmly replied taking Jim into her arms and kissing him. Although the American returned Natalya's affections, her instincts told her that something was wrong. She could sense the ineffable change in their chemistry. "Is there something wrong?" she suddenly asked feeling the sense of alarm nipping at her insides.

"Нет [Nyet]," Keating answered trying his best to disguise his unsettled feeling.

"I know there is," the Russian answered reverting to English. She was fully conscious of the other people sitting along the fountain's ledge and wanted privacy. "I know you too well for you to lie and get away with it!" she then added. "So tell me what's on your mind! Is it something I said or did?"

"No, nothing."

"Are you sure?" Natalya asked with concern since he had not denied that there was something on his mind.

"Yes, I'm sure. Believe me, there's nothing you could do wrong. You're the perfect girl. You're the woman I love," Jim answered trying to allay the Muscovites concerns.

"Я не знаю [I don't know]," Kalinina slowly exhaled, reverting back to her native tongue as she expressed her doubts. "For some reason I get the feeling you're holding something back from me. If there's a problem, please let's talk. I don't want some misunderstanding to come between us," she added, unconvinced of the American's answer.

"You must trust me. Nothing's going to come between us, Natasha," Jim reluctantly answered taking the Muscovite's hand and kissing it. "I won't let it. I love you too much."

"Пожалуста [Please]!" Natalya insisted. "Tell me what's on your mind. I must know."

Jim took a deep breath before beginning. "All right, since you must know..." he hesitantly surrendered. "You remember when we agreed not to discuss our work..."

"Да [Yes]," Natalya led him on, her interest piqued.

"Well, I guess my work's getting to me."

"How so? Is there something I can do to help?"

"I wish it were that simple," Jim Keating replied deeply pained at the decision he was going to make regarding the intelligence report. His heart was heavy. He was upset that the politics between their two countries had found a way to get into their relationship, a relationship he cherished more than any of the others he had previously had.

"It's all right," Natalya tried to comfort her troubled boyfriend.

"I wish I could tell you, but I can't," Jim exclaimed with sadness.

225

"It's all right. I understand," Natalya replied knowing there were some things they couldn't discuss because of their occupations.

"I really wish I could discuss it with you," Jim repeated. "I just hope this doesn't come between us," he then added.

"Don't worry. It won't. I still love you," the Muscovite woman answered taking the American into her arms and kissing him. "And I'll continue to love you."

"You're so kind. I love you too. I love you very much," Jim answered wanting Natalya to know his feelings for her had not changed.

"That's why I needed to know that it wasn't me. I couldn't go home tonight not knowing if I had said or done something to make you mad at me," Natalya declared pressing his body into hers. "At least now I feel better knowing it's work and wasn't me," she added kissing him.

"I relieved. I don't know what would've done if you weren't so understanding," the American answered, feeling better.

"I just want you to know that I'm an understanding person and if there's ever something bothering you – please, please tell me. And if you can't discuss it with me, at least let me know it's not me so I don't start worrying it was something I said or did."

"For now on I will," Jim agreed. "I don't want you upset at yourself or worried for no reason."

"Promise?" Natalya asked relinquishing him from her grip and playfully sprinkling him with a handful of water from the fountain's pool.

"I promise," he declared returning the Russian's favor.

"Good," Kalinina answered throwing more water on her friend. "You want to get wet?" she quickly added upon having water thrown onto her T-shirt. "I'll get you wet," she declared quickly grabbing his arms before he could throw more water onto her. She immediately pulled him into her body and rolled off the ledge into the fountain's pool.

"I don't believe you!" Jim exclaimed.

"Now we're really wet!" the Russian quickly answered kissing him as they laid in the fountain's pool.

"I see," he replied returning Natalya's kisses. Both were oblivious to the nearby people. "Я ты люблю [I love you]."

"Я ты тоже люблю [I love you too]," Natalya declared, briefly pulling her lips from his as they slowly rose and sat back on the fountain's ledge. "What we have is special and no one or nothing can come between us," the Russian then vowed. "Our love is eternal, sealed by our kisses under this fountain," she added as they again locked lips.

As both kissed for several minutes, listening to the romantic sounds of the gushing water, each could sense their relationship gravitating to a new level of greater love. Both could feel their unresisting hearts merging into one.

227

Chapter 26

As tension increased between Russia and the United States, the Kremlin began to unravel into to two increasingly hostile camps. Russian President Igor Meliacherov, his Prime Minister, Pavel Romanov, and his Defense Minister Yuri Likhovtsev joined forces in the aftermath of Valeri Sheremetev's assassination while the Foreign Minister, Sergei Kruchkov and the Kremlin's pro-Western economists took positions in staunch opposition.

The estrangement between the two factions grew deeper and began to take on personal dimensions when the Russian President presented the "Hero of Russia" Medal, the country's highest honor to Valeri Sheremetev's grieving widow. The Pro-Western faction issued unprecedented criticism of their President's decision hoping to steer their leader back to the West's side. Instead, Prime Minister Pavel Romanov flew to Kiev to meet with Belarussian and Ukrainian officials to discuss a possible alliance between the three countries.

Alarmed by the Kremlin's re-evaluation of foreign relations with the United States and Western Europe, Foreign Minister Sergei Kruchkov increased his contacts with the American Embassy and the White House. He was very concerned that he and the other pro-Western

Ministers would soon have no voice in Kremlin policy making and perhaps, even worse, be dismissed from their positions.

With the increasingly polarized sides moving towards a major ideological confrontation and the diminishing influence of Washington over Moscow, U.S. President Clint Stoker, his envoys to Moscow, Stephen Norcross and Robert Salerno, and the Russian Foreign Minister accelerated their plot to take control of the Kremlin. To the quartet, drastic action was needed or "Russia would be lost."

To further destabilize the Meliacherov Government, U.S. President Stoker with Kruchkov's blessings, telephoned Beijing to support China's territorial claims over Russia's southern flank. This was the same area where 45 years earlier the territorial giants had slip precipitously close to war when Soviet and Chinese forces exchanged fire along the Amur River. To buy time and gain power, Kruchkov was willing to sacrifice Russian land.

The area, first settled by Russian fur traders, had been in dispute since the reign of Regent Sophia (1682-89) when under the Treaty of Nerchinsk (named after Fort Nerchinsk where negotiations were held) Russia under duress (with their fort surrounded by 17,000 hostile Chinese soldiers and large numbers of heavily-armed junks preparing to attack) had ceded the entire Amur Basin to China to avoid war. The area remained under Chinese control until 1858-60 when Russian troops under Czar Nicholas I reclaimed their 380,000 acres of land from the declining Empire.

With Stoker's prodding, China suddenly demanded territorial concessions from Moscow. As Beijing made their demands, U.S. tanks and troops commenced ominous maneuvers in the near abroad (Georgia, Moldova, and the

ВЕСНА РУССКАЯ

Baltic States) and Poland. Warsaw even began to contemplate retaking Belarus's western lands, which they had lost during World War II.

With the growing instability and rising possibility of war, Russians became increasingly aware of their vulnerability. Moscow's earlier decision to destroy much of Russia's weapons and dismantle much of her armed forces looked more horrible every day.

History was again repeating itself as it had done so many painful times before – the Mongol invasion, defeat at the hands of the Turkish Beys, conquests by Swedish and Polish-Lithuanian States, invasion and destruction at the hands of Napoleon's Grand Armée, humiliation during the Russo-Japanese War, enormous suffering in World War II – all because in the words of Josef Stalin, "it was profitable to beat Russia." It was perceived that acts of aggression against Moscow went unpunished.

Russia again found herself in a pitiable plight. She was in the same state as two centuries earlier when the poet Nekrasov wrote, "Thou art poor and thou art plentiful, thou art mighty and thou art helpless, Mother Russia."

Fully conscious of the tightening noose around her borders, Russians began to feel a sense of growing fear. Families were again forced to contemplate the horrible losses and starvation their great-grandparents had enduring during World War II. Many angrily lamented their plight. Others wondered if their leaders had learned anything from their country's painful past. Some were so resigned, they wondered if "a Russian" was at all capable of learning. Like so many times in the past, Russia again found herself surrounded and at the mercy of hostile, foreign armies.

As the winds of war kicked up, Russian President Meliacherov scrambled to conclude an agreement with Belarus and Ukraine. It was this reason why Prime Minister Romanov had begun exploratory talks with the two countries.

In addition to wanting to enhance the security of Russia's periphery, Meliacherov also extended diplomatic overtures to other former Soviet States and East-bloc countries to gauge where they stood and if Russia had a chance to persuade them to choose neutrality. This angered and dismayed Washington.

With dreams of global harmony and international cooperation dashed, the world again found itself being torn apart in hostile spheres. Countries were forced to choose between Russia and the West. In the new cold war, Bulgaria and Slovakia took Moscow's side; the Czech Republic, Poland, and Romania took Washington's side; and Austria and Hungary declared neutrality.

Suddenly, although he had not intended it, U.S. President Clint Stoker found himself helpless to control the events he had precipitated. He had become a hostage to his belligerence and could not step back fearing that it would harm U.S. stature abroad and hinder Sergei Kruchkov's chances of taking control in Moscow.

As the world approached the precipice of war, Natalya Kalinina and Jim Keating found that their relationship had retreated into brief two and three minute telephone calls. Yet in spite of this, their love and loyalty to each other remained undying.

The global situation deteriorated further in early August when Belarus and Ukraine agreed to form a strategic alliance with Russia. Washington promptly retaliated sending additional troops and armaments to Europe and Asia. Moscow reciprocated dispatching a few

231

of her submarines and battleships within range of the North American continent. Before long, Russian and American submarines were engaged in high-stakes, dangerous cat-and-mouse, hide-and-seek games deep beneath the earth's oceans.

With the world's armed forces mobilized and poised for action, Russia (which had never been accepted as a full member of NATO nor had a full say), Belarus, Ukraine, Bulgaria, and Slovakia withdrew from the West's military alliance. The world's markets immediately suffered a massacre with the Dow Jones Industrials losing 440 and 690 points, respectively, on two successive days. Western Government bonds were also hammered with U.S. long-term notes losing an incredible 12½ points in one day. U.S. President Stoker and other Western leaders were suddenly forced to shut down their investment markets fearful of investor rage and that their economies were about to be plunged into deep recession.

After a month-and-a-half of global crisis and the high economic costs associated with it, the American President reluctantly offered to hold talks on resolving the festering dispute. With the prospect of a negotiated settlement and renewed hopes of avoiding a third world war, the West's markets stabilized when they were re-opened. All across the globe, people on every continent breathed a collective sigh of relief. There was a chance their leaders were going to be able to rein in the dangerous situation they had created.

Chapter 27

Early optimism soon faded when Washington refused to withdraw American troops from the near abroad unless Russia, Belarus, and Ukraine dissolved their new alliance and re-entered NATO with the understanding that they would unconditionally adhere to its directives. President Meliacherov rejected, knowing that Russia, without a veto, would remain powerless to influence policy in Western defense organization. In response, American negotiators refused to consider Moscow's requests and before long, talks were suspended bringing the world back to the brink of global conflict.

With talks ended, U.S. President Stoker ordered the Pentagon to re-target Russian cities with Intercontinental Ballistic Missiles (ICBMs). Back under the shadow of nuclear annihilation, Moscow had little choice but to reciprocate. Washington promptly condemned Russia's decision to re-target American cities.

As the world teetered closer to war, the United Kingdom joined the United States and also targeted Russian cities with nuclear missiles. However, when the Stoker Administration requested Paris to do likewise, the French President gave a firm "Non!" Before long, Germany, Belgium, Luxembourg, and the Netherlands joined France and refused to take sides. They were soon followed by Greece and Italy.

With Europe -- which had suffered major destruction and loss of life all across her lands during the two world wars of the 20th century – becoming unnerved, U.S. President Stoker was forced change course. In a nationally televised message, he somberly announced his intention to unilaterally withdraw American forces from the near abroad. Although the American President said he was making this "unconditional and benevolent move to preserve world peace which he cherished above all things" he had little choice. Several European Governments, unwilling to subject their citizens to another destructive war, had quietly warned him that they would expel U.S. troops if they were not voluntarily removed from the near abroad. At the same time, Stoker wanted to enhance the stature of his friend, Sergei Kruchkov so that he would have a better chance of attaining power. During his speech, U.S. President Stoker lavished praise on the Russian Foreign Minister calling his efforts to "resolve the crisis invaluable." It was Stoker's hope that with this "unconditional, unilateral concession," Kruchkov would become a hero to Russians.

Tensions eased considerably when U.S. forces began withdrawing from the near abroad. Confidence rose that the pre-cold war II peace could be restored to its original levels as the world retreated from the brink of war. Within weeks, following a staged "impromptu" meeting between the Russian Foreign Minister and U.S. President, Washington and London agreed to de-target Russian cities if Moscow agreed to reciprocate. Sergei Kruchkov agreed on behalf of his country and a week later, a tri-lateral treaty outlining this agreement was formally signed by the leaders of the United States, United Kingdom and Russia. Again each country's people were free of the shadow of nuclear Armageddon.

With the appearance of thawing relations between Moscow and Washington, the American President's hopes of building up the stature of his friend, Foreign Minister Sergei Kruchkov were realized. However, a major problem arose. Russians in even greater numbers saluted their President, Igor Meliacherov, who for the first time actually enjoyed significant popular support.

Knowing that his plans for Kruchkov's Kremlin takeover were still impeded, Clint Stoker began a new plan to elevate the pro-Western Foreign Minister to the Russian Presidency. As Stoker, American Ambassador and Deputy Ambassador Norcross and Salerno, respectively, and Sergei Kruchkov engaged in their covert scheme, the U.S. Embassy in Moscow became a hub of activity. CIA reports creating the illusion of a coup plot by the Russian Defense Minister, Yuri Likhovtsev, were manufactured and delivered to the Russian President. Other reports indicating KGB support for a Likhovtsev coup were also created and delivered.

With the deadline fast approaching for Jim Keating to hand his report documenting the Karelian uprising to the American Ambassador, he was forced to make a difficult decision. Out of love for Natalya Kalinina, he removed her name from the list of probable suspects. He also removed the names of Elena Potapova, whom he had met once and knew was her closest friend, and Valentin Makarov, her supervisor whom she admired. To suppress potential feelings of guilt, Jim justified his actions by repeatedly telling himself that "he did not work for Moscow and therefore had no obligation to present an accurate report that would go to the Russian Foreign Minister via

Ambassador Norcross, and then ultimately to the President of Russia."

Having completed his unenviable task, Jim Keating returned to his office wondering if his alterations would be discovered. Although he wanted to inform his girlfriend of the CIA mole in the Russian intelligence service who supplied the names for the "Karelian Uprising" Report, he declined. His conscience would not allow him to cost another man his life without reasonable cause – even if this person was a mole who could jeopardize his career. Because of his reluctance, the CIA officer braced himself for the potential fallout should the mole discover what he had done. Despite the threat to himself, Jim had no regrets. He was convinced that he had done the right thing – Natalya was out of danger and the United States had not been harmed by his actions. Out of love for the Muscovite woman, he was willing to sacrifice his honor, everything he had worked for, and if necessary, himself.

Chapter 28

A driving rain fell upon the gray, Moscow metropolis drenching people who ventured outside. All who could avoid going outdoors stayed in the confines of their dry homes reading or watching TV.

With the steady downpour, only a few scattered groups of tourists ventured into Красная Площадь [Red Square] to take photographs of St. Basil's Cathedral and the Kremlin's Spasskaya Tower. As the scattered tourists scrambled to and from their chartered buses, determined to fill their photo albums with memories of their trip to Russia, the country's leaders met only a few hundred meters away.

After the Russian Ministers had assembled in the Presidential Office, Foreign Minister Sergei Kruchkov, wasted little time in making his shocking announcement. "Igor, as we've agreed to six months earlier, I've obtained outside corroboration regarding the Karelian uprising. After reading the CIA reports, I must declare that my initial fears have been substantiated -- we cannot rely on the KGB's reports," Kruchkov, determined to accelerate his drive to power spoke as the heavy rain pelted against widow's glass.

"I'll take them," Russian President Meliacherov declared, relieving his Foreign Minister of the reports. "The Karelian uprising has been over for 6 months. As far as I'm concerned, that painful chapter in our history is closed," the President spoke, suppressing his irritation at Sergei Kruchkov for his continued reliance on Western sources, even after the world had teetered on the verge of third global war.

"Igor, are you implying that you won't follow up on these reports, because if you are, I must insist that you read them! You must know that there has been substantial KGB involvement in the rebellion!"

"I don't care. The matter's closed," Meliacherov firmly declared knowing that his stature had been greatly enhanced by his standing up to the West during the Global Crisis of a short time ago. Igor Meliacherov was determined to preserve his newfound standing among Russians.

"You must care!" Sergei Kruchkov protested.

"And why is that? I will not go back on my word and engage in witch-hunts and purges. That era is long behind us..."

"Are you telling me that you're going to let them get away?" Kruchkov interrupted.

"Да [Yes], I am! I won't dredge up the past to satisfy you or the West's leaders!"

"But if you let them get away, who is to say that there won't be another scheme aimed at destroying our Government, especially since we'll be viewed as weak," the Foreign Minister vehemently argued. "I'm not asking you to punish everyone, but you must set an example. Furthermore, you mustn't depend on people who can't be trusted. Sooner or later they'll make another attempt."

"I'll take my chances," Meliacherov replied with growing anger in his voice. "I won't discuss this any further. My decision is final!" the Russian President added, throwing the CIA reports into a nearby wastebasket.

"Very well, as you wish," the annoyed Foreign Minister gave in. "However, I have another report..."

"If it deals with Karelia in any way, Sergei, you had better be prepared to hand in your resignation. I won't tolerate any more insubordination on your part.

238

Furthermore, let me make this clear -- I was wrong to have agreed at your insistence, for an outside assessment of our intelligence services and their personnel, and I won't make that same mistake again. Because of your Western friends, we came damn close to war. I won't destroy our country for anyone," President Meliacherov vowed, determined to heed the demands of his own people.

"There's nothing here about Karelia," Kruchkov answered, momentarily taken aback by the Russian President's strong words.

"Very well, then proceed," Meliacherov urged his Foreign Minister after a brief pause.

"Mr. President, it is my sworn duty to warn you that one of your ministers, seated at this very table, is plotting to overthrow you," Sergei Kruchkov declared, sending shockwaves through the room. All immediately fell silent to devote give him their undivided attention. "For the last two months, Yuri [Likhovtsev] has been conspiring with rogue elements in the military and KGB to seize power and reverse our reforms.

"That's a lie!" the enraged Defense Minister rose to his feet and loudly objected.

"Silence! You'll have your chance to speak," the Russian President interrupted. "Can this be verified?" he then asked with concern.

"By whom? With agents of the KGB in on it, I don't know whom we can trust!" Kruchkov answered. "I can't even say how large this conspiracy is. That's why we must take immediate action before more join in and perhaps the military gets involved. Once they become involved, it'll be too late. We'll be helpless. Everything's outlined in this report."

"I see. Yuri, what have you to say to these charges?" the Russian President turned to his Defense Minister.

"Everything he says is a lie! I don't know what he's talking about," Defense Minister Yuri Likhovtsev spoke, his voice growing angrier at each additional word. "I tell you the SOB's lying! Believe me, if I had had any such notions, Красная Площадь [Red Square] would've been filled with tanks by now. You wouldn't be sitting in this office, least of all him!" Likhovtsev continued pointing at Sergei Kruchkov. "All he's trying to do is create a diversion because he can't live with the concept of `Russia for the Russians!'" the Defense Minister angrily attacked his pro-Western adversary.

"Don't tell me what I believe in," the equally irate Kruchkov shot back. "It's not I that is listed here! He angrily pounded his fist on the report, before sarcastically adding, "The only reason that your armies are not here is because you didn't know your plot had been discovered! Had you known, you would've acted before this meeting could be held!"

"Let me tell you this, Sergei. When I'm vindicated, I'll see to it that you will stand in front of a firing squad," Yuri Likhovtsev angrily vowed his revenge.

"Then you had better damn well have two lives, because you'll need them!" the Foreign Minister retorted.

"Okay, enough! I'll take the report," President Meliacherov finally interrupted the heated exchange between Kruchkov and Likhovtsev. "In the mean time Yuri, I'll have to ask you to take a leave of absence," Meliacherov continued. "I'm sorry, but these are very grave charges which must be investigated," the Russian President apologized. "I'll have the Constitutional Court look into it right away and unless

240

they rule against you -- I promise you, you'll still have your job."

"What do you mean? He must be arrested! He's too dangerous to remain free!" Sergei Kruchkov urged.

"Very well, to satisfy you, I'll place him under house-arrest," Meliacherov bitterly relented.

"That's not enough! Yuri must be imprisoned! We can't take a chance of him escaping. Besides, with members of our security forces involved in his plot, we can't afford anything less than maximum-security incarceration."

"House-arrest is enough. I'll stake my life on the loyalty and ability of the Kremlin Guards. I'm confident they're quite capable of performing their duties," President Meliacherov answered, refusing to modify his decision any further.

"How can you, after all our years together take his word over mine," the Russian Defense Minister inquired, with hurt in his voice.

"I have no choice but to look into this matter," Meliacherov repeated his apologies.

"You know he's lying," Likhovtsev quietly replied, resigned to his fate.

"I wish I did. But let me assure you of this, Yuri. If he's knowingly deceived me, there will be severe consequences," the President tried to reassure his long-time comrade, before turning to face his friend's accuser. "So Sergei, if you're not being truthful with me, you had better confess before I'm forced to place Yuri under house-arrest and relieve him of his duties. I want you to also know that I'm honored to call Yuri my friend, so you had better not be trying to drive a wedge in our friendship for your own personal gain or for whatever your motives might be."

"I'll stake my life on this report. An impartial investigation will fully corroborate the contents of this report,"

ВЕСНА РУССКАЯ

Foreign Minister Kruchkov firmly answered, enjoying the sight of his adversary's displeasure and discomfort.

"You had better, because if Yuri is found innocent, I'll have you shot!" the Russian President warned, before summoning two members of the Kremlin Guard to escort his friend, Likhovtsev to house arrest. "I'm really sorry," Meliacherov apologized one last time, psychologically torn apart about having to treat his long-time comrade with suspicion.

"It's all right. I don't hold you accountable. It is he whom I'll never forgive," Defense Minister Likhovtsev angrily declared pointing at the Foreign Minister, who taken aback by the Russian President's warning, sat in silence. "And when this is over, I'll relish watching his execution," Likhovtsev added before being escorted from the President's office.

When the meeting had been adjourned, everyone left in silence. Many felt sick to their stomachs and in no mood to talk. Once alone, the Russian President carefully read the CIA report documenting his friend's alleged coup plot. He was filled with dismay. "I don't believe it. This can't be," Meliacherov quietly uttered before filing the report. "I've known Yuri for too long not to know what he's capable of," the Russian leader reasoned, hating himself for having placed his Defense Minister under house arrest.

With pain and guilt weighing heavily on his conscience, Igor Meliacherov leaned back in his cushioned chair and closed his eyes. He desperately wanted to find escape from his torment, especially since he thought Russia's instability was over. The quiet pitter-pattering of raindrops dancing off the glass of his office window provided little solace. The gray Moscow weather only reinforced the President's agony.

Chapter 29

When the diesel train pulled in at Sergiyev Posad (formerly Zagorsk), twilight was giving way to night. A cool, refreshing breeze gently drifted through the small town situated 70 kilometers northeast of Moscow.

With the night chill gently settling in, Natalya Kalinina and her American boyfriend, Jim Keating quickly made their way from the train station to a nearby taxi stand. Both were eager to settle in the dacha that the Russian's supervisor had loaned them for the weekend. He loaned the small, wooden cottage to reward Natalya for successfully extricating the deposed Hawaiian Governor's daughter from the paradise Islands that he become a prison for her and to enhance his young agent's romance.

Although Valentin Makarov had offered use of the dacha to Natalya months earlier, she was unable to accept. With the world on the brink of war, Natalya and Jim had found it hard enough just to maintain phone contact with each other. A chance to escape to the solitude that the dacha offered was out of the question.

As they rode the cab, both thought about the weekend they would have all to themselves. It was a welcome relief from the politics that had mired their lives over the last few months. The escape to the Russian countryside would do them good.

243

ВЕСНА РУССКАЯ

"This is it," Natalya exclaimed as the taxi pulled up a narrow dirt driveway to the wooden dacha. As Valentin had warned in advance, it was certainly Spartan in nature. Nonetheless, Natalya and Jim welcomed its sight.

"Here you go," Jim stated, offering the cab driver a 50,000 Ruble note.

"Нет [Nyet], I've got it," Natalya declared, gently pushing the American's hand from the cab driver.

"Нет [Nyet], I insist," Jim protested.

"Very well," Natalya gave in, allowing her American boyfriend to hand the colorful note to the cab driver. "But on the way back, I get the tab," she declared as they got out of the taxi.

As Jim retrieved their luggage from the trunk and carried it to the dacha, Natalya made arrangements for the driver to pick them up late Sunday afternoon. Once the reservation was made, she ran up to the doorway. "You can't get in without me!" she teased her boyfriend, playfully hitting him. "I got the key!" she exclaimed waving the large, dark iron key in front of him.

"I guess I'll just leave," Jim replied, jokingly picking up his suitcase.

"Нет [Nyet]!" the Russian cried out grabbing him by the arm. "I won't let you!"

"As if I really was going to leave," Keating answered as Natalya unlocked and pushed the old wooden door open.

Although tired from their day's work and the slow train ride from Moscow, both gained a second wind of energy when they settled in the cabin. It was rejuvenating to alone with each other, away from civilization.

Having eaten a quick meal of chicken, mushroom soup, and Georgian bread before their departure from

244

Yaroslav Station, both munched on a quick snack of pirozhki. After an hour of quiet talk, both retired to the one bed that Natalya had freshly made for them.

"You love me, да [yes]?" Natalya who was now scantily clad asked as she pulled the covers over them.

"What kind of question is that?" Jim asked caught off guard.

"Just answer me. Do you love me?" the Russian insisted, gently placing her arm around him.

"Да [Yes] very much," the American replied, kissing her.

"I love you very much too," Kalinina answered as their lips converged. "I've been waiting for this day a long time," she added as they embraced.

"So have I."

"Finally we have each other all to ourselves," Natalya continued, gently unfastening his nightgown. "Now you're all mine," she declared placing her body on top of his body. They then locked lips and kissed again, each tightly holding the other. "Give me yourself," the Russian then exclaimed between breaths as she pulled down her undergarments.

"I'm all yours," Jim willingly surrendered, pulling down his boxers.

"And I'm all yours," Natalya replied as their bodies merged and they made love.

"I want you to know how special you are. You're the best thing to come in my life," the American declared.

"And the best thing that's ever happened to me. You're the only person I would give up my virginity to," Natalya replied, having surrendered her chastity. "You're mine forever," she declared feeling her pulse accelerate. She refused to settle for anything less as a tradeoff for her lost virginity.

ВЕСНА РУССКАЯ

"Да [Yes], and you're mine forever," Jim replied in agreement as both locked lips to seal their oath with a kiss.

As they kissed in silence, filled with passion for each other, they gently rolled over until Jim took the position that Natalya had occupied. With each passing second, their conversation diminished. Their pulses quickened, their breaths grew louder, and their kisses became more heated until, in harmonious unison, they reached the climactic moment they had been waiting for.

Even though their blissful moment could not be extended forever, Natalya and Jim continued to kiss and hold onto each other long after it. They embraced and kissed until their awareness imperceptibly drifted away into the unconsciousness of sleep.

Following their first night, the rest of the weekend went as a blur. Jim Keating could remember few of the monuments that Natalya had shown him during their daily walks even though some had been very famous such as the fortified Trinity Monastery of St. Sergius (founded in 1340) that consisted of the well-known, spectacular blue-and-gold domed Assumption Cathedral (built in 1554) and Trinity Church (where St. Sergius's remains were interred). It was easier for him to remember holding hands and kissing. Likewise, the food, people, and scenery of Sergiyev Posad left little impression on them. They had become too infatuated with each other to allow externalities to influence them.

Their minds only retained joyful memories of their interaction – of their spiritual (attained when Natalya and Jim playfully christened their relationship at the Miraculous Fountain within the confines of Trinity Monastery of St. Sergius) and corporal unions. With such happy memories, the weekend progressed too quickly. Natalya and Jim were filled with regrets on having to leave when the time came. Valentin's Spartan dacha, Sergiyev Posad, and all that surrounded it had become a magical paradise.

On the train ride back to Moscow, Natalya and Jim sipped glasses of champagne to celebrate the greater state of their loving union. When not sipping champagne, they held hands, kissed and hugged – all the while oblivious to their surroundings. At the same time, three other individuals – Robert Salerno, the Deputy American Ambassador, Sergei Kruchkov, the Russian Foreign Minister, and Gleb Chasov, the head of the Chasov Russian Crime Family – seated at Livan Restaurant on Улица Тверская [Tverskaya Street] sipped champagne to celebrate their own union.

"To Capitalism, America, and Sergei" Gleb Chasov offered a toast in badly pronounced English upon receiving a brief case filled with neat stacks of $100 bills from Robert Salerno. The payment represented consideration for Chasov's agreement to join Salerno's and Kruchkov's plot.

"To your good health and our partnership," the Deputy American Ambassador and Russian Foreign Minister chimed in, returning Gleb's toast.

Following their joyful toasts, with their business having been accomplished, the three men finished the remains of their Azerbaijani meals and left together. Before departing their separate ways, each embraced the other and bid farewell as family.

Two days later, a remote-controlled plastique explosive leveled a half-a-city block and its clusters of kiosks on the outskirts of Moscow. Scores of people – residents and shoppers alike were incinerated along with the Russian Prime Minister's chauffeured limousine that had been passing though on schedule according to the itinerary provided by the Russian Foreign Minister.

ВЕСНА РУССКАЯ

With Pavel Romanov dead, Sergei Kruchkov could feel the reins of power within his grasp. "One down, one more to go!" he triumphantly thought to himself. Aside from the Russian Foreign Minister and his tiny group of supporters, the rest of Moscow fell into a somber state of mourning.

Chapter 30

The days following the Russian Prime Minister's assassination and scores of innocent bystanders and residents that died with him were marked by public fear and trepidation. At the same, most in the Kremlin held a strong desire for revenge. No one knew who was involved or why the attack had occurred. Unsubstantiated reports and speculation regarding who was involved, how many were involved, and their motive worsened matters. There was a lot of impatience as the Moscow Police, KGB, and Constitutional Court conducted painstakingly vigorous, but slow investigations.

While the investigations were underway, guards were posted around the Kremlin grounds and Красная Площадь [Red Square] to prevent further attacks. A contingent of well-armed Kremlin guards accompanied the Russian President and other top-ranking officials at all times. At the same time, an Emergency Security task force consisting of KGB agents, police officers and Constitutional Court officials kept a vigilant watch on the armed forces. They were looking to detect any unusual movements that could be attributed to Defense Minister Yuri Likhovtsev's alleged plot to seize control.

With the investigation proceeding slowly, tensions between the two Kremlin camps heated up. On one side,

ВЕСНА РУССКАЯ

Foreign Minister Kruchkov and his pro-Western supporters demanded Likhovtsev's speedy execution declaring Romanov's death as sufficient proof of the Defense Minister's guilt in plotting a coup. On the other side, ministers closely allied with the President's thinking urged extreme caution. They were fearful of reviving Stalin's ghost and ultimately his blood era of "Great Terror."

During this trying time, Natalya Kalinina again found it difficult to find time to spend with her boyfriend. As a member of the Emergency Security task force, which also consisted of her supervisor Valentin Makarov and her best friend Elena Potapova, she was kept constantly busy. Demands for a speedy conclusion to the investigation left her little time to pursue her personal life. Mounting pressure from the pro-West camp to implicate the Defense Minister worsened matters.

Natalya found all of her hours occupied by relentless and thorough canvassing of Yuri Likhovtsev's family, friends, and associates. When she should have been sleeping, Natalya was attending lengthy nighttime meetings that stretched into the early hours of the next morning as each subgroup discussed its daily progress. Natalya, Elena, and her supervisor were consciously aware of the Defense Minister's sympathies for their RNR movement and thus wanted to proceed with extreme caution so as not to cause his unnecessary death.

Much to their relief as the investigation progressed, the evidence pointed towards the Defense Minister's innocence. It contradicted Kruchkov's CIA report that had been the basis for starting the investigation against Yuri Likhovtsev.

Two months after the investigation had begun, Yuri Likhovtsev was declared innocent and above reproach.

250

With the Defense Minister back at his post, the Russian Defense Ministry joined the Emergency Security task force to assist in finding the Prime Minister's killers.

With the Russian military again above suspicion and actively involved in the investigation, Natalya, much to her relief, again had time to spend with her American boyfriend. On occasional weekends, Natalya and Jim returned to Valentin Makarov's Sergiyev Posad dacha to enjoy quality time in solitude.

However, as Natalya and Jim reinvigorated their romance, relations between Moscow and Washington began to sour again. The deterioration was sparked by the arrest of Russia's pro-Western Foreign Minister. As President Meliacherov had bluntly warned on the day he had been forced to relieve his long-time friend of his duties and place him under house arrest, he took action. He was determined to reverse the humiliation and disgrace Yuri Likhovtsev and his family had suffered. With Sergei Kruchkov fired and under arrest, the Russian President vowed, "I'll have you shot!"

"You can't do this," the Foreign Minister vehemently protested. He was terrified at the growing prospect that he would have to live up to his words – having staked his life on the CIA report he had known was fabricated.

"I can and I will," Igor Meliacherov angrily retorted. "I'll make an example of you so no one else tries to have an innocent person put to death or maliciously deceives the country he swore to serve," the Russian President added handing his Foreign Minister over to be taken to Lubyanka Prison.

With Sergei Kruchkov behind bars beneath the KGB's headquarters, the Kremlin, in anticipation of his conviction, made arrangements for a public execution. While construction of wooden platforms was underway

ВЕСНА РУССКАЯ

near St. Basil's Cathedral in Красная Площадь [Red Square], U.S. President Clint Stoker backed by the leaders of the United Kingdom, Germany, and Japan demanded Kruchkov's immediate and unconditional release. They warned of serious reprisals if Moscow did not accede to their demands.

"Нет [Nyet]!" the Russian President defiantly answered, eager to make amends to his friend and to show the Russian people and the world that his country was no longer ruled out of a foreign capital.

Despite the Kremlin's stiffening resolve, U.S. Ambassador Stephen Norcross and his Deputy Ambassador, Robert Salerno flooded the Russian Government with clemency pleas and threats. "I won't be blackmailed!" the irritated Russian President declared, tossing a faxed warning into his wastebasket. "Take them all away," Meliacherov commanded his administrative staff. "I won't waste my time with this garbage!"

Although Sergei Kruchkov's confidence began to wane as the days -- which to him had grown increasingly short – passed leading up to his trial, he continued to tell himself that the Americans would come to his rescue. Newspaper accounts of the West's demands and threats lifted his spirits. However, at other times, the Foreign Minister's spirits sank into an endless abyss of depression especially when he ruminated in his confined quarters and heard the Russian President's words over and over again: "I'll have you shot!"

After two days of hearings in which an overwhelming preponderance of evidence attested to the Defense Minister's innocence and Kruchkov's guilt in attempting to frame him and cause his subsequent death, the pro-Western Foreign Minister was convicted and

252

sentenced to die. Although the way had been cleared for his execution, Sergei Kruchkov willed himself into a state of denial. Even though his chances were grim and his days numbered, he refused to believe that the Americans would not come through and save him.

Even when he was driven to the two blocks to Красная Площадь [Red Square] and escorted by armed guards to the platform to face his executioners and a massive crowd of 15,000+ people that also included the Russian President and Defense Minister, Kruchkov's faith in Washington remained unshaken. Only when his hands were bound behind a large sturdy post that supported his body and his eyes were blindfolded did the Foreign Minister's denial evaporate. When he was forcibly brought to reality he discovered his utter helplessness and the animosity and contempt Russian's harbored towards him. Amidst the sea of his own people, Sergei Kruchkov found himself isolated and all alone. Not even his ex-wife, whom he had badly hurt through numerous transgressions of infidelity, came to support him during his last moments. Her absence painfully tore at his sunken heart. Suddenly he could feel all the pain he had caused her. All the American women, the parties and the drinking had been for naught. His happiness had been a false illusion whose ugliness and evil became apparent has his death quickly approached. With the illusion exposed for what it was, Sergei Kruchkov was left with an empty, broken soul. His heart was filled with regrets.

"Ready your guns and take aim," the crisp words echoed in Kruchkov's ears, gripping him with fear of the unknown – the same unknown that he and his Western cohorts had condemned Prime Minister Romanov to, when they had arranged for and carried out his assassination. "There won't be a miracle," the thought haunted Kruchkov

ВЕСНА РУССКАЯ

as he was struck by the stark realization that the West, in spite of their intentions, was powerless to thwart Russian determination.

"Fire!" Sergei Kruchkov heard the loud crisp command followed by the loud crackling of nine rifles. Almost simultaneously, he felt an intense, rapid burning in his chest as the executioners' bullets tore through his heart and lungs. Within seconds, his badly compromised heart gave way and his bleeding lungs ceased inhaling.

With a pungent odor of burnt gunpowder wafting through the air, the large crowd stood and stared in silence. They watched as a doctor went up to examine Kruchkov's slumped body. Only after the doctor pronounced, "dead" did the crowd begin to slowly disperse in silence.

When Красная Площадь [Red Square] emptied, Kruchkov's body was left hanging from the wooden post where he had been fastened. It was left exposed to the elements and flies – a throwback to the Kremlin's medieval days when the remains of executed rebels and other enemies of the State had been chopped into pieces, burned, or left for the dogs. With Kruchkov's execution, blood had again been shed in Красная Площадь [Red Square] as it had been so many times before during preceding centuries.

"He'll die, Sergei. I swear to you," the Deputy American Ambassador silently vowed referring to the Russian President upon hearing the news of Kruchkov's execution.

Chapter 31

Tensions between the United States and Russia continued to rise in the aftermath of Sergei Kruchkov's execution.   With the Kremlin rejecting Washington's demands of having the World Court determine if President Meliacherov should continue in power or be tried for murder, the enraged American President severed all relations with Moscow. All American personnel in Russia were given one week to leave and the U.S. Embassy was ordered closed.

A misty drizzle fell from Moscow's leaden skies as Natalya Kalinina and Jim Keating slowly walked through Expo Park, holding hands.   Jim Keating's mind weighed heavily over the growing estrangement between their two countries as they made their way along the desolate pathways. His emotions and loyalties were sharply divided.

As they slowly reached the gushing waters of Friendship Fountain, where both had sealed their love, thoughts of the impending deadline gnawed at Jim's heart. He had seven days to decide whether or not to stay in Moscow. The repercussions from either choice were not pleasant.

"What 're you going to do?" Natalya Kalinina softly asked with concern, fully aware of Washington's decision to shutdown the American Embassy.

ВЕСНА РУССКАЯ

"Я не знаю [I don't know]," Keating answered, wishing that somehow he would wake up and discover that the Stoker's order had been nothing more than a bad nightmare.

"Please stay," the Muscovite quietly pleaded. She was fearful of losing him forever if she were to allow him to fly away from Sheremetevo. "I need you," Kalinina added, hoping to persuade her American boyfriend to stay. She was equally troubled by his dilemma.

"You don't know how hard this is on me. If I leave, I'll probably never see you again. I love you so much. I need you too," Jim agonized.

"Then, please stay. There'll always be a place for you with me," Natalya replied kissing him.

"I wish it were that simple, but if I don't leave, I'll not only lose my citizenship, but my whole family," the American answered with bitterness in his voice.

"Нет [Nyet], you won't," the Russian quietly answered, pulling him close to her.

"You don't understand. My father's a Senator and he'll support Stoker no matter what. When I tried to explain our situation to him, all he could say was,`follow your patriotic duty and come home!'" Jim continued, wishing his father had never been elected to the United States Senate. "The only thing he can think of is `patriotism,'" he sarcastically added.

"I'm sorry," Natalya answered, filled with sympathy for her boyfriend.

"And when I told him I wanted to stay for humanitarian reasons, he wouldn't hear of it. Instead of trying to understand, he warned me of severe reprisals if I didn't follow Stoker's directive!"

"What?"

256

"He said that I had two choices -- `either come home or be disowned!' I love my sister. I love my mom. I even love my dad, in spite of his shortcomings. I don't know if I could bear losing my family."

"How can he say that!" Natalya protested, enraged about the senior Keating's cruelty at making her boyfriend choose between her and his family. "If he cared for you, he wouldn't have said that. It's not fair."

"Tell me about it. With good ol' dad, it's country and honor, right or wrong. Nothing else matters. God forbid should I stay here and cost him some votes!" the American bitterly complained as an uncomfortable silence fell over them.

For several painful minutes, both sat in silence, listening to the gushing fountains, as water from the light rain trickled from their wet hair. With the rains growing steadier, both found themselves alone in the spacious park. Solitude, which had been their friend, had become their enemy. The loneliness only magnified their pain.

"I know it's hard," Natalya cautiously began not wanting to be stranded in limbo. "I wish it weren't so, but I need to know – what're you going to do?"

"I wish I had an answer, but I don't know," Keating painfully replied.

"Пожалуйста [Please], I must know," the Russian insisted.

"I need to think about it. It's too hard for me to decide now. My whole life depends on that one decision. If I stay, my father will never forgive me and..."

"But what about us?" Natalya Kalinina interrupted.

"Believe me, I don't want to lose you, but I don't want to lose my family either."

257

ВЕСНА РУССКАЯ

"Were our trips to Sergiyev Posad in vain? Was our love for nothing?" the Muscovite protested, thinking back to times when they had been joined in corporal union.

"Нет [Nyet], of course not," the American painfully answered, hugging his Russian girlfriend. "I love you too much."

"Then stay! We both swore we'd be each other's forever," Natalya complained, bringing up their vows.

"Да, Я знаю [Yes, I know], but what about my family? What about my country? We both also swore never let our country's politics enter into our relationship."

"Да [Yes], and by leaving you'll have broken that promise too!"

"And if you don't give me sufficient time to decide, you'll have broken your word," Jim Keating countered.

"Do you love me?" Natalya then demanded to know.

"What kind of question is that. I won't dignify such a cheap question with an answer, when you darn well know the answer," Jim retorted with growing irritation.

"Well, if you do, you'll stay," the Muscovite declared. "You'll have to decide where your loyalties lie. Are they with a living, breathing woman who can provide you with all the joys of life -- love, affection, companionship, friendship, and children, or with some abstract piece of land defined by arbitrary borders and ruled by a political elite who could care less about you and me! Answer me!" Natalya demanded upon being met with silence. "What will it be?"

Despite the Russian's insistence, Jim refused to reply.

"I want an answer," Kalinina demanded, firmly grabbing her boyfriend by the arms and holding him directly in front of her. "Make your choice. What will it be?"

258

"I need time," Keating firmly answered, suppressing his anger at Natalya's demands.

"I'm sorry you feel that way," Natalya slowly replied, gradually relinquishing her grip from the American's arms and slowly withdrawing from him. "I thought I knew you, but I guess not. I thought we had something special, but I guess I was mistaken. I guess it's over."

"Please try to understand. I love you..." the American protested.

"Please go. Please leave me alone," the Muscovite woman rejected her boyfriend's pleas.

"But..."

"Please go!" Natalya repeated.

"Well, then I guess it is over," Keating, having grown frustrated with the Russian's refusal to hear him out reluctantly concurred and turned and left Natalya by herself at the fountain.

Once in the solitude of her surroundings, Natalya was overcome by emotions. With their relationship torn apart and the emptiness of her pained heart hemorrhaging throughout her grief-stricken body, the Russian woman covered her eyes and sobbed uncontrollably. With the fountain's gushing intensifying the painful rupture of their relationship, Kalinina found herself glued to the spot and unable to leave. She was oblivious to the rains that had grown into a torrential downpour. He clothes and body were soaked.

With no one to comfort her, Natalya sobbed continuously. Her eyes grew red and irritated from the flood of tears that raged forth. "I wish I would just drown," the heartbroken Muscovite cried, momentarily becoming conscious of the heavy downpour as nearby puddles boiled under the barrage of rain.

259

ВЕСНА РУССКАЯ

"I don't want to live," Natalya told herself, slowly pulling her self away from the majestic fountain. "I hate this place," she cried out to the open, unsympathetic emptiness, before dejectedly dragging herself from the park into the sparsely crowded streets. As she made her way home, the stormy sky darkened with the approach of evening. The growing darkness reinforced the pain of her broken heart. "I wish I were dead!" she cried out in anguish with no one to hear.

Chapter 32

After having spent most of Sunday in bed dwelling in the comforting surreal world of dreams to escape reality's bitter pain, Natalya Kalinina found herself well enough to go to work on Monday. Although she felt stronger, Natalya was still haunted by loneliness. Seeing the picture of Jim Keating on her desk added further pain to her aching heart. Filled with renewed sadness, Natalya slowly and reluctantly removed the photograph and placed it in the bottom drawer of her desk having fought the temptation to dispose of it all together.

As Natalya gradually closed the drawer, she silently wished for a miracle. She thought back to the day when the American had intervened on her young cousin's behalf in Красная Площадь [Red Square] on New Year's Day.

Several kilometers away, Jim Keating shared Natalya's sadness. He sat slumped over at his desk reminiscing on their once happy relationship. He could remember the first day he had gone over to the Russian's house. "How could I have been so stupid," he angrily scolded himself. "Now I've lost the woman I love," Jim lamented having realized that if his family truly loved him, they would have understood.

With a debate whether or not to call Natalya Kalinina to try to patch things up raging through his mind,

ВЕСНА РУССКАЯ

Jim found it difficult to do his work. He found it impossible to maintain concentration when reviewing reports that had been given to him by his subordinates.

Filled with pain and not knowing what to do, Keating reluctantly called his younger sister, Michelle in New York. Wanting advice, he poured out his troubles to her.

"I'll always love you," Michelle promised her brother. "I don't care if you stay in Russia; you're still my brother," she continued. "You'll never find another woman like Natasha. Call her and apologize," she urged.

"Do you think there's really a chance we can make up?" Jim asked.

"You must try. I'm sure she'll understand. We're all human and make mistakes. Sometimes we hurt those we love when we don't mean to," Michelle tried to comfort her brother. "It can't hurt by trying. But if you don't at least try, you'll never know what could've been and you'll never forgive yourself."

"I guess you're right."

"I am right. Like it or not, dad will have to get over it. As for mom, I know she'll always be there for the both of us, no matter what dad tries to say, so promise me you'll call Natasha."

"Okay, I'll call her," Jim responded.

"When?"

"In a day or so."

"No today, right now," Michelle demanded. "You two don't deserve to be alone for another day or so. So promise me you'll call her as soon as we get off the phone."

"Okay, I promise," Jim answered taking a deep breath. "But that doesn't mean it'll work."

262

"Just try and be optimistic," Michelle urged.

"I will, but…"

"You'll work it out. I know you will. The two of you have put too much in your relationship to just throw it away," Jim's sister declared. "You have to try."

"I will. I promise."

"Good. Then I guess I'll say 'goodbye' so you can call her," Michelle replied before wishing her brother luck and getting off the phone.

Immediately upon replacing the receive, Jim became conscious of the time. In his sadness, he had forgotten about the conference he was supposed to attend with the American Ambassador and Deputy Ambassador. Though eager to follow his sister's advice, Jim knew the phone call to Natalya would have to wait.

After getting up and walking to Stephen Norcross's office, Jim reached for the door knob. As he clasped the knob he heard something that made his hand freeze.

"We've got four days to liquidate Meliacherov," he heard Ambassador Norcross telling his Deputy Ambassador, Robert Salerno. Filled with curiosity and disgust, the CIA officer listened in on the conversation without opening the door.

"Don't worry, it'll be taken care of," Salerno answered.

"I am worried. Actually I'm very worried. In four days we'll be out of here and then it'll be impossible for us to avenge Sergei," Norcross spoke referring to the executed pro-Western Russian Foreign Minister. "And besides, if we fail, that'll be the end of our careers. The President won't reassign us."

"I assure you, everything's set in place."

"It better be, because if we fail, you're the one who's going to be doing the explaining to the president.

Just remember, nobody can be permitted to hurt the President's friends or family and get away with it."

"As I said, everything's in place," Robert Salerno reiterated. "Tonight when Meliacherov and his wife retire to bed, they'll be poisoned!"

"How? By whom?" Norcross asked concerned that Kruchkov's execution had left their allies badly shaken.

"By Dimitri Pleshkov, the head of Russian Presidential Security," Salerno declared. "I've set up his account in Geneva and paid Gleb's [Chasov] men to get him safely out of the country to his new residence in Lisbon."

Needing to hear nothing further, Jim Keating knew what he had to do as he quietly retreated back to his desk. He was determined to prevent the assassinations. Ignoring security protocol, he picked up the phone and dialed Natalya's KGB number.

"I don't want to talk to you," Natalya Kalinina immediately exclaimed upon hearing the American's voice. She was still deeply hurt by his reluctance to choose her.

"Listen, it's very important," Jim immediately cut the Russian off.

"If it's about us, I don't want to hear it. You've already hurt me enough!"

"I would like to talk about us, but..."

"Нет, нет, нет [Nyet, nyet, nyet]!" Kalinina quickly interrupted.

"Just listen," Keating pleaded.

"Нет [Nyet], I will not!" the hurt Russian stood her ground.

"I'll meet you outside Детский Мир [Children's World] in 30 minutes. Be there!" Jim, pressed for time instructed Natalya as he ignored her words. As he spoke, Keating felt a hot sweat break from his pores.

"Why should I?"

"Just be there," he repeated before hastily adding, "I must go" and then handing up the phone before the Muscovite could inquire any further.

"I'm going out for a little while," Jim told the Embassy's receptionist as he headed for the elevators.

"You can't. the Ambassador issued standing orders that no one leave," the receptionist protested. "It's too dangerous out there."

"I guess I'll have to chance it," Keating quickly replied as he hastily stepped into the elevator's cabin. When the doors closed and the car proceeded to its destination, Jim found himself enveloped by intense fear. His heart pounded and his shirt became soaked with sweat. "Come on," he told the elevator, knowing that the receptionist would inform the Ambassador of his decision to defy his orders and that the Ambassador would in turn contact the Embassy's Marine guard.

Once out of the elevator, the CIA officer hastily exited the Embassy building. "Open the gates," he instructed the Marine guard as he tried to retain his composure.

"We're under instructions not to allow anyone in or out," the Marine sergeant firmly replied. "Ambassador's directive."

"Just open the damn gates," Keating angrily ordered. "I'm on official CIA business and if you don't open them, the Ambassador will have your head. Call him if you insist!" Jim demanded, silently praying that the sergeant would not call his bluff. He was then filled with panic when the sergeant obliged and instructed one of his men to contact the Ambassador. "Just stay calm," the CIA officer silently commanded his tense nerves. "You'll find a way out of it," he tried to reassure himself as he felt his body being crushed by an invisible pulverized of claustrophobia with every glance at the closed gates. He felt like a caged animal seeking freedom.

"I can't get through," the Marine told his sergeant. "The line's busy."

"That's because he's still on the line with the President about my mission," Jim immediately replied. "So if you want to disobey your Commander-In-Chief and thwart his operation, go ahead. I'll go back and tell the Ambassador myself," Keating added knowing that the only reason the Ambassador's line was busy was because the receptionist was reporting him.

"Very well, go ahead," the Marine sergeant reluctantly gave in, pressing the button to open the remote-controlled gates. Simultaneously as the iron gates began to slide open, the Marine post's phone rang.

"It's now or never," Jim thought to himself, barely squeezing through the tiny space as the Marine sergeant called him back.

"He's already out!" Jim heard one of the Marines yelling into the phone's receiver as he ran down the street.

"Suddenly a barrage of automatic shots rang out. Know that his life was in danger, the CIA officer ran into Станция Баррикадная [Barrikadnaya Station]. With a group of Marines in pursuit, Jim weaved his way through the crowds and managed to jump onto the subway just as its doors were closing.

Only after the train slid away from the platform, accelerating as it went, did Jim Keating breathe a sigh of relief. From a distance through the train's fogged-up window, he could see several startled Russian police officers approaching the American Marines.

Despite his escape, the CIA officer knew that he was not safe. He was fully aware that his conversation with Natalya on an unsecured line had been recorded. "Just let her be there," Jim silently prayed as the subway pulled into Станция Лубянка [Lubyanka Station]. Almost simultaneously as the train doors slid open, the American pushed his way through the crowd of passengers standing in front of him, apologizing as he went.

Jim's heart pounded as he made his way onto the street in front of the yellow, concrete children's store. Filled with anxiety and gasping for breath, the American scanned the street in search of Natalya. To his dismay, she was no where to be seen.

At about the same time as Jim searched for the Russian agent, another trained pulled into Станция Лубянка [Lubyanka Station]. It carried Robert Salerno. "He must be stopped!" the Deputy American Ambassador heard Norcross's orders echoing in his head as he made his way across the platform with a weapon hidden under his trench coat.

"Where are you?" the American silently implored, not wanting to remain in front of Детский Мир [Children's World] any longer than he had to. As he searched the street with growing anxiety, he caught sight of Robert Salerno emerging from the metro station's glass doors.

Before Jim Keating could move, the Deputy American Ambassador pulled out his gun. Seeing Salerno's finger on the trigger, the CIA officer drew a deep breath and pulled out his weapon. Although he was reluctant to get in a shootout because of the nearby crowd of pedestrians that included many children, Jim had little choice. If he did not act, he would be killed.

ВЕСНА РУССКАЯ

As a shootout ensued, Robert Salerno was suddenly struck in the back of the head with Natalya's bullets. Though the Russian agent's actions had been solely motivated by desperation to save her ex-boyfriend, she felt no sadness when she recognized the identity of his attacker. She held Robert Salerno partially responsible for having put her through the steep depression she had suffered following her first case two years ago. She could also still remember the arrogance and hostility he had extended towards her during their first and only meeting. If anything, she felt a sense of satisfaction upon viewing the Deputy American Ambassador's crumpled figure.

"Спасибо [Thank you], Jim began knowing that the Russian had likely saved his life. Nonetheless, although he was relieved at seeing the Russian, he asked with a tinge of protest, "Where have you been?"

"I'm sorry," Natalya softly apologized embracing the American. "I didn't know if I wanted to see you. I'm so sorry," she repeated, slowly releasing Jim from her grip. Her feelings for the American had not died. As the Russian relinquished her hold, she noticed blood on her hands. "You've been shot!" she cried out with alarm. Not knowing the extent of his injury made tears well in her eyes.

"Never mind," Jim replied, for the first time becoming aware of the pain emanating from his wound. Prior to Natalya's statement, the rush of adrenaline that had ensued from his escape and desire to foil the planned assassination of Russia's President had suppressed his pain.

"No, you need help," Natalya protested reverting to English.

"There's no time for that! Your President is in grave danger. He's going to be assassinated tonight," the American went on.

"By whom?" Kalinina asked while radioing instructions for an ambulance. "Sit down," she softly urged, gently pushing him to the sidewalk. "Just take it easy," Natalya then added, kneeling besides him. Although increasingly concerned at the American's labored attempts to breathe, the Russian tried to comfort him. She took his hand and held it tightly in hers. "It'll be all right," she softly added, trying to reassure him.

"Dimitri... Pleshkov... " Jim slowly answered, ignoring Natalya's words. As he spoke, Jim struggled to pronounce his words. Blood forced by the loss of pressure in his chest, seeped up his trachea and into his mouth. The American was slowly drowning in his own blood.

"Just please hang on," Natalya pleaded. "I can't live without out. I love you," she added, terrified at the prospect of losing him.

"Forgive me," Jim implored the Muscovite woman.

"I forgive you," Natalya answered without hesitation. "Please forgive me."

"You've done... nothing."

"Please forgive me," Kalinina repeated.

"Very well... I forgive... you," the American slowly grasped for words. "You don't... know.. how much... I... love you,"- he then added struggled to hug Natalya as swirling darkness closed in on him.

"I love you too," Natalya quickly replied, pressing his wounded body into hers. "I love you," she softly repeated with tears rolling gently down her cheeks. "Please God, if you can hear me – please don't take him from me," the Muscovite silently prayed as she watched her boyfriend's condition deteriorate. "Talk to me!" she suddenly commanded Jim, becoming acutely aware of his silence.

"I... can't," he struggled to get the words out as he closed his eyes.

"Don't do this to me!" the Russian demanded with panic sweeping over her. "Talk to me!" she repeated, softly slapping him in desperation to keep him conscious.

"I... can't," Jim repeated before crying out, "Watch out!" as he caught sight of two CIA cleaners advancing on them.

Despite his warning, shots rang out as Natalya spun around and drew her weapon. Almost simultaneously as the Russian fired her gun, she felt a stab of pain tear through her left shoulder. An even greater explosion of pain ripping through her right elbow immediately followed it. With her arm shattered, Natalya's hand lost its grip on her weapon. Her gun fell to the pavement rendering her defenseless.

Knowing they were at the mercy of brutal, well-trained killers assigned the unenviable task of "cleaning up messes" when operations didn't go smoothly, Jim, fighting to retain his last bit of consciousness summoned all of his remaining strength. He picked up his gun and fired through the swirling dizziness, mortally wounding one of the CIA agents. As the attacker fell to the ground, Elena Potapova and a group of KGB agents, having heard the gunshots and rushed from their offices across the street, killed the remaining cleaner.

"Are you all right?" Elena asked her best friend filled with concern.

"Да [Yes], but please help my boyfriend," Natalya insisted as an ambulance and several police vehicles arrived.

Natalya quickly relayed the assassination plot to her friend and the other KGB agents who surrounded them as paramedics treated their wounds. "We've got him stabilized," one of the paramedics announced as they were lifted into the ambulance. "Спасибо Дорогой Господь [Thank you Dear God]" Natalya quietly expressed her gratitude, holding her boyfriend's limp hand in her good hand. Tears of relief streamed from her eyes as they rode the ambulance to the hospital.

Chapter 33

A light snow quietly coated Moscow in a serene white, as the Orthodox Christmas approached. Inside the brilliant, golden-domed Annunciation Cathedral of the Kremlin, once the Czar's House of Worship, Natalya Kalinina and Jim Keating were married to each other in front of a large crowd that included the Russian President, Igor Meliacherov who had bestowed "Hero of Russia" honors on them a day earlier at the Great Kremlin Palace. Other guests included, Valentin Makarov, Natalya's KGB supervisor, Yuri Likhovtsev, the Russian Defense Minister who succeeded Pavel Romanov, various other Russian Government officials and KGB staff, along with Erica Lew's family, Aimee Kualani, and the newlyweds' families. Natalya's best friend, Elena Potapova served as the bridesmaid while Jim's brother-in-law served as the best man. — — —

Following the wedding, the group walked through a brightly decorated passageway into the Great Kremlin Palace, once the residence of Russia's Czars. The wedding reception was held in the spacious St. George Hall, which was usually reserved for State banquets. As everyone joyfully dined in the renaissance atmosphere they were surrounded by stucco-molding and twisting columns, each supporting a laurel crowned allegorical "Statue of Victory." The hall was filled with these intricate columns. Both newlyweds felt special happiness knowing that Jim's father had, in the end, found it in his heart to accept their marriage and attend the ceremonies.

During the dinner, the grateful Russian President awarded the newlyweds two dachas. One was on the outskirts of Moscow and the other was in Suzdal. Natalya and Jim planned to make the former their residence and use the latter as a vacation retreat.Natalya and her husband returned to Expo Park a day later, having finally found a moment to themselves. As they slowly walked through the soft snow, both thought about the future. With Russia in pursuit of real reform, Natalya and Jim planned for their family since in good conscience they no longer had to wonder if bringing children in the world could be morally justified. Russia re-nationalized her resources that had been swindled away by so-called foreign "entrepreneurs." Existing stock certificates were voided and new shares were issued to reverse the iniquities caused by greedy speculators who had preyed on the population when they were most vulnerable. Russian employee-managed and owned companies that had prohibited outsiders from purchasing their stock were exempt from Moscow's reissuance policy. Physical property consisting of homes, dachas, and land were returned to their original owners and/or their descendents (prior to the breakup of the Soviet Union) in cases where the "holders" refused to adjust their original payment to constitute just compensation. Abandoned property or land and housing belonging to owners that could not be located were transferred to the transferred to the homeless.

Already, with prices rolled back to realistic levels, an emerging market built on honest principles of free trade and

ВЕСНА РУССКАЯ

Russian social-capitalism (the pursuit of ingenuity and profit in conjunction with recognition of and just wages for the invaluable contributions and worth of each and every citizen) and a new Ruble backed by her vast supply of precious metals, Russian standards of life improved dramatically. To ensure past mistakes were not repeated, the Kremlin refused to accept foreign currencies on a fiat basis, the crime that had allowed the "Elite 7" to swindle much of the world though unjust currency manipulations.

Russians for the first time in decades began to shed their pessimism. With their newfound optimism, the nation's the demographic implosion was reversed. The country was no longer in peril of becoming a "Russia without Russians".

Shortly after the Meliacherov assassination plot and the murders of the Russian Prime Minister and civilians who died with him, the full extent of the crimes and individuals involved were exposed. The United States Congress then impeached President Clint Stoker who subsequently resigned. With a new President and the commencement of damage control to mend fences, the U.S. Government withdrew troops from Hawaii and granted the Island Paradise independence. The West then adopted new global monetary standards to enhance world standards of living and protect national currencies from future manipulation. With global interdependence it made sense to protect international economic stability since repercussions from one country were felt in many others. And with the application of identical standards for every country, Russia and a good part of the world got a second lease on life. They were offered a new opportunity for peace, growth, and cooperation. And with the Stoker administration gone, Russia and the United States resumed contacts paving the way for another try at friendship.

"Soon we'll have children of our own," Natalya and Jim spoke, eagerly envisioning their future family while watching a group of children playfully sledding in the snow. A few lingering flurries, gently drifted through the air, sprinkling the newlyweds' hair as they kissed and held each other in the greatest affection. "There truly was a God," Natalya had come to believe after all that had happened. Miracles were possible and with "new hope" radiating throughout the planet, both dared to dream of the better world their children would inherit.

ISBN 141200418-7